phtw

PUFFIN BOOKS

D1512101

APR -- 2016

Dan Abnett is a multiple *New York Times* bestselling novelist. He is the fan-favourite author of over thirty Warhammer and Warhammer 40,000 novels, and has sold nearly three million copies in over a dozen languages. He has also written for franchises such as *Torchwood*, *Primeval* and *Doctor Who*. When he's not being a novelist, he writes screenplays and video games.

In collaboration with Andy Lanning, Dan has scripted some of the most famous superhero comics in the world, including *Iron Man*, *Thor* and *The Guardians of the Galaxy* at Marvel, and *Superman*, *Batman*, *The Legion of Superheroes* and *Wonder Woman* at DC Comics.

Dragon Frontier is Dan's first book for younger readers.

DRAGON FRONTIER

DAN ABNETT

PUFFIN

PUFFIN BOOKS

Published by the Penguin Group
Penguin Books Ltd, 80 Strand, London WC2R ORL, England
Penguin Group (USA) Inc., 375 Hudson Street, New York, New York 10014, USA
Penguin Group (Canada), 90 Eglinton Avenue East, Suite 700, Toronto, Ontario, Canada M4P 2Y3
(a division of Pearson Penguin Canada Inc.)
Penguin Ireland, 25 St Stephen's Green, Dublin 2, Ireland (a division of Penguin Books Ltd)
Penguin Group (Australia), 707 Collins Street, Melbourne, Victoria 3008, Australia
(a division of Pearson Australia Group Pty Ltd)
Penguin Books India Pvt Ltd, 11 Community Centre, Panchsheel Park, New Delhi – 110 017, India
Penguin Group (NZ), 67 Apollo Drive, Rosedale, Auckland 0632, New Zealand
(a division of Pearson New Zealand Ltd)
Penguin Books (South Africa) (Pty) Ltd, Block D, Rosebank Office Park, 181 Jan Smuts Avenue,
Parktown North, Gauteng 2193, South Africa

Penguin Books Ltd, Registered Offices: 80 Strand, London WC2R ORL, England

puffinbooks.com

First published 2013
001

Written by Dan Abnett
Story and concept by Dan Abnett and Andy Lanning
Text copyright © Dan Abnett and Andy Lanning, 2013
Chapter-head illustrations by Benjamin Hughes
Chapter-head illustrations copyright © Puffin Books, 2013
All rights reserved

The moral right of the author and illustrator has been asserted

Typeset in Baskerville MT Std by Palimpsest Book Production Ltd, Falkirk, Stirlingshire
Printed in Great Britain by Clays Ltd, St Ives plc

Except in the United States of America, this book is sold subject to the condition that it shall not, by way
of trade or otherwise, be lent, re-sold, hired out, or otherwise circulated without the publisher's prior
consent in any form of binding or cover other than that in which it is published and without a similar
condition including this condition being imposed on the subsequent purchaser

British Library Cataloguing in Publication Data
A CIP catalogue record for this book is available from the British Library

ISBN: 978-0-141-34296-2

www.greenpenguin.co.uk

MIX
Paper from
responsible sources
FSC™ C018179

Penguin Books is committed to a sustainable
future for our business, our readers and our planet.
This book is made from Forest Stewardship
Council™ certified paper.

ALWAYS LEARNING   **PEARSON**

For Alexander Dembski-Bowden – there be dragons!
– D. A.

For my wife, Lynne, my girls, Rachel and Lucy,
and for my mum and dad – while my head is in the
clouds, you guys help me keep my feet on the ground
– A. L.

PROLOGUE

I have a story to tell you.

Many years ago I found myself at the beginning of it. I was a child then, lulled by the nodding rhythm of a westbound wagon.

It seems so far away now. I see the start of the story as nothing more than a group of tiny figures on a distant plain. They are blurred by the heat, moving across the landscape, just specks upon a giant world.

When we travelled west, we had already been told the land was vast. We expected it. Pioneering fellows had gone ahead of us, bold as you please, all the way to the end of the land. They journeyed far enough to see the ocean that waited on the other side.

Until you see it with your own eyes, you don't truly know what a great distance looks like. It felt as if the land went on forever. That's what people said. We were in the middle of a great land, under a greater sky, and there was nothing beyond the horizon except another horizon, and then another.

Our wagon train, assembling for departure outside St Louis, Missouri, seemed grand and rowdy, but once we entered the West it seemed to be reduced to a tiny thread by the sheer size of the country. We were like ants among the crumbs on a fancy cake plate, the glassy dome of the sky above our heads. We were tiny and we were insignificant. Whole days, whole weeks passed by without the sense that we had taken a single step.

Some of us saw the ocean, eventually. Some of us did not. Some of us made homes in the middle of the great distance, and only knew the ocean through stories and pictures.

Some of us found that 'West' was a constant, and the land did go on forever. Then our imaginations, already numbed by the scale of our adventure, had to contend with the greatest distance of all, and the wonders contained therein.

I will do my best to make an account of them.

The year was 1850.

1

Julius Greengrass clung to the lip of the cockpit, his hands sweating as he heaved and kicked, and tried to climb back to safety.

He could feel his heart thumping in his chest. It wasn't supposed to happen this way. One last burst of effort, and the top half of Julius's body was in the cockpit, while his feet continued to dangle. He pulled hard on the lever set in the floor of the cockpit of the magnificent flying machine. Then he reached out and yanked on the handle that controlled the left wing, making it spread out to full stretch. The flying machine levelled off a little, and Julius swung his legs over the lip of the cockpit and safely inside.

He reset the winch and switched his attention to the right wing. The brass handle had sheared off in the collision with the silver gondola of the evil captain's hot-air balloon. Exasperated, Julius had no choice but to haul himself back on to the lip of the cockpit. In a matter of a few anxious seconds, he was standing high on the contraption's back. The wind flapped at his jacket and stuck his trousers to his legs as the machine hurtled into a steep bend. He grabbed the joint and pushed hard with the heel of his hand, locking the right wing.

Finally, both wings of the flying machine were at full stretch as the last of the steam that propelled the brass and tin beast streamed from its nostrils.

The clouds around Julius were grey and black, and heavy with water. They were his biggest worry because the machine needed the sun to fly. Without its rays, the engine would die, and the great beast would plummet to earth. Julius feared that he would plunge to his death. He must stop the evil captain from ruling the great city of Atlantis, forever. There was nothing for it: he must gain control of the machine and steer it into the last of the sunshine.

Julius saw a long beam of light cut through the clouds at an angle to his right. He began to paddle the pedals in the bottom of the cockpit, stalling on the left and then pedalling hard on the right so that the machine glided towards the sunbeam.

Another bead of sweat appeared on Julius's young forehead, and he pushed away a damp curl of blond hair, blowing hard up into his face to prevent the sweat from dripping into his eyes. Then the sunlight hit his face and gleamed off the golden carapace of the cockpit. In another moment, the machine's engines began to tick over slowly.

Julius used the burst of energy from the sunbeam to flex and flap the wings, working hard to adjust the wingtips so that he could gain the optimum amount of lift. The sunbeam broadened above him, and then the carapace in front of Julius dulled in the failing light.

He must pull around again, back into the sunbeam, so that he could gain enough lift to recharge the magnificent flying dragon's engines and land before dusk.

Suddenly, the machine lurched sideways as the guide-wire on the right wing snapped free from its anchor point. It whipped through the air, narrowly missing Julius's face. He dragged himself up on to the wing to secure the rogue wire. The wing wasn't just shiny metal, it was also slick with moisture, and, as his weight began to tip the wing, Julius lost control and slid down its entire length.

'Aaaaahh!'

Julius flew off the great, segmented, brass dragon wing, its surface glittering with droplets of water. At the last moment, he twisted his back and thrust out an arm. His hand grasped the guide-wire as it whipped over his head. He swung through the air, clinging to the wire. He flipped over and flew past the dragon's head at the front of the flying machine, before crashing into the cockpit floor. His back slammed hard into the pedals, but he never let go of the guide-wire.

He had done it. Julius Greengrass had gained control of the machine.

He steered the great brass dragon back under the sunbeam, and, when it had recuperated a little, he managed to gain enough lift to leave the clouds below him and come out into the low angle of the last of the sun.

The great yellow ball of flame was beginning to fall through *the clouds, its lower curving edge disappearing into a grey fog. The cloud was forming a mist low over the ground. Soon, the sun would duck below the cloud layer, and there would be no more fuel for his flying machine. He must come down to earth fast, before losing all power and falling out of the sky to certain death.*

'Jacobs,' said a faint voice, somewhere in the distance. 'Jacobs, can you hear me?'

Jake Polson looked up from the book he was reading. It had taken him a moment or two, but he finally realized that his father was riding his horse next to the wagon and talking to his son.

'Sorry, Pa,' he said.

'You and your stories,' said Jake's father. 'Maybe we'll see the elephant today, neh, Jacobs?'

With a wink and a laugh, Pa pulled on the reins and trotted Jeremiah ahead to join the lead wagons.

Jake Polson, sitting on the driver's bench of their covered wagon, laughed in reply, but only out of habit. He was hot and weary, and his pa made the same joke at least once a day. One foot up on the side-board, elbows on his knees, Jake flicked the reins. It was not as if Gertie or Bertie, the two sturdy oxen, gave a hoot about what he did. Jake was convinced they'd maintain their steady, plodding pace even if he lashed them with a whip or fired Pa's old musket in the air.

Most of the other families in the wagon train didn't bother riding in the driver's seat. They preferred to walk alongside the wagons or, if they were lucky enough to have them, ride their horses or mules. Jake was allergic to horses. He started sneezing and coughing if he stayed near them too long, and his eyes turned red and swelled up.

Pa, who was a doctor, had told Jake it was his job to drive the wagon and look out for his ma and his eight-year-old sister, Emmie. Jake knew his pa was trying to make him feel better by inventing a job for him. The oxen didn't need driving, and his ma and Emmie, who were taking a nap in the wagon, didn't need looking after.

Jake desperately wanted to ride, even on an old horse like Jeremiah. The other boys laughed at him behind his back for not being able to. What sort of pioneer would he make if he couldn't even ride a horse? He reached into the wagon for a canteen of water and took a long drink. It was baking hot under the afternoon sun, and the rocking and bouncing of the wagon made him feel seasick, despite them being as far from any ocean as it was possible to be.

'We're riding a schooner across a sea of dust,' his pa joked, 'but it'll all be worth it when we see the elephant, neh, Jacobs?'

Over the last six months, Jake had often heard people talk of the mythical beast. Elephant sightings were reported almost daily at the beginning of the journey, when folk were full to bursting with anticipation at setting out west. Lately, the remark had become something else.

'That desert is the Great Elephant of the route, and God knows I never want to see it again.'

It had taken Jake a while to realize that they weren't referring to an actual elephant, that herds of wild pachyderms weren't roaming the prairies with the buffalo. They might have been, for all he knew. Jake was a city boy, born in St Louis, Missouri. When he'd asked about the elephant, his pa had laughed and ruffled Jake's hair, which always irritated him. He was thirteen, after all. He was grown-up.

'There's no elephant, Jacobs,' his pa had said in his deep voice, his Scandinavian accent lending his words great importance. Back home, before they had been obliged to move, it had made people take his diagnoses and remedies seriously. 'You'd have to travel all the way to Africa or India to see such noble creatures, neh?'

'Neh' was Pa's favourite word. Depending on how he said it, it could mean almost anything.

'Why an elephant, Pa?' Jake asked. 'Surely a buffalo would make more sense?'

'Ha!' his pa cackled. 'Jacobs, always the scholar. Everyone has seen a buffalo, neh? Not everyone even knows what an elephant looks like! A farmer rode his wagon to the circus. Upon arriving, he encountered an elephant, which so terrified his horses that they overturned his wagon. "I don't give a hang," declared the happy farmer, "for I have seen the elephant!'"

Jake wondered what they would really do if they saw an elephant. He decided they'd probably shoot it and have a cookout every night for a month.

The steady jolt and sway of the wagon rocked Jake into a daydream as the world passed him by. There was nothing new to see, no one new to speak to and nothing new to do, just like every other day on the long trek west.

2

Jake was woken from his daydream when the rhythm of the wagon was broken by several little bumps. They weren't from the well-trodden road but from someone moving around behind him.

Jake's mother emerged from the wagon, carrying a tall beaker of milk and some hard tack. She handed them to Jake, and then straightened her dress and smoothed her hair. The little brooch that Pa had given her for her birthday caught the light. It was a circle of bright green enamel leaves, interlocked like fish scales, with a perfect ruby at the centre, and Ma wore it every day they were on the trail, as if it was a lucky charm.

'Drink your milk, Jacob, it'll make a man of you,' said his mother, pushing at a lick of hair that had fallen across his forehead.

The milk was too warm and creamy on such a hot afternoon, but Jake drank it to please his mother. Then he drew the sleeve of his shirt across his face, before she could fuss over him again. He cleaned

10

away the milk-moustache, but left a grimy smear on his cheek where the dust on his shirt met the sweat on his face.

Jake's mother dropped deftly off the side of the wagon. All around them, women and children began to appear, refreshed after their naps. Emmie was one of the last. When she ducked out under the canvas flap of the wagon, their mother reached up and helped her down. Soon, she was running around with the other children.

Jake scowled. The children were noisy, and the women's chatter was irritating. He wished for the hundredth time that he could ride with the older boys, but that was never going to happen. His eyes itched at the mere thought of being near a horse. All Jake wanted to do was forget that he was on the wagon, sitting behind Gertie and Bertie, jostling along, and crossing the country, day in and day out.

Jake had read the book twice already. He hadn't planned to open it again so soon, but, of the few things he had been allowed to bring with him, this was his favourite. Space was at a premium on the wagon, so he had left behind almost half of his clothes, which he didn't mind so much. He and Emmie had been allowed to keep their favourite toys, though, including the rag doll that Emmie was seldom without.

Books were heavy, so most families packed only the family bible. Pa believed in the value of education, but, in the face of necessity, they had given their books to the schoolhouse, all except for Jake's favourite. He wriggled it free of his pocket. The bright red bookcloth had worn to the colour of old dried blood, the edges of the pages were dark with trail dust, and the corners of the cover were bent from long use. Jake could hardly read the words on the spine, but he didn't care; he knew what they said:

FIRE BEYOND THE CLOUDS
BY
H. N. MATCHSTRUCK

H. N. stood for Hubert Neville, and Jake believed that Hubert Neville Matchstruck was the greatest writer in the world.

Never mind Pa and his elephants, he thought. *I'd much rather fight one of Mr Matchstruck's marvellous monsters!*

He had got to the part where the magical flying machine, part soaring bird and part steam engine, with a twinkle of magic thrown in, was heading into the clouds. Julius Greengrass was the young hero on-board, fighting to keep it aloft. The fate of the great city of Atlantis was in his hands, but he was in great danger. Young Julius must manoeuvre the craft through the thunderheads and into the sunshine that propelled its mechanism. If he failed, the machine would plummet to the earth and he would die with it.

Jake picked up reading where he had left off and was soon deep in the magical world of H. N. Matchstruck once more.

Without warning, one of the wagon wheels hit something hard in its path, throwing Jake viciously to one side. His hat dropped down over his face, and he was thrown from his seat. *Fire Beyond the Clouds* tumbled out of his hands and under the wagon. Jake threw the reins over the bar in front of the driver's bench and jumped down, but he was too late. There was another jolt as the rear wheel ran over his book. He dashed to the back of the wagon, bent in the dust and retrieved his book. It was battered and dirty, and the spine had been so badly crushed that some of the stitching had come loose.

Jake could feel the prickle of a blush on his neck. He felt stupid and childish, because his book was one of his few belongings. He was angry at Gertie and Bertie and the wagon for ruining his book, and he was fed up with the endless trek west. Most of all, he was angry with his Uncle Jonas. If he hadn't gambled everything away, including the family's reputation, they wouldn't be here now.

Jake kicked a plume of dust from the ground in frustration and then ran back to jump on the wagon, which Gertie and Bertie were pulling steadily onwards.

3

As the long day fell into a slow twilight, the wagons began to gather in a smaller area than their usual camp gathering.

There had been a hundred wagons when they'd left St Louis in the spring. That number had swelled to three hundred when they reached the staging post at St Joseph, Missouri, in May. At its largest, there were almost twelve hundred people making the trek west and only two doctors.

Jake's father, Doc Polson, had tended to hundreds of scraped knees and bumped heads. He'd set four broken arms and fixed dozens of sprained ankles before people got used to hopping on and off the moving wagons. He'd also salved a couple of dozen scalds and burns, he'd sat up with a child with croup for three nights, and he'd even delivered two babies, with the help of Aunt May, the midwife.

The wagon-train numbers had been stable for eight or ten weeks, and then the caravan had divided at Fort Hall. Two-thirds of the wagons set off on the

California Trail, while the Polsons and four hundred other folk took the Oregon Trail. Doc Polson was the only doctor in the group heading for Oregon, but, since the wagon train had divided, he was much less busy. The wagon-trainers had settled into an easy daily pattern and suffered fewer accidents. The summer weather had been kind, and only a few unfortunate incidents had broken the day-to-day routine. They had escaped the terrible threat of cholera entirely.

Today there was a buzz running up and down the long line of the caravan, and all anyone could talk about was the next river crossing. Back east, rivers had been crossed on bridges of wood or even stone, which looked to Jake as if they had been there forever. The bridges were safe, and, although the wagons had to cross one at a time, the train wasn't slowed down too badly.

Some rivers ran very fast or very deep, or had banks that were too steep or beds that were too rocky. It was too dangerous for anyone, except perhaps for some of the hardiest of the Native Americans, to cross them. All of the native tribes lived with the land more closely than the immigrants ever had or ever would. They were experts, but there were some rivers that even they would not dare to cross when they were running as full and fast as they were this fall.

They were heading for a fording place on the Snake River, on their way to Emmet's Crossing. It should be safe, but it was also something exciting to look forward to. Most rivers could be forded where the waters were slow enough and shallow enough for a horse or a wagon to cross on foot. Fording places were most often found upriver and where the river was widest.

The Oregon Trail had been trodden by thousands of feet, hoofs and wheels before them, and Doc Polson and the other elders of the families had no doubts that the wagon train would cross the river safely. The staging post had been set up by pioneers long ago, and the men had built several sturdy scow rafts, which could carry a wagon each and cross the river without anyone or anything even getting wet.

When the wagon train reached the crossing place, Jake couldn't wait to get down. Doc Polson, Mr Hogarth and Pa Watkiss, who was the oldest man and the most experienced traveller in the wagon train, approached the men repairing one of the scow rafts. Meanwhile, Jake, Buck and a couple of the other boys walked down to the river to take a good look at it.

The water was brown and churning, and they couldn't see the opposite riverbank in the fading light. It looked as if the crossing might be dangerous, after all. A surge of excitement buzzed through Jake's head as he imagined what Julius Greengrass would do, faced with the torrent of spuming grey-brown water, frothing white in places. He drew closer to his father, to listen to the negotiations.

'A man could build a house for what you're asking,' said Pa Watkiss. 'I should know, I've done it twice.'

'That's the price,' said the heavy-set scow man, with the brush of thick stubble.

'It's more than we can afford,' said Jake's pa, deep in thought.

'Should've considered that before joining the caravan,' said the man with the stubble, turning to the blond man next to him, who simply nodded. When Stubble-man had his back turned to him, the blond man winked at Jake, gestured with his head and slowly turned to walk away. It was obvious to Jake that the two men weren't on friendly terms.

'I won't be held to ransom,' said Pa Watkiss, pulling his hat firmly down to shade his eyes, without managing to hide the angry line of his mouth.

'Do as you please,' said Stubble-man. 'The river's high and running fit to bust. It's a dangerous business crossing her, and a man deserves to be paid well for taking the risk.'

'It's not the wagon,' said Doc Polson, 'but why so much to transport the horses?'

'You can ride a horse,' said Stubble-man, crossing his arms over his barrel chest in defiance, the hair on his wrists almost as thick as the hair on his head.

Jake could see that he wasn't going to lower his prices.

'Simple folk ride wagons and use their two good feet to walk the trail. If you can afford to ride a horse, you can afford to pay for it to cross the river,' he said. 'Even the strongest horse would struggle to get safely across under its own steam. Paying the fee is smarter than losing the horse.'

Doc Polson looked down at his shoes. He could never keep such a close eye on all of his patients if he didn't have his horse.

'Of course,' said Stubble-man, 'if you sold me the horse, you could afford to cross with the wagon.'

Jake didn't like what he was hearing. He ducked under Mr Hogarth's arm and came up behind his father.

'Pa,' he said, but his father wasn't listening.

'Pa,' he said again, a little louder.

'In a minute, Jacobs,' said his pa. 'I've got to work this out for the best, neh?'

Jake tugged on his pa's coat-sleeve, trying not to draw too much attention to himself.

Doc Polson sighed.

'Excuse me for one moment,' he said. He led Jake back towards the wagons. 'What is it, Jacobs?' he asked.

'You might not have to cross here,' said Jake. 'There might be another way.' He turned to look back at the scow men. Stubble-man was still speaking to Mr Hogarth and could not overhear them talking.

'Well, my boy, what is this wonderful idea of yours, neh?' asked his pa.

'It's over here,' Jake said, suddenly spotting what he was looking for.

Doc Polson followed Jake into the darkness upstream of the scows. He caught up with him just as he reached the blond scow man.

'Can you help us?' Jake asked.

'They work together, son,' said his father. 'Don't turn working men against each other.'

'Loyalty's one thing, Doc, but your son's right,' said the blond man, offering his hand to shake. 'The name's Gene Bell, and I can tell you that Hog Harry's a greedy old fool. He'll lose us business if he puts the prices up every time we have a bit of rain. Besides, if people try to cross by their own efforts, someone's going to die sooner or later. I've been in the water, more than once, myself.'

'Then what do you suggest?' asked Doc Polson.

'It'll put a few days on your journey, and it's not without its own risks,' Gene began.

'Go on,' said Jake, clearly excited by the prospect of an adventure.

'If you follow the river upstream ten miles or so, you'll find another fording place. That's not the risky part, though.'

'Spending all of my money and losing my horse is a risk, neh?' asked Doc Polson, encouraging Gene to speak up.

'It's Native country,' said Gene. 'They're good men, and they'll help you to cross the river for a fair price, or for trade or barter.'

'That doesn't sound so risky,' said Doc Polson. 'Yours is the risk when your friend Hog Harry finds out you're turning away business.'

'The Natives aren't the risky bit,' said Gene, leaning in, as if he was telling some sort of secret.

Jake couldn't help taking a step towards him, so that he could hear better.

'It's the forest and the creatures they say dwell there,' said Gene. 'It's all rumour . . . conjecture my wife calls it, not that she'd ever venture into that territory. She likes it safe, like most folk.'

'What forest?' asked Jake, his eyes widening. 'What creatures?'

'You've never heard tell of the Thunderbird?' asked Gene.

'It's a Native legend, neh?' said Doc Polson.

'The Thunderbird is more than a legend,' said Gene. 'They say that it lives in the forest and that the greatest storms follow in its wake. Its wings span yards and yards, and the beat of them sounds like thunder.'

'Is this your big risk?' Doc Polson asked. Then he

turned to Jake and ruffled his hair, saying, 'Not so risky as losing my horse, neh?'

'They take it seriously,' said Gene, 'and you will too, if you've half the sense you were born with.'

The smile on Doc Polson's face faded.

'How should I take this Thunderbird seriously?' he asked. 'How can I keep my family safe?'

'Stay out of the forest,' said Gene, 'and woe betide anyone that lights a fire in the sight of a Thunderbird. Fire makes them angry, and when a Thunderbird's angry the whole world pays.'

'We'll steer well clear of the forest, hope for good weather and eat our stored provisions so we don't have to light a fire,' said Doc Polson. 'If we want for warmth, we'll spread an extra blanket, neh?'

'We won't light any fires?' asked Jake, a little disappointed that he might not see the Thunderbird if there was no fire to draw it near.

'We won't go in the forest, and we won't light any fires,' said his pa. 'We don't want to risk the Thunderbird's wrath, neh?'

'So,' said Jake, 'the Thunderbird's just another elephant.'

'Neh?' asked his father.

'Something else I won't get to see,' said Jake, stuffing his hands in his pockets, dropping his chin and walking away as disappointed as he had ever been.

4

When they set off upriver the following morning, there were eight wagons. The Polsons couldn't afford to take their horse on the scows, and Doc Polson wouldn't leave Jeremiah behind. Pa Watkiss said the devil could take him if he was going to pay so richly to cross a river. Hogarth was reluctant to pay for the scow, but he decided he must think first of his family, and get them and their wagon safely across the river. Besides, he had only his wagon to worry about.

Pa Watkiss had built his wagon. It was just long enough for him to sleep in it, all five feet six inches of him, from the toes of his boots to the crown of his hat, and barely wide enough for him to roll over. It was not more than half a wagon, but Hog Harry still wanted to charge Pa Watkiss the full fee for the crossing.

Several of the single men also opted to cross the river further upstream. This was a rare opportunity for them to be pioneers, and they longed for an adventure.

Jake's pa promised the wagon-trainers that he'd catch up with the rest of the caravan as soon as he could, so they wouldn't be without a doctor for too long.

The vast majority of the wagon-trainers prepared their vehicles and animals, and jostled for the best position to get an early ride on the scows. Soon, there was no one left to say farewell to. Doc Polson mounted Jeremiah, and, at the head of his own small wagon train, the doctor led the way, waving his hat in the air to signal his direction.

Jake was proud of his father and proud of his own position as driver of the lead wagon. He knew that no amount of encouragement would make Gertie and Bertie walk faster than their usual pace, but he urged them on anyway.

Within a few hours of leaving the fording place, the path began to narrow and wind. There was a gradient, and Jake could feel the front of the wagon tilting upwards as the ground rose in front of him.

The wagon-trainers had chosen to travel single file, spread in a long, thin line across the countryside. Now the little train travelled single file along the rocky path because it must. Doc Polson followed the river upstream, with the water to his right. The air was fresh and dry. The women and children walked in a group towards the rear of the wagon train, just in front of the boys, riding their horses.

Jake leaned back to check on his mother and sister, just as Emmie stumbled and dropped her doll. His ma shook the dust out of the rag doll's skirts, while Emmie watched, her face serious.

Pa pulled up on his horse beside them.

'How's that doll, Emmie?' he asked. 'All the better for having such a caring keeper, neh?'

'She's all dirty,' said Emmie, holding the doll up to show her father.

Doc Polson slid down off Jeremiah and patted his daughter's head above her long blonde braids.

'The path's getting steep, so why don't you get in the wagon, neh?' he asked gently.

Jake watched them catch up, and then his ma lifted Emmie quickly on to the wagon, before hopping up beside her son.

With everyone safely on-board a wagon, or mounted on a horse or mule, the wagon train proceeded up the winding path that continued to narrow and steepen with every turn.

As the day wore on, and the trees cast longer shadows, the wagon train slowed down. The terrain was getting rougher, and Doc Polson would not take any risks with his family or with anyone else. He wasn't even sure he was doing the right thing. Maybe they should have paid the ferryman, after all.

When they reached the top of the trail, it was late

afternoon and the light was fading. The land to the left was steep and heavily wooded, but, to the right, it opened out. The river curved away, and Jake could see for miles.

They planned to cross the river the next day, and there was plenty of work still to be done. If water got into the wagons, all the dried supplies would be ruined: the flour would be useless for cooking with, the hay mattresses would be impossible to sleep on, and blankets, quilts and clothes would all have to be dried. It was much easier to guard against the water now than it was to solve the problem of water damage later.

Jake's father set Pa Watkiss to lighting a fire at the centre of the circle of wagons. They could use it to melt the wax to waterproof the wagons, and, when that was done, they could cook supper on it. Pa Watkiss called on the young riders, and in no time at all he had a pile of wood and kindling to set a fire, and a ditch dug to build it in.

Jake eyed the fire, remembering what Gene Bell had told him about attracting the Thunderbird. He thought about going over to say something, but quickly changed his mind. It would be just another reason for the older boys to tease him about flying creatures and make-believe.

In fact, they would be right to tease, because Jake believed that the Thunderbird might be his only chance of a proper pioneering adventure on the boring Oregon Trail. Thinking about the Thunderbird made Jake Polson feel a little bit like his hero Julius Greengrass, and that had to be a good thing.

5

Everyone worked hard for the next two hours, stoking the fire, sewing splits and patches on the canvas canopies, and then melting wax for the wagons and painting it on.

When they were travelling, it made sense to have to hand all the things they would need to use every day, including things for eating and washing, and extra clothes against the early-morning chill. Items such as sacks of flour and potatoes were packed in the bottoms of the wagons, where they stayed for most of the journey. For the crossing, it was important to pack things that couldn't be damaged by water lowest in the wagons, with more perishable items like flour on top.

Pa Watkiss kept the fire burning while everyone worked, and there was a happy atmosphere in camp. Jake's ma began singing while she waxed the stitches on a patch of canvas, and soon everyone joined in. Pa Watkiss got up from beside the fire and pulled his fiddle out of the back of his wagon, ready to strike up the next tune.

As the sky turned a dark blue-grey, the moon began to rise like a milky disc almost at eye level, large and full. Jake had a bag of flour over his shoulder, ready to heave it back into the wagon, when the music suddenly died away. A tall, lean man, with skin the colour of a glorious sunset and hair longer and straighter even than his mother's, approached the camp. Jake watched while the man kicked dust into the firepit, burying the flames under loose soil that began to smell of scalded earth.

Jake had heard of the Native Americans, like everyone else. He had even seen some at a distance, but this was the closest he had ever come to one of them. The man wore a band around his head, keeping his hair in place, and another around his arm. He wore trousers down to his shins made of soft leather, like buckskin, and matching shoes that seemed to fit his feet like the best wool socks Jake's mother knitted.

The Native worked quietly but determinedly, while everyone watched, frozen, for a minute or two. Then Doc Polson made an odd tutting sound, and the spell was broken. Jake breathed a sigh of relief and dumped the sack of flour in the back of the wagon. Then he hurried to stand beside his father and get closer to the fascinating stranger.

The man lifted his head, pointed into the sky and made a sweeping gesture with his arms, waving them elegantly. Jake knew, immediately, that the man was impersonating a great bird. He was warning them about the Thunderbird.

That was when Jake saw the strange markings on the Native's left arm. He had seen a tattoo once before, on an old sailor's arm, but it had been crude, as if drawn by a child. The fine curving lines on the Native's arm made a shape like a featherless bird's wing. A long, serpentine tail wrapped around his wrist, but Jake had never seen a bird with a tail like that. The skin around the tattoo was puckered and yellow as if it had been badly burnt. The Native also wore a cuff of leather thongs strung with beads and feathers with a ruby at its centre, just like the one in Ma's brooch.

Without thinking, Jake ducked under his father's arm and began kicking dust into the flames. He kicked with enough gusto to cover the Native's feet in the reddish dirt. Jake looked in horror at what he had done, and the man looked down, and then at Jake.

Jake's heart thumped in his chest as the man bared his teeth, but then he realized that he was grinning. Jake felt the colour in his cheeks rise in an embarrassed flush.

'I bet Julius Greengrass wouldn't do such a stupid thing,' he said under his breath.

'Neh?' asked his father.

'Nothing, Pa,' Jake mumbled. 'I just remembered what Mr Bell said, about the fire and the Thunderbird.'

'I don't think we need worry about flying beasts, Jacobs,' said his father. 'That book has filled your head with foolish ideas again, neh?' Then he turned to the stranger and gestured for him to sit. Doc Polson waved the others away to prepare the camp and finally sat down to talk to the Native, with Jake lingering at his side. He was surprised to find that the man spoke very good English.

6

Jake felt restless that night. He was excited by the stranger and by the prospect of crossing the river with him, and he was still curious about the magical Thunderbird.

Most of the time the wagon-trainers slept under the wagons or close to the fire, but the fire had been put out as darkness fell, and there was a chill in the air.

'I'm frightened,' Emmie told Jake.

'What are you frightened of?' asked Jake.

'Of the dark,' said Emmie, 'and the funny man.'

'It's going to be exciting,' said Jake. 'You'll see.'

'Will you sleep in the wagon with me tonight?' Emmie asked. 'Will you tell me a story?'

He looked at her, but could only see her huge, blinking eyes in the darkness, and he felt sorry for her.

'All right,' he said. 'What story do you want?' They shared lots of stories that their parents had told them when they were very little, and which Jake sometimes told to Emmie when she was sad or frightened.

'Tell me one of Uncle Jonas's stories,' said Emmie. 'He always told the best stories.'

Jake gritted his teeth for a moment. 'Yes, Emmie, he did,' he said, helping his sister into the wagon, 'but I don't think Pa would like that.'

Emmie was fast asleep before Jake had finished his story, and he found himself lying in the darkness thinking about his pa and his uncle Jonas. He knew that his pa had lost all of his money and his reputation in St Louis because of his brother's gambling. Jonas Polson was 'no better than he should be', in his mother's words.

Jake had loved Uncle Jonas because he was jolly and he played with the children as if he was one of them. He had even read a chapter of *Fire Beyond the Clouds* to Jake one evening. Jake did not understand how his uncle could be so jolly and lovable, and then cause so much trouble.

Jake wrapped a blanket around his shoulders and hopped off the back of the wagon to find his father.

'What are you doing out of bed?' Pa asked, placing a hand on his son's shoulder.

'I have a question,' said Jake.

'Jacobs,' said his father, 'this can wait until the morning, neh?'

'But you'll be busy in the morning,' said Jake.

'We will all be busy in the morning,' said his father,

leaning against the high back wheel of the wagon. 'Now, ask your question, if you must.'

'Uncle Jonas,' said Jake.

Pa chuckled low in his throat.

'Why do you laugh about him?' asked Jake. 'I hate him, and I don't even know why.'

'You hate him because he upset your ma,' said Pa, 'and that is a good enough reason.'

'Why don't you hate him?' asked Jake.

'The thing you have to understand about Uncle Jonas,' Pa began, 'is that he is mostly a child. It is not so good to be a child and play games when you are a man. In the end, someone will pay the price, and it's almost never the man-child.'

'You paid the price, Pa, didn't you?' asked Jake.

'Your uncle played a lot of games on the casino boats. He loved to gamble and he loved to win,' said Pa.

'Did he win?' asked Jake.

'Sometimes,' said his pa.

'But not enough?' asked Jake.

'No, Jacobs,' said Pa, 'not nearly enough.'

'Did you gamble with Uncle Jonas? Is that why Ma was so cross?'

Pa laughed out loud, and the sound of it travelled around the little circle of wagons in the darkness. He stopped short, conscious that he was filling the silence with his laughter.

'No, Jacobs,' he said. 'The idea of a doctor gambling is absurd. We have to gamble with life. We have to wager that one treatment will work better than another. I could never gamble for fun . . . never for money.'

'So how did you lose your money, Pa? And why did patients stop coming to you?'

'Because a man's reputation is tied to the people he loves, and my fate was tied to your uncle Jonas. When he could not pay his gambling debts, I paid them for him. I was shunned because I was a gambler's brother and I would not disown him.'

'Then he is a bad man, and I should not love him,' said Jake.

'Of course you should love him,' said Pa.

'I will only love you from now on . . . You and Ma and Emmie.'

'Ah, my lovely Emmie,' said Pa. 'I stood behind my brother, and, if Emmie ever needs it, you must stand behind her, neh?'

'No matter what?' asked Jake.

'No matter what,' said Pa.

'I don't understand,' said Jake.

'One day you will.'

Jake looked for a moment at his pa and wondered how one man could be so wise.

'Now, off to bed with you,' said Pa, 'and off to bed with me, neh?'

7

The morning was bright and clear. They all dressed and ate as quickly as possible, because crossing the river would take all day, and there was no time to waste.

Everyone got in their wagons, mounted their horses and stowed the last of their belongings. Jake looked up from the reins of his wagon to see the Native sitting astride a tall, black-and-white Appaloosa horse. He was on the track closer to the forest than the river, but it appeared that Pa trusted the man enough to follow him.

As they rode out, Jake could hear the stamping of oxen and the baying of horses, muffled and at a distance. He looked out across the valley below and saw the wagon train they had left behind making its way across the treacherous river. The water was churning grey and white, the riders and scow handlers were calling to each other, the oxen were lowing and the mules braying. There was a lot of noise and fuss, and Jake wondered how long it would take the train to cross the river. Jake's pa had promised they would all cross in one day, no matter how hard they had to work to do it.

The wagon train travelled for about an hour, all eyes on the unfolding scene below. The people and horses were no bigger than ants on the horizon. The wagons were like toys carved for tiny little hands, but the noise and dust and the swell of filthy water seemed real enough.

After an hour, the view of the scow-crossing was lost, and, half an hour after that, the Native slid off his horse and tied it loosely to the nearest tree. Soon, all of the men had dismounted.

The river stretched out wide before them. The water was moving quickly, but it was clean and clear, and Jake could see the riverbed when he looked into it.

The Native examined the river carefully for a minute or two, and then pointed at one wagon after another, and at the horses and mules in turn.

Pa Watkiss was to be the first to cross. His wagon was the smallest, so if it made the crossing safely, the others should be fine. Pa Watkiss was a seasoned old man, and he'd be the most capable of judging the fording. If it wasn't safe, he'd be sure to turn back, and none of the others would be placed in harm's way.

Pa Watkiss's ox, whom he'd never named because

he thought it sentimental to name God's creatures, adjusted her position, and Jake's pa tried to coax her into the water, but she shied away.

The Native mounted his horse, rode up to the ox and took a firm hold on her yoke. The ox stepped one tentative hoof and then another on to the bank down into the water. The river was wide and the bank was a gentle slope, so the ox was soon perfectly at home. Pa Watkiss looked behind him at the others still on the riverbank. He doffed his hat and grinned as if to reassure them that the going was good.

Pa Watkiss's little wagon was the first safely across the water. The river was deep in places, and everyone gasped once or twice as the water came up almost to the tops of the wagon's wheels. Finally, Pa Watkiss and his wagon were safely on the other side of the river, and he was soon emptying the contents of his home out on to the grass. He separated the dry from the wet and laid the wet out to dry. Then he began to pack up his wagon again. He waved every so often, and the children on the opposite bank waved back, enjoying the game, but the people in the water were far too busy to join in.

By the time Pa Watkiss had finished crossing, the riverbed had been churned up, and Jake could no longer see through the water, which had turned brown and cloudy.

Two horses helped to steer the next wagon across,

and the Native remained in the water all the time. Once or twice, he was up to his saddle in fast, swirling water, but it didn't seem to bother him.

The Polson wagon was the third to cross the river. Ma and Emmie were in the back, and Jake was up front, driving. Pa rode his horse closer, to reassure Jake and to help steer the wagon, even though Jake thought he could manage the oxen on his own.

The wagon tipped and rolled its way into the water, and one of the wheels made an alarming creaking noise. Jake was suddenly nervous, and he clutched the reins tightly, until his knuckles were white. Then he looked over at his father. Doc Polson looked serious, but nodded at his son to reassure him that all was well. Jake was suddenly very glad his father was at his side.

Soon, Gertie and Bertie were up to their necks in fast-flowing water, and Bertie began to bray in a sorrowful tone. The riverbed dipped away beneath them. Suddenly, the wagon jerked and rocked as one of the back wheels hit a boulder.

Jake urged the oxen forward, but, when they tried to pull, the wagon twisted away from them, creaking again in an alarming fashion. Suddenly, there was a deathly, high-pitched scream, and then Doc Polson began to shout.

'Get out!' he yelled.

As the wagon made a thunderous creaking noise,

Ma thrust Emmie out of the canvas flap at the back of the wagon and into her father's arms. Then Ma jumped into the water. She plunged in up to her waist, the current whipping strongly at her legs. Jake had the odd sensation of watching his ma's skirts drifting up, sitting on the top of the water, swirling around her in a great circle of pink flowered cotton.

She was wearing one of her best dresses, complete with the little green enamelled brooch with its fiery red eye. It was a momentous day on the trail, and she'd worn the brooch because nothing could happen to it unless it happened to her first. As Jake watched his ma, stranded in the water, it crossed his mind that, however beautiful the brooch, it wouldn't count for anything if his ma wasn't alive to wear it.

Ma had stretched her arms out to either side of her, trying to keep her balance in the currents that threatened to drag her under. Then she was pulled into the arms of a slightly embarrassed young man and hoisted up behind him in his saddle, safe and sound.

Jake was about to breathe a sigh of relief when he realized Bertie and Gertie were still struggling with the wagon. It continued to twist and creak, and gave a mighty shudder as all the things carefully stacked inside began to shift and roll. He yanked frantically on the reins, trying to make Gertie pull and straighten up the wagon. The sheer weight of the vehicle and the added momentum of the water were too much for the ox, and the back of the wagon began to tip.

Suddenly, Ma's sewing box and best quilt fell off the back, and Pa shifted Jeremiah out of the eddy he was caught in to try to get closer and salvage his property. Then a large barrel of dried meat tumbled over the side of the wagon, breaking the ropes that held the canopy in place. The canvas cover whipped back against the side of the wagon, making a slapping noise like a huge wing beating.

Jake was thrown clear of the wagon as the back wheel finally rolled over the stubborn boulder. The movement was sudden and violent, and Jake's cry was drowned out by the braying of the frightened oxen. As he flew through the air, Jake saw the Native surging through the water towards him, his horse kicking up brown spray all around him.

'Jacobs!' Pa shouted.

Jake hit the cold water hard, and the air was knocked clean out of his lungs. His mouth had been wide open and halfway through the sort of scream that Emmie might make. Consequently, his lungs and stomach were soon full of dirty river water. He twisted and turned through the fast-moving water, desperately trying to right himself, but it was several moments before he could raise his head out of the rushing water. He emerged, gasping for air.

Jake saw his father fighting against the flow of the water to reach him, while the Native went to the aid of the oxen. Just as Jake began to catch his breath, the tailgate of the wagon fell open and splashed him again, covering his head and face in more cold water. Keen to get out of the river and on to dry land, Jake struck out to swim towards the back of the wagon.

The fast-flowing water made swimming impossible, and Jake felt it dragging him downstream. Struggling, he reached out a hand and grabbed hold of the rope that had fixed the cover of his wagon in place. The rope was slick and rough, and it scorched his palm as he clung to it.

More of the family's belongings began to trickle out of the back of the wagon. Pa's second-best boots soon sank, but one of Ma's shawls spread in a beautiful arc across the water, just as her skirts had done, swirling with the eddies in the river.

Then Jake saw his beloved copy of *Fire Beyond the Clouds*. He watched as the red cloth cover darkened almost to black, and the pages began to yellow and swell. He reached, instinctively, for the book with his free hand, but it was pulled away from his grasp by a spiralling current of water. When it bobbed back to the surface, the book was a yard further downstream.

Still hanging on to the rope, Jake waded in the direction of the book, feeling his way through the rocky riverbed with his feet, and trying not to be tugged away by the strong currents. He willed himself to find the strength to rescue his most prized possession. Some of the stitching had been torn when the wagon had rolled over the book. Now pages began to separate from the binding and drift off in the water.

As Jake reached out one last time, in despair, a tiny little head bobbed out of the water between his hand and the book. He gasped for a moment and then realized that the hair was yellow wool, sewn into a round calico head. It was Emmie's beloved rag doll.

In another moment, the rag doll and the book sat next to each other in the water. Beyond them, Jake could see another eddy current, taking the water down to the riverbed in a spiral. It would surely take the doll or the book, and they would be lost forever. In one swift movement, Jake grabbed the doll by its hair, and the book disappeared, just as he knew it would.

8

Doc Polson pulled his son out of the water and carried him up the slope of the riverbank, while the Native steered the wagon safely to dry land.

Ma and Pa stood over Jake as he sat on the ground, catching his breath and still holding Emmie's rag doll. Ma had a blanket wrapped around her own wet shoulders and was ready with one for Jake. She spread the blanket to cover as much of her son as possible and fussed around him, while Pa carried Emmie, who had managed to escape a soaking.

Jake's little sister held out her hands for her doll. He handed it to her absent-mindedly. He had more important things to think about than her silly doll. *Why did I save the rag doll when I could have rescued my book?* he wondered.

Pa Watkiss had already prepared and lit a fire, and Jake spent an hour or two sitting close to it, wrapped in his blanket. Once or twice, someone tried to speak to him, but he didn't feel like talking.

By the end of the afternoon, all of the wagons,

people and animals were safely across the river. The Native was paid for his services and disappeared beyond the treeline. The only incident had been Jake losing control of his wagon, and it made him feel foolish, even though it could have happened to anyone.

Jake didn't speak much over supper, not even to Emmie, who kept trying to thank him for saving her doll. He just shrugged her off, and she went back to her mother, confused and sad.

'It's time to snap out of it, Jacobs,' said his pa. 'Be kind to your sister, neh?'

'I saved her stupid doll, didn't I?' asked Jake.

'You did a wonderful thing,' said Pa.

'I did a stupid thing!' shouted Jake. 'Why didn't I save my book? Why did I have to save stupid Emmie's stupid doll? Why did we have to cross the river? Why did we ever join the stupid wagon train?'

'You know why,' said Pa.

Emmie began to cry quietly into her ma's shoulder, and Ma looked at Jake, clearly hurt by his outburst.

'It's all because of your stupid loyalty to your stupid brother! I hate Uncle Jonas and I hate you, and I hate this stupid wagon train!' said Jake.

'Apologize to your ma,' said Pa, his face as stern as Jake had ever seen it. 'Apologize to me.'

Jake stood his ground and said nothing. Today

45

proved that he was still a boy when he already felt like a man, and he was humiliated.

'Then go and tend to the animals, Jacobs,' said his pa. 'Come back when you have something to say for yourself.'

Jake pulled his hat on, buttoned his jacket and threw the blanket over his shoulder. Then he turned and walked away.

Fine! He'd tend to the animals and camp out, and he wouldn't be in the wagon when they woke in the morning. *That'll show them*, he thought.

Away from the heat of the fire, Jake kept himself busy with the animals, hoping the work would keep him warm. Besides, he was more than a little worried about the fire. The Native had kicked over their fire the night before for very good reasons, and the flames seemed much too bright in the darkness.

It had been a long day and Jake's adventure hadn't been quite what he'd been hoping for. He was horribly tired and part of him wanted to climb into the wagon where he'd be warm and comfortable with his family. Another part, a bigger part, was too proud to go back. So he shook out his blanket and lay down against Bertie's back for warmth.

9

Jake woke with a start. His heart was thumping, and he was on his feet and looking around before he was fully awake.

The air was split by the pained cry of some beast that Jake didn't recognize, but he knew, instinctively, that it was the sound that had woken him. He looked up into a sky that was glowing an odd greenish colour. The light was intermittent, not like sunlight at all, or moonlight for that matter.

The animals were restless, and Jake wrapped his blanket around his shoulders with slightly shaking hands and strode over to calm his father's horse. Jeremiah was rearing and pulling at the rope that tethered him to a tree for the night.

Jake took hold of the rope and tried to comfort Jeremiah. The horse's eyes were wide and bright, and his nostrils flared. Heat rose from his sweating neck. The air was filled again with the wild cry, and Jake felt the terror in Jeremiah's quivering flanks. He also felt the sweat of his own palms and looked quickly around to see what predator had come in the night to taunt and frighten the poor creature. Then Gertie made a sudden high-pitched noise, not at all like her usual grunting and lowing but more like a cry of pain or anguish.

Suddenly, the green light in the sky intensified, and there was a loud cracking noise, like the canvas cover of a wagon flapping in a high wind, except that the sound was deeper and slower and more like a throb. Then a gust of sudden wind swept Jake off his feet. Face down on the ground, he lifted his head as high as he could, only to see a flash of glowing light and a ball of fire bursting from the camp.

The wagons! thought Jake. *The wagons are on fire!*

He tried to get to his feet, but the rolling ball of heat kept him on the ground as a gust of hot air whirled over his back. As soon as it passed, Jake sprang to his feet, patting himself down quickly to make sure he wasn't on fire. He was trembling, and his legs felt weak, but he took a deep breath and ran towards the wagons to help his family.

Screams started to shred the night. Men, women and children, all shouting or crying, slipped from their wagons and began to beat frantically at the fires with their quilts and blankets.

Pa Watkiss, in his long, red underwear and heavy boots, beat at the canvas cover of his wagon with his jacket. There was no hope of him quelling the flames, but he had to try to save his little house on wheels and all his belongings. Suddenly, the whole thing lifted two or three feet off the ground in a hot explosion. Jake threw himself flat on the ground where he lay still for several long seconds before he began to scramble towards the wagons.

Before he was five yards closer, crawling through the gritty, warm earth on his belly, another wagon burst into flames, and then another. Fireballs descended out of the sky, rolling towards Jake like orbs of lightning, flashing white-hot and turning the night sky green. He struggled to his feet, leaning into a hobbling run to try to get to his family and get them out of there.

'Ma!' he shouted. 'Run!'

The rumble of flames, cut through with the screams of the animals and the frantic cries of the people in the camp, filled the night air.

Jake felt the ground beneath his feet quake and shudder. At first, he thought it was something to do with the fire and destruction that was happening all around him. Then he heard Gertie make that noise again. The animals panicked, pawed frantically at the ground, and then began to stampede, desperate to flee their fate.

Jake ducked and threw himself on the ground, covering his head with his hands. No one ever survived a real animal stampede in the wild with thousands of buffalo on the plains, but Jake desperately wanted to believe that he might survive this stampede of oxen and a few horses and mules.

He could not help looking up when he heard a horrendous screech. Bertie was flying through the air, wide-eyed and screaming. Jake was so horrified by what he saw that he ducked his face back into the dust. A loud thud, a few feet in front of Jake, made him jerk open his eyes. Bertie's severed head, the eyes wide and milky and the tongue lolling out, rolled to a halt right in front of him. Jake thought he was going to be sick.

Then he heard another scream.

Ma needs me, Jake thought, clambering to his feet and running as fast as he could towards his wagon. It was on fire, and his ma and pa were beating at the flames with blankets. Emmie was nowhere to be seen, but Jake was sure that his ma had made certain she was safe, even if she only had her doll for company. For the first time since it had happened, Jake was not sorry that he had plucked the rag doll out of the water.

Not looking where he was going, but intent on getting there, Jake ran headlong into something that seemed to have fallen out of the sky right in front of him.

The object was hard and rounded and very big, like a great curving wall. There was also a smell, one that Jake recognized. He was forced on to his backside, and he sat for a moment, trying to identify the stench. It was the rotten-eggs smell of the sulphur that his pa used to treat wounds.

Without warning, the great curved wall began to move and shift in a sinuous way, like some huge snake. Flames from the latest explosion filled the sky with light, and Jake saw that the thing was black and grey, and made of solid flesh. It had a beautiful, iridescent pattern on its surface, like the prettiest of fish scales, only bigger . . . much, much bigger.

Then the air moved again, and Jake tried to get away from the beast, shuffling a pace or two on his hands and backside. Suddenly, he stopped, in wonder and fear.

Was this his elephant?

A great pointed head swung into view, and Jake was confronted by a living eye as big as his face. It blinked and stared, and the pupil dilated in a great purple iris. The eye blinked at him again, and then moved out of view. Then a great maw swung up, opening to reveal neat rows of huge, pointed teeth.

The smell from the thing's throat came suddenly and strongly, and Jake was knocked over by the stench of sulphur. It was so strong that he wondered if it was keeping him conscious when he was sure he should have fainted. His heart beat so hard that he could hear his pulse throbbing inside his head, and, once again, he was staring so intently into the eye that the edge of his vision was blurring. Then the thing exhaled, and its very breath sent Jake flying.

He thought that he must be dead or dreaming, or, maybe, that he had died in the grip of some terrible dream. Then he was cold and falling, tumbling with that familiar feeling.

His eyes opened, and he saw green strands of river-weed and tiny grey dust particles suspended in a brownish liquid. He was in the icy-cold, fast-flowing water of the river for the second time in one day.

The first time it had cost him his book. This time he honestly believed that the river had saved his life.

Once Jake was over the shock of the cold water, the adrenalin ebbed away, and he felt himself drifting off. He dreamed about his mother and the beautiful brooch that Pa had given her. He dreamed of the great black pupil in its vast purple iris, and, in his dream, he saw a person looking back at him, a human. He stared and stared until he could no longer hold back the urge to blink.

10

The first thing Jake felt when he awoke wasn't the pain in his back, although his back was sore, and it wasn't the jolting gallop of his ride, although he was certainly being jolted. It wasn't the chill of his wet clothes or the dread of losing his family to a fire. It wasn't the searing heat in his arm or the throb of blood in his head from his position bent double with his backside in the air.

The first thing Jake felt when he awoke was the tickle in the back of his throat, the itch in his nose and the hot swelling of his tongue. The first thing that Jake wanted to do when he woke up was sneeze.

In the end, he had no choice. He sneezed hard, twice, banging his head against firm flesh with a short, smooth covering of tough hair. He felt a broad hand on his back, spreading a little warmth, and he heard the single word 'Rest', spoken with a calming accent.

That was all.

The second time Jake awoke, he wished he hadn't.

The pains in his arm and back were worse than ever, he was still cold and damp, and his face was so swollen that he could barely open his eyes. Then he heard what he thought might be words, coming from behind and above his head. With all the strength he could muster, and despite feeling like his back would break, Jake lifted his head to see where the voice was coming from.

The face above Jake's, with its fine dark skin, its glossy hair and its grim mouth, reminded him of someone, and, although he couldn't have explained why, it made him feel safe. He closed his eyes and then blinked them open again. It was the same man who had come to Pa's camp and helped the little wagon train cross the river. Jake wanted to ask a question, but, by the time the Native realized he was awake, Jake's shoulders had slumped back over the side of the horse, and he was once more unconscious.

The third time Jake awoke, he was lying comfortably on his back, swathed in a layer of blankets and skins. Someone was squeezing his hand and speaking to him gently, and he could feel warm, sweet breath on his face. His face did not feel as tender as it had done when he was being jolted over the horse's back. Jake's horse allergy mostly subsided once he got away from them, but he had many other ailments.

'It's smoky,' he said before he'd even opened his

eyes. Beyond the smell of sweet breath he could detect woodsmoke, a smell like almonds roasting, yeasty bread and ripe fruit.

'Rest,' said a light voice with the same calming accent that he'd heard before.

He looked up into a pair of black, gleaming eyes in a smooth-skinned, noble face.

'The smoke is medicine,' said the girl.

'I can't go near horses,' said Jake, relaxing and breathing the fine veil of smoke that hung in the air. He inhaled deeply, allowing the velvety smoke to soothe the back of his nose. Then he breathed out through his mouth so that the same smoke rolled over his sore throat and swollen tongue. He felt better almost immediately. He blinked twice, and even his eyes seemed less sore and dry.

'Good,' said the girl.

Jake took this to mean that he should continue to breathe deeply. The next time he exhaled through his mouth, a wispy trail of smoke hovered around his lips. He crossed his eyes in wonder, trying to look at it. The girl laughed.

'I'm better,' said Jake, trying to lift himself up on his elbows. Then suddenly he felt weak and hot and had to lie back down.

'The fever will return,' said the girl, 'and your arm and hand are not healed.'

Jake lifted his left arm. It felt strangely numb, but

he vaguely remembered a searing pain there. His arm was encased in a thick gooey bandage, like the poultices that Pa and Aunt May used to treat cuts and burns.

'Pa? Where's Pa?' asked Jake, suddenly frantic.

'You are safe here,' said the girl. 'There was a fire and you were hurt.'

'Who are you?' asked Jake.

'My name is White Thunder,' said the girl. 'I am of the Nimi'ipuu people. My father is our medicine man.'

Jake had stopped listening. He was thinking about Pa Watkiss's wagon and of landing in the water. He had flashes of a huge purple eye as big as his face. He blinked hard to shift the image, knowing that it must have been a dream.

On the third day, White Thunder's father, Tall Elk, changed the poultice on Jake's arm and examined the lines and curves of the vivid blisters beneath. The scars would be as elegant and as complete as any he had ever seen.

White Thunder was right: the fever did return, brighter and hotter and fiercer than ever. Jake bucked and twisted in agony under his blankets on the floor of the teepee. The air was thick with smoke, and he could hear a low, sonorous moaning that reminded him of the Native's voice. Then he remembered that he hadn't seen his family for so long that he couldn't keep track of the passage of time.

Sweating and thrashing, Jake opened his eyes to see bright, yellow lights among the sweet-smelling smoke that filled the room. The low moan was like a chant or a song, and he saw feet pounding the floor close to his head. The feet were the colour of pecan nuts and were ornamented with beaded, tasselled ankle cuffs. The feet wove intricate patterns, hopping and stamping in rhythm to the chanting. Jake looked up, but he could not see who they belonged to in the pall of smoke.

When he awoke again, he felt a strange sensation on the skin of his chest, a tickling feeling, followed by sharp stings. He opened his eyes to see brushes made of feathers and leaves smoothing a sheen of perspiration from his torso. He breathed the smoky atmosphere and smelled the salt tang of his feverish sweat.

His dreams were of green skies and of birds with scales instead of feathers. He dreamed of breathing fire and of flying. He dreamed of brown-skinned strangers riding on the broad necks of massive Thunderbirds. He dreamed of blood-red eyes staring deeply into his soul. He dreamed of his ma too, and of Pa and Emmie. He dreamed of magical storybooks and of rag dolls that came to life.

One day, he dreamed that he lay still for a very long time while White Thunder's gentle voice sang him the strangest lullabies. He dreamed that, while she was singing, someone was writing or drawing pinpoint patterns around his wrist and up his arm. He felt a million pinpricks and a thousand scratches, almost as if he had pins and needles in his arm for hours at a time. The next time he awoke, the memory was so vivid that he looked at his arm. It was covered in the poultice that smelled of herbs and mosses, and was wrapped in bandages.

Sometimes the teepee was filled with smoke, but sometimes Jake thought the inside was swarming with Thunderbirds. Then he would blink and realize that the Thunderbirds were painted on to the skins that made up the walls of the teepee.

Once he opened his eyes to find a huge scaled snout pushing its way around the door-flap, snuffling and snorting. He blinked and it was gone, but he could hear a voice outside scolding. There was a whiff of smoke in the air, despite there being no fire in the teepee. Moments later, the Native who had helped them cross the river was hovering over him.

'Hello,' said Jake. 'You're . . . You helped us cross the river.'

'My name is Yellow Cloud,' said the Native guide.

'But clouds aren't yellow,' Jake said, and then he

thought better of it. 'Except the ones in my dreams.'

'Ah . . . dreams,' said Yellow Cloud, as if there was some sort of mystery. Jake wondered if the Native had misunderstood the word.

Jake had seen other people delirious with fever, when his pa had treated them, but he had never suffered himself. Lying in the teepee, he often felt that he didn't know the difference between his dreams and the real world. He felt so peculiar, and he saw such surprising things, and yet sometimes they seemed so real that they made him gasp with wonder.

The next time Jake awoke, he was in a frightful panic. He almost pushed White Thunder aside in his struggle to get out of bed and run to his pa. He stumbled around outside on weak legs, his knees wobbling beneath him. Then he caught sight of where he was, and his eyes widened in wonder and his mouth fell open.

He stood on a plateau so high, he could see for miles. The sky was streaked pink and orange, and the sun hung like a great yellow ball right in front of him. Jake saw a crowd of teepees with their animal-skin coverings and a corral full of beautiful Appaloosa horses, not at all like Jeremiah, the old nag his pa rode.

He wandered over to a group of men fixing

arrowheads to newly cut shafts with lengths of leather cordage. They looked up, but did not seem surprised to see him.

Jake turned to apologize to White Thunder and saw the most extraordinary sight. Just as there was a corral for the horses, there was also a corral for an altogether different group of creatures. Jake thought that he was seeing things, that his fever would rush back into his head and cause him to faint.

He did not want to faint in front of White Thunder, and he did not want to go back to the teepee. He wanted to look deep into the creatures' eyes and see what he had seen on the night of the fire . . . what he thought he'd seen.

Are these the creatures that set fire to our wagon? Jake wondered. *What happened to Pa and Ma and Emmie? I must find them, I must!*

He watched several Native men feed the creatures fish from baskets woven with designs of Thunderbirds. The beasts were vast and scaled, with long tails and huge heads. They looked like lizards with wings. No, they didn't look like lizards or birds, even though that's what the Natives called them. Jake remembered his favourite book, and he knew that he had read descriptions of creatures just like the ones in the corral. He knew that he had seen a linocut print of exactly the same creatures in *Fire Beyond the Clouds*. Jake knew that these were not

Thunderbirds because he knew that these creatures were dragons.

Just at that moment, a dragon dropped out of the sky right in front of him, landing gracefully and bringing its head down to Jake's level.

Yellow Cloud stepped between Jake and the dragon, and the boy was sure the Native had been riding the amazing beast. The Native guide took a leather thong from around his wrist with a bright red jewel at its centre. Jake saw the jewel glinting in the light and was reminded of his mother's brooch with its green enamel scales and its brilliant ruby. Then Yellow Cloud raised the bracelet high above his head and spun it in the air. Jake was amazed by the clear, high-pitched whistle that it emitted.

The creature that had startled Jake, rooting him to the spot with awe and wonder, lifted its head. Then it turned towards the whistle and backed carefully away from the boy.

Jake's eyes sparkled, his throat tightened and his head felt as if it was full of hot cotton wool. Suddenly, he was sweating all over, and his head was spinning. He felt as if he was going to fall off the plateau, over the cliff and into the bright yellow sun. His eyes rolled back, his knees buckled, and he fainted, right in front of White Thunder.

He didn't hit the ground because Yellow Cloud scooped him up in his arms and carried him back into the teepee. As the Native guide laid him on the matting, Jake opened his eyes. For just a moment, he saw Yellow Cloud's left arm close up. The tattoo in the shape of a dragon's wing extended the whole length of his arm, with its tail circling his wrist. The tattoo was a series of delicate lines, but the spaces between looked like faded yellow burn scars.

The next night, Tall Elk, the medicine man, worked on Jake from twilight almost until dawn, but his fever would not break. Jake's skin was boiling hot, but he shivered with cold. He sweated so much that Tall Elk struggled to feed him enough water to keep him alive, and he was as pale as a ghost, except for the bright red spots high in his cheeks and the pink glaze of his bloodshot eyes.

Jake's head was full of visions of dragons and of glittering, silver fish being thrown into their gullets. He dreamed of being bundled through a blue-black sky, wrapped in skins. He dreamed the smooth, dry scales of a dragon under his hands and the weight of Yellow Cloud's body at his back. He dreamed the view over a flying dragon's head.

Then he was falling, swooping down off the plateau, making huge lazy circles in the sky before seeing a cluster of lights in the distance below. The sun began to paint a hazy pink line on the horizon, against the ridges of inky blue mountains.

Jake dreamed the rush of air cooling his fevered

brow and the dragon's smoky exhalations wafting past his face. He dreamed that he was flying over a cluster of wooden buildings with firm dirt roads between them. He dreamed the sounds of a cock crowing and a woman scolding. Then he felt strong arms around him and the jostle and jolt of a pair of legs running beneath him.

He tried to look up, but his neck was unbearably sore, and his eyes burned. He felt hot and cold, and every muscle ached, and he couldn't fight the urge to surrender to the falling sensation that swept over him.

Jake grew limp in Yellow Cloud's arms, as the Native dashed the last hundred yards to the nearest house.

The blacksmith was already stoking his fire for the day's work. His wife was in the kitchen, preparing his breakfast and lighting the stove. When she saw the Native with the child in his arms, looking so pale and ill, she dropped everything and called her husband to help carry the boy into the house.

She turned to speak to the Native, but she was too late. Yellow Cloud left just as soon as he knew that Jake would get the help that he needed among his own people. Tall Elk had done his best, and now it was up to the local doctor to use his modern medicine to save the boy.

11

'Bring him into the forge,' said Elizabeth Garret, 'and fetch Doc Trelawny. Wake him if you have to.'

Elizabeth Garret was a fierce little woman with a tight bun under her house cap. She had been a mother for long enough to know when a child needed more than just a mother's love to get well.

Pius Garret was a surprisingly small man for a blacksmith, but he made up for his lack of stature with a tough, tight-muscled body and a good deal of dexterity. He worked harder and longer than he needed, not to impress, but because he loved his job. Pius Garret had grown up the son of an Irish jockey, travelling the racecourses of the Emerald Isle and never settling down. It mattered to him to be at the centre of a community, and this community was growing fast.

Elizabeth Garret put a kettle on to boil, filled a dish with cold water and, armed with a pile of neatly folded flannels, went to work making the boy comfortable.

As she tripped past the ladder to the loft where her three children slept, Elizabeth called to them to get up quickly and fend for themselves.

Eliza, the Garrets' thirteen-year-old daughter, was downstairs and in the forge before her father had come home with the doctor. She was wearing an old shirt of her father's and bib-overalls. In fact, if it wasn't for the braids that kept her hair tidy, she might have been mistaken for a boy.

'What's happened, Mama?' she asked. 'Papa's bacon isn't cooked and there are no eggs.'

'Interruptions is what's happened,' said her mother. 'You'll find enough eggs under Gwen and the girls, and you know very well how to use a skillet, young lady.'

'What interruptions?' asked Eliza.

'Never you mind what interruptions,' said her mother. 'Sort out the boys and fix breakfast, and we can talk once I've sorted this out.'

'If anyone can sort out interruptions, it's you, Mama,' said Eliza, and then ducked out of the way, laughing, as her mother threw one of the wet flannels at her.

'For goodness' sake put a dress on before you go off to school, or Miss Ballantine will frown at me long and hard the next time I see her,' said Elizabeth Garret.

The truth was that the last thing on Mrs Garret's

mind was what the schoolmistress would think of her daughter's overalls. She was much more concerned about the pale, lifeless boy whose brow she was mopping.

There was a good deal of banging and bustling as Doc Trelawny hurried in, his black doctor's bag carried before him. He took off his hat and coat before he crossed the forge to Jake, and offered them to Garret to put away. Then he leaned over the boy to take a closer look at him.

After peering into Jake's pale face, Doc Trelawny said, 'Well, I'll be darned if this isn't Lars Polson's boy. I knew Doc Polson back in St Louis. I'd heard they were heading west on the trail. I'd stake my reputation this is his boy. I never thought to see a survivor, and certainly not one I'd recognize.'

'Survivor?' asked Mrs Garret.

'The fire down at the river crossing, ten days since,' said Doc Trelawny. 'You never saw such a thing, and not enough bodies to bury.'

Two boys suddenly rushed into the forge, almost falling over each other to see what was going on.

'Eliza said there was interruptions,' said one of them. It was impossible for anyone but his family to know that Michael was speaking and not his identical twin brother, David. Their teacher, Miss Ballantine, knew them apart because David held his pencil in his left hand, a habit she was trying to shake him of, despite his mother's protestations that she couldn't see anything 'sinister' in it.

'Away, boys,' said Garret. 'The lad needs air.'

The boys stepped back to stand one on either side of their father. Despite being only eight years old, they stood almost shoulder-high to him, but they respected him the same as if he'd been seven feet tall.

'Besides,' said Mrs Garret, 'we don't know what's the matter with him, and he's got a fever fit to burst.'

Jake rolled his eyes up and opened his lids. He could see a woman's face close to his, but it didn't look like the girl who'd been looking after him, so it must be . . .

'Ma?' he asked.

'Poor boy. He's delirious,' said Mrs Garret, and she shushed him and put a fresh flannel on his forehead.

'I'll need to look for injuries,' said the doctor, 'so let's get him undressed.'

Ten minutes later, Jake Polson had been thoroughly examined and wrapped up in blankets. His skin was clammy and pale, but there were no obvious injuries apart from some bruises on his back and shoulder that were beginning to fade.

'Now, let's take a look at that arm,' said Doc Trelawny.

'This doesn't look like your work,' he said to Mrs

Garret as he began to take away the bandages and examine the bitter-sweet-smelling poultice beneath.

'It was done before the Native brought him here,' she said.

'They must have found him that night and taken him to the settlement to tend to his wounds,' said the doctor. 'Perhaps the tribe felt responsible for the fire. Maybe there are others.'

'Others?' asked Garret.

'There were bodies missing. The fire was fierce and blazed for half the night, but there should have been more evidence of the dead. If the Polson boy survived, perhaps others did too.'

'We could get up a party,' said Garret. 'We could go in search of more survivors.'

'I'm sure if there are more survivors, they're in good hands,' said Doc Trelawny. 'Let's just worry about the boy for the time being.'

Doc Trelawny was confident he would find the cause of Jake's fever under the poultice. Then he peeled it back and gasped as he discovered the medicine man's tattoos. He was shocked by them at first, but the delicate lines pricked into Jake's skin with the inks made from soot and plants didn't look sore. The burns running the length of Jake's arm had not completely healed, but the skin was a healthy colour, and it was not inflamed either. Doc Trelawny carefully turned Jake's arm this way and that until he had thoroughly examined all of it.

'What have they done to the poor child?' asked Mrs Garret.

'It's quite extraordinary, isn't it?' asked Doc Trelawny. 'It's beautiful work, though, and they've done no harm to his skin. It's clean and smooth, and there's no scabbing at all.'

'I've never seen the like of it,' said Garret.

'The Native guide has something the same,' said Elizabeth. 'I saw it when he put the boy in my arms, but why would they do such a thing to a child?'

'I don't know,' said Doc Trelawny, 'but they are religious people with a great many rites and traditions. They would not tattoo the boy to do him harm.'

Doc Trelawny laid Jake's arm on the outside of his blankets. Jake's left hand was closed in a tight fist, apparently the only muscles in his fevered body that were capable of tensing. Doc Trelawny firmly unwrapped Jake's clenched thumb, and then his fingers. It soon became obvious that the skin of his palm was damaged. It was puffy and purple, and puckered at the edges of a crusting yellow scab. Doc Trelawny could feel the hand throbbing as he released the fingers. He held it side by side with Jake's right hand and noticed how discoloured and swollen it was.

'Look,' said Doc Trelawny. 'The boy's got poison

in his blood and no mistake. We must clean and dress the wound. A leech or two should do the trick. Then it'll be up to you to manage the fever and make sure the boy gets enough to drink and a little to eat.'

'It's so swollen,' said Mrs Garret.

'That's not the worst of it,' said Doc Trelawny. 'If the colour doesn't improve, we might have to amputate a finger or two before this is over.'

Pius Garret swallowed hard, clutching the doctor's coat and hat so tightly that he was almost wringing the life out of them.

'Don't just stand there,' said Mrs Garret. 'Fill the large dish with water from the kettle, and, once we've cleaned this lot up, we'll get the boy to bed.'

Eliza popped her head around the forge door. 'Breakfast, Papa,' she said brightly.

'And set a place for the doctor,' said her mother. 'He'll be ready for a good breakfast by the time we've finished.'

Doc Trelawny and Mrs Garret took great care cleaning the wound, removing the crusty scabs and draining the infected areas. The hand looked worse, but Doc Trelawny didn't want to leave any infection behind. When he had finished, the wound was smeared in a soothing salve, made by Doc Trelawny's wife, and covered up. Then the hand and arm were wrapped in the boiled rag bandages.

When they were finished, Garret carried the boy up to the loft and settled him in Eliza's bed.

Jake's fever stayed with him all day. Elizabeth Garret sat with him and kept replacing the cooling flannels on his forehead. Jake cried out for his mother once or twice, and he said 'White Thunder' once too, but Mrs Garret had no idea what it meant.

12

The following morning, Pius Garret woke up before the first cock had even had a chance to crow.

He forgot he had a mysterious sick boy in his loft, but when he remembered he listened at the foot of the stairs. The loft was quiet, and Garret hoped that his wife had got some sleep. He stoked the fire in the forge and made coffee, and the first cock crowed.

'Cock-a-doo–'

'Aaaaaaahhhhh!'

Garret flew up the ladder when he heard the scream, and Jake was still screaming when the black-smith reached the loft.

David and Michael were clutching each other, and Eliza was staring at Jake with huge eyes, holding her blankets tightly against her chest as if they would shield her from harm. Jake was sitting bolt upright, the scream still coming from his open mouth, while Mrs Garret shook him gently by the shoulders and talked quietly to him.

'You're going to be all right. You're in a safe place. We want to help you,' she said.

Pius Garret gave Jake a stern look as he crossed the room to his sons. He ruffled David's hair and patted Michael on the shoulder. Then he looked over at Eliza who smiled at him and loosened her grip on her blankets.

'He's scared,' Pius told them. 'You would be too if you found yourself in a strange house without Mama.'

Jake stopped screaming and turned, wide-eyed and alert, to Mrs Garret.

'There, there,' she said. 'It'll be all right, you'll see.'

Jake was thin and weary after the ten long days of his fever, and Doc Trelawny had insisted he needed to rest, but Mrs Garret had to almost force him to lie down.

Once he had calmed down, Pius took the twins' hands and led them across the room.

'Come and say hello,' he said. 'You too, Eliza.'

Soon, the whole family was clustered around Jake. Once they had all been introduced, Jake listened while Garret told him what they knew about his family.

'They're dead?' asked Jake, pressing his lips together so that they did not tremble.

'The search party found two bodies, both young

men,' said Garret. 'The damage was serious, so there might not have been a lot of remains, but it seems unlikely.'

'So where are Ma and Pa and Emmie?' asked Jake.

'We don't know,' said Mrs Garret, putting an arm around Jake. He shrugged it off.

'If they're dead, I want to know!' shouted Jake, bright spots of colour appearing on his cheeks, but not from fever this time.

'The Native guide –' began Mrs Garret, trying to answer Jake's question and soothe his anger, but, as soon as he heard the words, he went into a rant.

'The dragons will get you!' he shouted. 'They'll fly back here, and they'll burn your house down, unless you tell me where my ma and pa are.'

'I thought his fever had broken,' said Garret.

Mrs Garret tried to place a hand on Jake's forehead. His fever had broken during the night, but his face was very red, and he was speaking gibberish.

'There are no dragons,' Garret said firmly.

'The Natives keep them in a corral. I saw one in the teepee too. They call them Thunderbirds, but there's no such things. I don't know why they call them that. They're dragons . . . Like horses, only bigger and greener and –'

Mrs Garret couldn't bear to listen to Jake's delirium any more. She grabbed his shoulders and shook him firmly. Jake looked at her for a moment, stunned, and then lay back on the pillow.

'I'm tired,' he said.

'Sleep,' said Mrs Garret kindly, pulling up his blankets.

'So . . . many . . . dreams,' said Jake, drifting off to sleep.

13

When he had finished his day's work, Pius Garret went to sit with Jake while Mrs Garret rested, for she had been with him all day.

Upstairs, Jake woke with a start.

'Where am I?' he asked quietly. 'Where are Ma and Pa and Emmie?'

'You're in the forge house at McKenzie's Prospect,' said Garret. 'You remember. We talked about . . .'

'The fire,' said Jake in a sad, quiet voice. 'There was a terrible fire. I saw Ma and Pa trying to save the wagon.' His eyes widened. 'The dragons,' he said, his voice even quieter, as if he dared not say the word.

'Dreams,' said Garret. 'You had a terrible, burning fever. The Native brought you here to get better.'

'White Thunder looked after me,' whispered Jake. 'I was hot, and I saw dragons, and then I fainted.'

'You're much better now,' said Garret.

'White Thunder,' said Jake again, 'and Yellow Cloud, with the dragons.'

'Yellow Cloud brought you here,' said Garret. 'He rides a horse. I know because I taught him to shoe his horses when one of them was lame.'

'There were dragons,' said Jake again.

'Only in your imagination,' said Garret. 'The Natives breed fine Appaloosas, the finest I ever saw. I won't have you talking about dragons any more, do you hear me?'

Garret wasn't angry with the boy, but he was concerned for him. The fever could do terrible things to a person's body or mind.

'He brought me here?' asked Jake.

'He acts as contact between the Natives and the local towns and settlements along the river,' said Garret.

'He helped us to cross at the fording place, before the fire,' said Jake.

'I'm sure that's right,' said Garret, relieved that the boy finally appeared to be talking sense. He began to say that Jake could stay with them for as long as he needed, but Jake had other ideas.

'I can't stay here,' he said. 'I have to find out what happened. I need to know everything about the fire and what happened to my family!'

'You mustn't get your hopes up,' said Garret.

'There's been no sign of your parents and your sister . . .'

Jake's face fell and he looked pale and fragile. 'You think they're dead, don't you? Pa and Ma . . . and Emmie . . .' he asked, sniffing hard.

There was nothing for it. Garret gently put an arm around Jake's shoulder and handed him a handkerchief. Neither Garret nor Jake noticed when Eliza put her head around the door to ask if her father would come downstairs for his supper.

Eliza watched for a moment and then ducked back out of sight. A whole flood of emotions welled up in her. Her brother, Daniel, had died of cholera when he was about Jake's age. They had buried him on the trail, before they even reached McKenzie's Prospect. Her father had missed Daniel so badly that Eliza had tried to fill his place, but he still clearly pined for his lost son, and now he had his arm around another boy, a stranger.

Eliza's face burned with feelings that she didn't understand, but she knew that she hated Jake. She hated him for coming into their home, taking her bed and for taking her brother's place in her father's heart.

She coughed and knocked so that her father knew she was there, before she put her head around the loft door again.

'Supper's ready, Papa,' she said, trying to sound

cheerful. 'Mama says it's the best bean stew she ever tasted.'

'Good girl,' said Garret, not looking up. 'Bring me a bowl of it and some bread, and I'll eat it sitting here.'

Eliza wanted her father to look up, to see the scowl on her face, but he didn't. He simply kept looking down at Jake, lying in her bed.

14

McKenzie's Prospect had started out as a one-horse trading post.

That all changed when Nathan McKenzie made his home there and built a mercantile and a saloon bar to entice the traders to stay a while. Several of them did. They named the little town McKenzie's Prospect after its founder and built a landing stage on the bend of the river.

Within a year or two, Main Street was named, and pretty soon people were building on Second Street. Old Doc Thompson had swelled the town numbers again when he decided to stay, and, when he'd been on his last legs, his nephew, Doc Trelawny, over from St Louis, had looked after him. Eventually, he'd taken over the doc's surgery and built a second storey on the house for his wife and children. He'd been the town's doctor for nearly two years.

McKenzie's Prospect was bustling. Some of the first buildings had been replaced by bigger ones with steps up to verandas to keep the dirt out and tether posts for horses. The mercantile store was the biggest emporium for a hundred miles, supplying the wagon-trainers on their journeys west, and there was always someone drinking in the saloon.

The settlement was not as big as St Louis, or as comfortable, but Main Street was flat and level, and wide enough for two carriages to pass. Large parts of it even had new boardwalks, so that pedestrians wouldn't step in front of the wagons and carts that rode up and down the street all day long.

There was plenty of good farmland to the east of the town, and folks settled to a decent life, farming and trading. Nathan McKenzie was happy to take the credit for the town's prosperity. He had made a good deal of money out of the place and his businesses, but he was an ambitious man who believed that he could make anything happen. He spent his days sitting at the counter of the mercantile store, resting his bad leg, while his nephew did all the work. He spent his evenings in the saloon bar, welcoming folk to his town and finding out who was doing what.

Eight or ten days after arriving in McKenzie's Prospect, Jake was allowed out for the first time. His arm was still bandaged, and Elizabeth Garret still changed the dressing on his hand every day, but the swelling had gone and the flesh was pink again. Jake's fever was a thing of the past. It was the first time Jake had been in a town for months and he was desperate to get out of the house. He was also desperate to talk to people and to try to find out what had happened to the wagon train, and to his parents and Emmie.

He was grateful to the Garrets, and he had grown very fond of them, but he had too many questions about the Natives and the dragons, questions that the Garrets couldn't answer.

Jake and Garret rode into town in the blacksmith's cart to pick up supplies from the mercantile. They lived close enough to walk, but Jake was still weak and Garret needed the cart to drop off some of his finished wares. He pulled his cart up outside the mercantile and walked up the steps with Jake. The boy didn't need his hand holding, but Garret stayed close. He couldn't bear the idea of anything happening to Jake, after the terrible time he'd had.

Nathan McKenzie sat at the end of the counter with a pipe in his hand. He didn't smoke much, but spent a lot of time filling his pipe, tamping down the tobacco and lighting it. Then he'd set it down and let it go out. He'd scrape out the unburnt tobacco and put the pipe in his pocket, and twenty minutes later he'd begin the ritual all over again.

'Blacksmith,' he said by way of a greeting when Garret walked into the store.

'Mr McKenzie,' said Garret.

It was unusual for the most important man in town to greet the blacksmith, but today Pius Garret had brought the wagon-train boy with him. Nathan McKenzie always liked to know exactly what was going on in his town.

Lem Sykes, Nathan McKenzie's nephew, smiled his awkward, crooked smile at Garret.

'Give you a hand to unload, Mr Garret?' he asked.

'Sure, Lem,' said Garret. Then he turned to Jake. 'Will you be all right finding something to look at?'

'I'll be fine,' said Jake, smiling at Garret. When he felt surer of himself, he might ask Mr McKenzie if he knew anything about the fire, but he wanted to get an idea of the man first.

Jake looked at the broad shelves that ran around the room, filled with everything from pickling vinegars to honey. Barrels of corn and flour stood in front of the counter, and there were sweets in jars beside the cash register. Guns hung from hooks, with knives in a cabinet beneath. One wall had shelves full of cloth, sewing notions, skins, shoes and boots, but Jake didn't care very much for them. Immediately to the right of the door, however, there was a rack that Jake was interested in.

Frontiersmen and homesteaders didn't have much time for reading, but McKenzie's Prospect was home to a schoolhouse, and some of the ladies could find time for a dime novel or a story magazine.

Jake stood in front of the rack that housed a dozen or so books and a display of magazines. Most of them were only homespun tales or romances, but Jake did take one book off the shelf. He turned to the title page and was about to read it when a large hand fell heavily on his shoulder.

'So, who might you be, young man?' asked Nathan McKenzie, as if he didn't know.

'It's that boy,' said a gruff voice before Jake could answer for himself.

The odd growl made Jake jump so hard that McKenzie's hand fell off his shoulder. Jake ducked away from the man and looked around, eyes wide, for whoever had spoken. He hadn't realized there was anyone else in the store, and there was something oddly familiar about the harsh voice. Jake thought, for a moment, that he was hearing a ghost.

'Been with the Injuns, they say,' added the voice.

'Let the boy speak,' said McKenzie.

'Pa . . . Watkiss?' asked Jake, realizing who the voice belonged to and feeling relieved and excited all at once. If Pa Watkiss had found his way to the town, maybe there was hope for the Polsons, after all.

'Ain't nobody's pa,' said the voice as a head appeared over the lip of the counter. It had a mop of red hair and a grizzled beard the same colour. Then there was a sound of rummaging about, and a small man with a barrel chest walked around the counter to stand next to Nathan McKenzie.

Now that Jake could see him, he realized he'd been wrong. This man was even shorter than Pa Watkiss and much scruffier. Pa Watkiss had prided himself on his neatness and taken great pleasure in his make-do-and-mend philosophy. This man didn't appear to have mended anything for five or ten years. He hadn't had a shave or trimmed his hair or beard for a year or two, and he didn't look like he'd washed his hands for a month.

'Sorry, sir,' said Jake, blushing at his mistake, and secretly very disappointed.

'Trapper Watkiss,' said the grubby little man, wiping a hand down the filthy front of his shirt, as if making ready to offer it to the boy for him to shake.

McKenzie's eyes lit up, suddenly interested in the boy again.

'Don't frighten the lad,' he said, 'and keep your grubby hands to yourself.'

'Didn't mean nothing,' said Watkiss, looking for a pocket to stuff his errant hand into.

'I'm not frightened, sir,' Jake said. 'I just thought . . .' Then it dawned on him. 'Trapper Watkiss?' he asked, looking carefully at the scruffy little man.

'Come to think of it,' said Trapper Watkiss, 'I had

a brother once. Long time ago. Haven't seen him since . . .'

Jake waited, expecting this Mr Watkiss to summon up a date. He didn't.

'Not since Missouri,' he said after a pause. 'Thought he was dead.'

Trapper Watkiss said this in a very matter-of-fact tone, but suddenly Jake's face felt hot with excitement again. Maybe there was a connection, after all.

He swallowed hard and said, 'I think he is.'

'Well, there you are then,' said Trapper Watkiss.

'Take the book if you like it,' said Mr McKenzie.

Jake looked at his hands. He'd completely forgotten about the book. His father's voice rang in his head, 'Neither a borrower nor a lender be, and be in debt to no man.'

'No thank you,' said Jake, putting the book back on the shelf.

A hand fell on Jake's shoulder again, but this time it was Pius Garret's firm grasp, and Jake sighed with relief.

'Are you all right?' asked Garret.

'Fine,' said Jake.

'You've met Mr McKenzie and Trapper Watkiss, I see,' he said to Jake in a voice that sounded somehow stern.

'He's old friends with Trapper's long-lost brother,' said Mr McKenzie, and then he laughed at his joke.

He took his pipe out of his pocket and, with the help of a sturdy walking stick, made his way back to the stool at the end of the counter.

Pius Garret stepped up to the counter and took a liquorice stick out of one of the jars. He handed it to Jake and said, 'Why don't you go and sit in the cart while we load her up? Lem can put this on my bill.'

'Thank you,' said Jake, and left the mercantile. Nathan McKenzie made him feel uneasy, and it was clear that the blacksmith didn't like him any better. He also had mixed feelings about Trapper Watkiss. Jake knew Pa Watkiss's bite had been every bit as bad as his bark and decided that the same must be true of his brother. Still, the connection might prove important in finding his family.

The cart was soon loaded, and Garret thanked Lem for his help and took up the reins for the ride home.

'Are you all right?' Garret asked Jake. 'Did Mr McKenzie bother you?'

'Who is he?' asked Jake, chewing on his liquorice.

'McKenzie's Prospect is named after him,' said Garret. 'He was a trapper, before he set up a trading post right here, on the bend of the river. He was working for the Hudson's Bay Company, still is. You've heard of them, I suppose?'

'Yes,' said Jake.

'He's got a finger in every pie in the county,' said Garret, 'and he's always looking for new ways to bring folk to town and make money.'

'Is that good or bad?' asked Jake.

'Probably a bit of both,' said Garret. 'His new scheme's got a lot of folk hot under the collar. He claims there's gems in the mountains, and he's looking for prospectors to set up camp and start mining.'

'Is that what Trapper Watkiss does?' asked Jake.

'McKenzie used to work alongside Trapper, until the accident,' said Garret. 'I suppose you noticed McKenzie's walking stick?'

'Yes. He's got a bad leg,' said Jake.

'Trapper rescued McKenzie from a grizzly bear. Frightened it off by wailing at it, they say. Carried McKenzie with his half-chewed leg all the way to a doctor. Saved his life, although his leg hasn't been much use ever since. Give him his due, McKenzie always makes sure that Trapper is well looked after.'

'Is he still a trapper?' asked Jake, wondering if Trapper Watkiss might be able to track down his family.

'He's mostly just an old man,' said Garret. 'He spent so long in the mountains alone that some folk think he's half mad with cabin fever. What's all this about his brother now?'

'I mistook his voice for someone I used to know,' said Jake. 'We called him Pa Watkiss, and he had red hair too. I suppose I hoped he'd survived the fire. I saw his wagon explode.'

'Old Trapper tells tales about the Natives,' said Garret, changing the subject. 'Back in the old days, him and his crew got lost on an expedition. He was the only one that came down off the mountains. Some say he ate the other trappers to stay alive. He had a fever when they brought him down, said he'd seen dragons. Still claims it's true when he's got a drink inside him.'

Jake looked around suddenly at Pius Garret, clutching his arm.

'Dragons?' he asked.

'That's what he says,' said Garret, smiling at Jake. 'Says that bracelet he wears proves it.'

'Bracelet?' asked Jake.

'Of course, the old man talks a lot of nonsense, but he's got some old Native beads on a thong around his wrist. He's a superstitious old goat and still searches the mountains for the Thunderbirds . . . the dragons, as you call them. You see, you're not the only dreamer in these parts. Just you remember, though, young man: it is all just dreams.'

Jake sat quietly next to Garret and chewed his liquorice, thinking all the time about Ma and Pa and Emmie, and about the dragons and the wagon train. Somehow, it all had to add up to something.

Garret kept an eye on the boy, but assumed that he was just exhausted from the day's outing.

When they got home, Mrs Garret said that Jake must go to school with Eliza and the twins the next morning. It was a half-day holiday so a morning of school shouldn't be too tiring, and it would get him used to the idea. Jake was prepared to do as he was told because the Garrets were so kind, but he was determined not to stay in McKenzie's Prospect for long. He was adamant that he would find the dragons responsible for the wagon-train fire and work out exactly what had happened to his family.

15

The next day, Jake walked to the schoolhouse with David and Michael. The twins had always been inseparable, and they used to follow their brother Daniel around like a pair of puppy dogs. They wanted to make sure that Jake was taken very good care of.

Eliza scooted out of the house with a book under her arm before her mother could even scold her about wearing a dress, and Jake and the twins did not see her on the road to school. Jake had loved Emmie and missed her terribly, and girls had always liked him well enough, so he was surprised that Eliza avoided him whenever she could.

The schoolhouse stood on its own piece of land a quarter of a mile to the east of the town. The building had been paid for by Nathan McKenzie and raised by the community, and Miss Ballantine, the first teacher, had arrived six or seven months ago from back east.

The schoolhouse had one large room with big

windows on both sides and a high veranda, so that Miss Ballantine could watch the children at play during recess. There was a long flight of steps down to the dirt road, and, even several hundred yards away, Jake could see a pretty woman standing on the top step ringing a handbell. The peal of the bell brought children running from all directions, and Michael and David urged Jake to hurry so as not to be late.

Jake stumbled while he found his feet, but enjoyed the little burst of speed up to the school and the dash up the steps. Then someone swung a heavy book from a strap, thumping it into the back of Jake's legs, as if trying to trip him up on purpose. If David hadn't caught the book, Jake might have fallen down the steps.

Once inside, the teacher and the new student stood at the front of the classroom with long benches and desks spread out in front of them. The youngest children sat at the front, and the oldest at the back, boys on the right, girls on the left. Jake noticed a large lumpen boy sitting on the last seat on the right, and realized that he was the one who'd knocked into him with his book. The boy was dressed in Sunday-best clothes, and he looked uncomfortable, and too big for school. He even seemed to have the beginnings of a moustache on his top lip.

'This is our new student, Jacob Polson, from St

Louis,' said Miss Ballantine, patting Jake lightly on the shoulder. 'I hope you'll make him very welcome as he's all alone in McKenzie's Prospect.'

David, who was sitting in the third row, thrust his hand into the air.

'Yes?' asked Miss Ballantine.

'He's not alone,' said David.

'He's got us,' said Michael.

'Very well,' said Miss Ballantine, still smiling. 'Just for today, Jacob may sit with you, but tomorrow he'll have to sit with the older boys, where he belongs.'

The morning passed in a flurry of copying sums and calculating the answers. Most of the children had slates with chalk and rags, but some of the older ones used paper and pencils. Then came handwriting. The younger children were given pencils from a beaker on Miss Ballantine's desk. The oldest used penknives to cut feathers into writing tools, and the last two rows of desks even had inkwells for dipping the pens into.

Jake enjoyed the maths, and he was happy enough to do a writing exercise with a pencil. He was even amused by David's tongue darting out between his lips as he concentrated on writing with his right hand. He switched the pencil to his left hand when he thought that Miss Ballantine wasn't looking.

Jake sat on the classroom steps during recess. He was not allowed to run around because of his recent illness, and his hand and arm were still bandaged. Besides, recess gave him time to think about his plan for finding the dragons. While he was thinking, Jake kept an eye on the big lumpen boy with the starched collar and moustache. He soon realized that the boy was a bully with a little clutch of cronies, and he was surprised to see Eliza speaking to him. In fact, she spent at least five minutes apparently deep in conversation with the boy.

Miss Ballantine rang the bell for the end of recess, and Jake waited for David and Michael.

'Who's that big boy?' he asked as they climbed the steps.

'Ugly, isn't he?' asked David, whispering behind his hand.

'That's Horace McKenzie,' said Michael. 'He's almost as mean as his dad.'

'And twice as ugly,' said David and Michael together.

'Quiet, please,' said Miss Ballantine. 'In honour of our new student, we're going to have a spelling bee. So thinking caps on, and everybody stand up.'

There was a rustle and shoving as everyone stood up.

'Would someone like to tell Jacob the rules, please?'

A dozen children put their hands up, but Miss Ballantine didn't pick any of them.

'Horace McKenzie,' she said, 'as the winner of

our last spelling bee, please recite the rules of the competition.'

Horace McKenzie huffed a huge sigh and then began to recite, in a surprisingly high, squeaky voice.

'Every child will be asked to spell a word,' he said. 'If he spells it correctly, he remains standing. If he misspells it, he sits down and the next child is asked to spell the same word. The last child standing wins.'

'That is correct, Horace, thank you,' said Miss Ballantine. She looked at the first child on the left-hand side and said, 'Louisa-May, your word is "small", as in, "My kitten is very small." Please spell "small".'

Half an hour later, only three children were still standing. Jake felt rather foolish standing in the third row, surrounded by smaller children. He didn't like to turn around, but he knew the two other people still in the competition were Eliza Garret and Horace McKenzie. Neither of them seemed to like him very much.

'Eliza Garret, your word is "bronchitis", as in, "The doctor diagnosed Billy-Bob's cough as bronchitis." Please spell "bronchitis".'

'B-R-O-N–' Eliza began. She counted the letters off on her fingers and then continued. 'C-H-I-T-U-S, bronchitis.'

'That is incorrect, Eliza,' said Miss Ballantine. 'Please sit down.'

Jake didn't dare turn around, especially when he heard Eliza huffing and the creak of her bench as she sat down too hard, clearly annoyed.

'Jake, your word is "bronchitis",' said Miss Ballantine.

'B-R-O-N-C-H-I-T-I-S, bronchitis,' said Jake.

'That is correct,' said Miss Ballantine. 'Horace, your word is "pneumonia", as in, "Billy-Bob's bronchitis turned into pneumonia." Please spell "pneumonia".'

Horace began to spell. 'P-N-U-M–' Then he hesitated before beginning again. 'P-N-U-M-O-N-I-A, pneumonia,' said Horace.

'That is incorrect, Horace,' said Miss Ballantine. 'Please sit down.'

'But . . .' Horace began.

'Sit down, Horace,' said Miss Ballantine in a firm voice that Jake hadn't heard before.

Jake was the only person still standing in the classroom. He desperately wanted to turn around to see the look on Horace's face, but he didn't like his chances if he did.

'Jacob,' said Miss Ballantine, 'if you spell your next word correctly, you have won this morning's spelling bee. Good luck. Jacob, your word is "pneumonia".'

Jake took a deep breath and concentrated hard. He could see every letter in his head, and he let out his breath and spelled the word.

'P-N-E-U-M-O-N-I-A, pneumonia,' he said.

'That is correct,' said Miss Ballantine. 'Well done, Jacob. Let's all give Jacob a big clap.'

Jake felt rather foolish and began to blush as the other children applauded politely, all except for David and Michael, who clapped as hard as they could.

Miss Ballantine dismissed the class, and they filed out, one row at a time, beginning at the back. Jake watched as Eliza stomped past his seat, head down, arms around her book, looking cross. Then Horace scuffled past, wrestling his two thuggish cronies.

'Beaten by a baby,' he heard one of them say, punching Horace in the arm.

'Don't you worry,' replied Horace, 'I'll soon show him how to get beat.'

'Quietly, boys,' said Miss Ballantine.

When it came time to dismiss his row, Miss Ballantine asked Jake to stay behind.

'You can wait for Jacob outside,' she said to David and Michael. 'You had a good first day,' she said when the classroom was empty.

'I was just lucky,' said Jake.

'You're a bright boy,' said Miss Ballantine. 'Don't let them pick on you. You're new, and it isn't always easy –'

'I'm fine,' said Jake, interrupting Miss Ballantine, even though he didn't like to. He'd been taught that it was impolite to interrupt, and he liked Miss Ballantine and didn't want to seem rude. He knew, though, that she was treating him differently because he'd lost his family, and he didn't want her pity. Besides, he hadn't worked out what had happened to them yet, and he still hadn't found out about the dragons.

Jake looked around for something to distract Miss Ballantine and noticed the book on her desk. He thought he recognized the cover, so he picked it up.

'That's not for school,' said Miss Ballantine, holding her hand out for the book.

It was covered in red linen bookcloth, and Jake was strongly reminded of another book. He turned the spine towards him so that he could read what was written there in gold:

THE FROZEN TUNDRA OF KORATH
BY
H. N. MATCHSTRUCK

'I love this book,' said Jake. 'Matchstruck is my favourite author. I prefer *Fire Beyond the Clouds*, though, because the villain's more interesting and the ending is stronger.'

'Don't give away the plot,' said Miss Ballantine. 'I haven't read it yet.'

'Sorry, Miss,' said Jake, blushing and handing her the book.

'That's all right,' she said. 'It's good to find someone else who loves Matchstruck as much as I do. Have you read *Flame Trees of the Antipodes*?'

'I've read them all,' said Jake, 'at least twice. I hope he'll write another.'

'I'm sure he will, and, in the meantime, you can reread your favourites.'

Jake remembered losing his book in the river. Then he remembered Emmie and his ma and pa, and he felt ashamed for thinking about the book. His face flushed and he dropped his head.

'I'm sorry,' said Miss Ballantine. 'Is everything all right?'

'We left a lot of books in St Louis,' said Jake, 'and I lost my copy of *Fire Beyond the Clouds* in the river. That was before . . .'

'It's a terrible thing to lose your family,' said Miss Ballantine.

'It's worse knowing that the last words you said to them were hateful,' said Jake, sagging down on to the nearest bench.

Miss Ballantine produced a clean handkerchief from her dress pocket and handed it to Jake.

'You shouldn't think about the bad times,' she said. 'There must be lots of good times to remember. Your parents loved you, and your sister too.'

'I just feel so dumb thinking about losing that stupid book,' said Jake. He folded Miss Ballantine's handkerchief defiantly into a little square. He'd cry when he knew for sure that his family was dead and not before.

'Don't feel that way. A good book or a cup of hot milk keeps us all going when we're sad,' said the teacher. 'In fact . . .'

Miss Ballantine stepped over to the bookcase behind her desk with its dictionary and encyclopedia and primers, and bent down to the row of clothbound books on the bottom shelf. She ran a finger along the titles until she found the book she was looking for and pulled it out.

'Here you are,' she said, handing Jake a copy of *Fire Beyond the Clouds*. 'This should help to cheer you up.'

'I couldn't,' said Jake.

'Yes, you can,' said Miss Ballantine, 'and, when you've finished reading it, bring it back and I'll lend you another. We'll call it the library, you and I.'

Jake finally left school twenty minutes after everyone else, so he wasn't surprised that the twins had gone, and the patch of ground in front of the schoolhouse was empty. It didn't matter. He knew his way back to the forge, and the walk would give him time to think about Ma and Pa and Emmie and what had happened to them, and about the dragons too. The Garrets didn't like him talking about the dragons, but he had to know if they were real, and he had to find out whether they had something to do with the wagon-train fire.

Jake tucked the book into his jacket pocket. The jacket had belonged to Daniel Garret and was a little short in the sleeves. Then he bound down the schoolhouse steps and began to walk to the forge, his head still full of unanswered questions.

Ten minutes later, Jake was halfway home when he was suddenly knocked sideways by a blow to the head. He managed to stay upright after staggering for a moment or two, and then he put his hand up to his head where a clod of wet mud had stuck to his hair. He started trying to clean himself up.

'Hahahaha-hehehehe!' The laugh was high-pitched, almost like a shriek. Jake wondered whether a girl had thrown the mud, and Eliza immediately popped into his head.

'Hehehehe!' The laugh suddenly sounded very familiar.

'Who's there?' shouted Jake. 'Is that you, Horace McKenzie?'

Three boys came out from behind a clump of rhododendron bushes, roaring with laughter, and started taunting Jake.

'Ooh, listen to me spelling all the big words,' said Will Hunt.

'Aren't I the teacher's pet?' mocked John Waldo. 'Aren't I a little bookworm?'

'I've got all the best stories,' said Horace in his squeak, as the boys surrounded Jake. 'No, wait, they're not stories. They're real!'

'Nasty, horrid dragons,' said John.

'Boohoo! The nasty dragons killed my mommy and daddy!' said Horace, pretending to cry.

'The fire-breathing dragons killed my family and the Natives let them . . . Boohoo!' said Will.

Jake was not going to let a bully like Horace McKenzie get the better of him, even if he was outnumbered. He did the only thing he could do. He turned to face Horace and stared him right in the face for several seconds. Then he launched himself at the big boy's body as fast as he could, running the few paces between them, head down.

Jake's head ploughed into Horace's belly. He wrapped his arms around the bully's thick waist, and the two boys fell over in a tangle of arms and legs.

16

David and Michael Garret planned to wait for Jake, after Miss Ballantine kept him behind. They hadn't reckoned on their bossy sister.

'What are you doing?' asked Eliza as David sat down on the schoolhouse steps.

'Waiting for Jake,' said Michael. 'Miss Ballantine kept him behind.'

'We're walking home with him,' said David.

'No, you're not,' said Eliza. 'You're walking home with me, right now. Mama's waiting for us.'

'She's waiting for Jake too,' said David.

'We'll tell her he's been kept behind,' said Eliza.

Her voice sounded urgent, so the twins did as their sister told them. They'd been home for five minutes when Mrs Garret began to fret.

'I wonder where Jake's got to?' she asked no one in particular.

'We'll go see,' said Michael, jumping up from the table with David following suit.

'Go with them, Eliza,' said Mrs Garret. 'Lunch can wait a few minutes.'

Eliza and the twins went back the way they'd come until they reached a fork in the road.

'You go that way,' said Eliza, pointing to the left, 'and I'll go this way, and we'll soon find him.'

The twins shrugged, and they went their separate ways to look for Jake.

Jake's fists landed in the soft fat of Horace's body twice, three times, but the blows seemed to have little effect. Then Horace grabbed hold of Jake, pinning his arms to his sides so that he couldn't punch the bigger boy. Jake wriggled and kicked, and Horace's grip loosened. Horace hit back with two hard slaps to Jake's chest. They stung, but there was no real strength behind them.

Horace wasn't tough; he was just bigger than most of the other kids, and that was why so many of them were scared of him. He was a bully.

Jake grabbed Horace low around his middle and pushed him over, at the edge of the muddy road, while Will and John cheered Horace on. Jake was determined to get the better of Horace, and he was sitting on the boy's chest when he thought he heard someone in the bushes at the side of the road. Jake looked up and saw Eliza's face peering at him.

Jake thought about shouting out, but Horace was

fighting hard to turn him over. As he battled to keep the upper hand, Jake caught Eliza's eye. She looked right at him for a moment, and Jake thought she might try to help him, but her expression didn't change. Then she simply turned and walked away. She wasn't going to come to his rescue, after all.

Fine! I don't need rescuing! Jake thought. He didn't need rescuing because Horace was a bully, or because his stories about dragons had made him a laughing stock, and he didn't even need rescuing because he had lost his family and he didn't know if he'd ever see them again. Jacob Polson could look after himself.

Eliza hurried back to the fork in the road and called her brothers. They came running back to her and stood panting as she explained what had happened.

'I've seen him,' she said. 'He's walking home with Horace McKenzie. He's made a new friend, and he doesn't care about you any more, so we'd better just go home.'

David and Michael looked at each other, confused, but Eliza was already stomping off back down the road home.

Jake was so distracted by his anger at Eliza that he let his guard down, and, before he knew it, he was being pinned down while Horace punched his belly. Jake squirmed, but the bullies held him tight.

He twisted his body away, and Horace's next blow bounced off his hip bone.

'Argh!' shouted Horace, stretching the fingers of his sore hand and trying to shake out the pain. Jake began to fight harder.

Will held Jake by the left arm, while John held his right. Jake pulled and dragged on his left side, realizing that Will was weaker than John. Will held on tight, but Jake fought so hard that something had to give way. Jake twisted hard, and suddenly his arm sailed through the air, ripping the left sleeve clean off Daniel's jacket, leaving it hanging in Will's grasp. Jake was finally free.

Jake's left fist flew across his body and connected with the side of John's head, sending him sprawling. Will tried to grab hold of his left arm again, but stopped in his tracks. He gasped and stared at Jake. Horace followed Will's stare, and, as soon as he had recovered, John also noticed that they were all unnaturally still and quiet. Jake was the last to look at his left arm.

He had been wearing one of Daniel's short-sleeved shirts because it was the only one that fitted, and the sleeve of Jake's borrowed jacket was still in Will's hand.

The bandages that had covered Jake's arm for the last three or four weeks had come loose with all the pulling and grabbing, and had collected around

Jake's wrist. He pulled them free. The bandage on his hand remained in place because Mrs Garrett changed it regularly and was an expert at tying a bandage.

Horace, Will and John each took a step forward to get a closer look at Jake's arm. Jake stared too. This was the first time he could remember seeing his arm since the fire. It was covered in the flaming scars from the fire, but it was also covered in the beautifully tattooed outlines of a long curling tail around his wrist and a beautiful wing reaching all the way up his arm. He had a tattoo just like the one he'd seen on Yellow Cloud's arm. Perhaps some of his dreams had been real, after all.

The boys stood mesmerized for several long seconds. Then Horace blinked and huffed, and threw a fist at Jake's gut. He caught Jake unawares, knocking the wind out of him with the lucky punch, and the spell was broken. Jake's knees buckled under him, and, clutching his stomach, he fell to the muddy ground.

Horace laughed his nervous, squealing laugh, and the other two quickly joined in. They danced around their fallen victim for a moment or two, and then they ran away, shrieking and giggling.

Horace turned back once and yelled, 'Freak!' before running off to join his cronies.

Jake got his breath back, and then he gathered

up the torn sleeve and pulled it back up his arm, trying to cover up the tattoo. He had never felt so ashamed or so angry in all his life, but at least now he was forced to do something, and he knew exactly what that something was going to be.

17

Jake was determined to leave McKenzie's Prospect.

Mr and Mrs Garret had been very kind, and he liked Miss Ballantine, but Eliza must have told Horace McKenzie and his cronies about his dragon stories and made him a laughing stock. Besides, two things mattered to Jake more than anything in the world: knowing what had happened to his family, and finding the dragons. There didn't seem to be any hope of getting answers to any of his questions if he stayed in the little town.

Jake knew that he would miss Michael and David, who in some small way made up for the loss of Emmie, but he knew they would manage without him. Besides, Emmie might still be alive somewhere, and, if she was, it was up to Jake to find her.

Jake thought hard about what to do next, and then he headed for the schoolhouse. It had no near neighbours, and, since school was over for the day, there should be nobody there to see him. Jake was determined to head west, but he knew that he couldn't go anywhere without supplies. He had no intention of seeing Eliza again, and the Garret house would be full of people all afternoon, so he couldn't go back yet for the things that he needed for his journey, or for a meal, despite his hunger.

As he walked back to the schoolhouse, Jake thought about getting what he needed from somewhere else. He'd need warm clothes, a blanket and a compass to help him on his way. He'd have to take food too. He thought about taking a gun with him, since he planned to head for the forest. He might need to defend himself against wild animals or even hunt for food.

Most of the houses in town would have all of those things, and the mercantile too, but that would mean stealing, and Jake couldn't bear to add 'common thief' to the list of things the local people probably called him. If he took the things he needed from the Garrets, at least he could convince himself he was only borrowing them. So Jake decided to go back to the forge much later, when the house was quiet.

Jake had seen Miss Ballantine lock the schoolhouse door with a large key, so he didn't try to get in. He didn't want to be seen by anyone who might pass by, so, on his hands and knees, he crawled under the schoolhouse steps. They were sturdily built of wood, but the steps had no risers, so Jake could sit behind them and still see anyone nearby through them.

They, on the other hand, would not see him unless they looked very hard.

Jake took Miss Ballantine's book out of his pocket, made himself comfortable and settled down to read. He'd only read a page or two before he realized that he wasn't really reading at all because he was too busy thinking about his next adventure.

Jake didn't know where or how far away the Native settlement was, except that it was west of the town, but he felt sure he would find the landmarks from his dreams, if he looked for them hard enough. He felt sure that when he was free of McKenzie's Prospect, the landscape would open up and guide him back to the Natives.

He had so many questions, and it seemed to him that the Native camp held all the answers. If Doc Trelawny's talk of the lack of bodies was to be believed, anything might have happened after the fire. Ma, Pa and Emmie might still be alive, and, if they had all been killed, Jake was determined to find out how they had died and take his revenge.

Jake put the book down and pulled the sleeve off his left arm. He traced the lines of the tattoo down from his shoulder and around his wrist, and marvelled at it. *Why is it there?* he wondered. Part of him wanted to be proud of it, but then he thought about Horace calling him a freak. Jake had seen tattoos on Yellow Cloud and Tall Elk, but why did they think he was like them? He wasn't a Native.

Then Jake began to wonder what was under the bandages around his left hand. It was still sore, though, and he didn't want to risk being ill again, so he decided to leave well alone. Surely Mrs Garret would have told him if there was something beneath the bandages, but then why hadn't she talked to him about the tattoos?

Jake felt that he should trust no one until he found out whether his family was dead and why he had the tattoo. He wanted proof of what was real and what was make-believe. He had dreamed of someone drawing on his arm, and felt the pins and needles as he'd been tattooed. He'd thought it was a dream and yet here he was with a tattoo the length of his arm. What else could he prove was real?

Could Jake prove that there were dragons?

18

Jake was startled from his thoughts by the sound of distant voices and booted feet walking around in front of the schoolhouse steps, apparently with some purpose. He heard the single word 'Jake' spoken in a low voice that was also somehow gentle. It was Pius Garret's voice, and, for a moment, Jake was sorry not to answer his call.

A few minutes later, David and Michael ran around the schoolhouse calling his name, but neither of the twins checked his hiding place under the steps. The boys called out to their father in unison, 'He's not here, Papa!' Then they were gone, scampering back to their father's side in the fading light.

When he could no longer hear footsteps, Jake crept out from under the schoolhouse steps and dashed across the open ground in front of the school. He kept to the shadows and out of sight as he hurried back to the forge.

The house was lit up, but, as he hovered nearby, Jake could hear no sounds inside. There was no light in the forge, and he couldn't hear Eliza or Mrs Garret in the kitchen, so perhaps they'd joined the search. Jake could not think of a single reason why Eliza would look for him, since she was clearly responsible for telling his secrets to the other kids. It didn't matter. He was just glad she wasn't home.

The door was not locked, and Jake went into the house. He took a good wool blanket and spread it on Eliza's bed. He looked at Daniel's pyjamas folded on the pillow and blessed Mrs Garret for her kindness, but he didn't want to dwell on that. He took the clothes that he'd arrived in and one of Garret's old forge jackets, and placed them on the blanket. He realized that he'd arrived in their home with almost nothing.

Jake bundled up the blanket and took it downstairs. He took the end of a loaf of bread and the last of the ham, complete with its bone, off the dresser. Then he took three crisp, green apples out of the fruit bowl. Next, he opened the dresser drawer and found a good gutting knife and a compass with a cracked glass. He also took a ball of string and a bodkin. He wasn't sure what he'd use them for, but they were the sorts of objects that Pa Watkiss always said would come in useful one day. Jake felt sorry about taking the compass because he knew that David and Michael played exploring games with it. One day he'd return it and tell them of his own adventures.

Jake tied the blanket carefully around the things in it and slung it over his shoulder like a sack. It wasn't heavy, but it was clumsy to carry.

He looked at the rifle that hung next to the kitchen door. He'd never seen anyone use it and didn't even know if it fired properly. He'd been taught to shoot, of course. He wasn't a kid. He didn't like the idea of shooting anything, though. He'd only ever shot at targets. His Uncle Jonas had taught him to shoot at bottles standing on a wall, but he'd never even shot at rats. He'd been on the trail for weeks, but the men, or the older boys on their horses, had carried the guns.

Jake started to take the gun from its hook, but thought better of it. Besides, he thought he heard something and decided to leave quickly. He ducked across the yard into the shadows of the line of trees opposite and listened. He heard nothing. He looked back across the yard and noticed that a chink of light was visible where he'd left the door ajar. It couldn't be helped. That chink of light was the last Jake expected to see of the Garret house or any other house in McKenzie's Prospect for a very long time.

He adjusted the blanket sack on his shoulder and, keeping to the shadows, Jake Polson spared a final thought for the town and the people that had taken him in and headed west.

19

It was twilight, and the sun hovered low over the western horizon, showing Jake which direction to take, so he wouldn't need the compass.

The dirt road out of town took Jake the first three miles and the first hour of his journey. He had missed lunch and was hungry, but he was determined not to stop until nightfall. He'd make camp when it was properly dark.

He checked the compass, to be sure he was still travelling west, and veered off the dirt road on to a footpath that soon became steep as it wove up through rocky ground. Four miles from the forge, Jake ducked beneath a branch to follow the path into woodland.

He wasn't sure how far he'd walked, or what the time was, but it was getting too dark to continue, and his right hand was sore from carrying the bundle over his shoulder. Twenty or thirty yards from the path, Jake unwrapped the blanket. He'd stayed warm enough while he was walking, but now that he'd stopped he realized how cold it was. He took off the jacket with its torn sleeve and put on Garret's forge jacket, which wasn't torn and was a better fit.

Jake looked at the objects in the blanket and wondered whether he'd be able to make a fire. He'd never lit a fire on his own in the dark and damp, and he didn't much like his chances, but he thought he'd better try. Then he remembered the scow man talking about the dangers of the forest and warning against lighting a fire. The memory only made Jake more determined. He wasn't afraid of dragons.

Autumn leaves had begun to fall from the trees, and he foraged in the undergrowth for twigs and sticks, but everything was damp. Jake looked around for dry kindling, but it was proving impossible to find. Besides, he wasn't sure how he'd strike a flame. He knew it could be done with a couple of sticks of dry wood, but Pa had always used a flint and tinderbox, and Jake didn't have either of those things. He felt foolish for forgetting them.

Scouting around, Jake found a more comfortable site for his camp. It was sheltered and there was a wide log to sit on, rather than the damp earth. He sat on Daniel's old jacket and ate some of the bread and ham. He was getting colder, and he only had the jackets and the blanket to keep out the chill of the night. He'd only brought the scraps of clothes he'd been wearing when he'd arrived in McKenzie's

Prospect because they were his only real belongings. They weren't good for much.

Jake looked at the knife and realized that he might have the tools to make a spark, after all. He rummaged around in the undergrowth until he found a small jagged stone that would fit neatly in his palm. Then he took the knife in his right hand and struck the stone with the edge of the blade. He was right; a spark did fly off the blade. It was only then that Jake remembered he'd need tinder and firewood.

Jake put the stone in his pocket and the knife back in the ham. He scooped some of the undergrowth away to build the fire on the bare earth. He thought about making a little ring of stones, like Pa Watkiss always did, but his fire would only be small, and, as long as there was nothing flammable nearby, it should be safe.

Jake arranged the sticks that he'd gathered in a lopsided cone-shape and pushed some dead leaves into the centre. None of the material was dry enough to use for tinder; Jake didn't want to tear up the jackets or the blanket, and he couldn't bear to sacrifice his own clothes. Then he realized that the bandages on his left hand were dry, and he reasoned that they were only old rags cut up, so were of little use to anyone else.

Carefully, Jake began to unwrap Mrs Garret's bandages. He wound the cloth from his left hand on to his right, so that he could rewrap the left hand without the bandages getting dirty in the process. When he had taken off about half of them, he could see the edges of dark brown scabs, and the new skin was very pink. A wave of nausea hit him and suddenly taking off the bandages didn't seem like such a good idea. So he stopped. He bit through the cloth and secured the end of the bandage on his left hand. Jake made a little heap of the cloth and held it in his left hand with the stone. He bent close to the little pile of twigs, and pulled the knife out of the ham and wiped the grease off on his trousers.

Jake struck the edge of the stone with the knife blade. Nothing happened. Jake struck again and again, and then several more times in quick succession. He was beginning to feel frantic, and there was still no spark. He took a deep breath, and he heard his father's voice in his head saying, 'More haste, less speed, Jacobs, neh?'

Jake took another breath and struck the stone once with the blade. Nothing happened. Then he struck the blade against the jagged point of the rock. Two great sparks flew in different directions. Neither of them lit the bandage tinder.

Jake turned the stone in his hand and rearranged the bandage. Then he struck the blade against the stone once more, and another spark flew. It caught on the rags and began, very slowly, to curl the cloth.

Jake brought his hand up close to his face, and he could just see the beginning of a flame. Holding the rags in his fingers so that the bandage around his hand wouldn't catch light, Jake blew gently on the little flame. Then he smiled broadly as the tinder caught. He placed it in the base of the fire and bent down on the damp earth to blow on the flame some more.

Jake thought that he would get nothing more than the ragged smoke that began to drift out of the little pile of sticks. Then the leaves at the centre of the fire began to shrivel up, and a couple of the sticks began to turn black, even though Jake couldn't see any real flames.

He persisted with his efforts and soon had a proper fire lit. Even though it spat and popped with the dampness of the fuel, the fire made him feel much safer and much more confident. He had a sudden, sharp memory of the Native kicking over the fire in the wagon-train camp and smiled to himself. He didn't want to keep the dragons away. He wanted to find them.

Next, Jake took out Daniel's old jacket. He wanted to wear it under Garret's jacket to sleep in, but the torn sleeve would make that difficult. Then Jake remembered the string and the bodkin, and he set about sewing the sleeve back on to the jacket. By the time he had finished, he was ready to sleep. He put on Daniel's jacket and then Garret's, buttoned both up as far as he could and pulled the collars up around his neck. Then he wrapped himself in the blanket and rolled as far under the log as he could manage, so that he was protected from the weather.

Jake's day had begun with his first morning at school and ended with the little fire in the woods, miles away from his home of the past couple of weeks. He closed his eyes and thought about Pa and Ma and Emmie, and hoped, more than anything in the world, that he might one day see them again.

20

The Garrets met back at the forge house just in time for supper. Pius Garret had spent most of the afternoon looking for Jake, and they were all beginning to worry.

Eliza hoped against hope that Jake would appear for his supper, none the worse for wear. She and her mother had gone back to where she'd last seen Jake, but there was nothing there, and when they called Jake's name there was no one to hear. Eliza said nothing.

Mrs Garret and Eliza had then gone to find Horace at his aunt's house. Nathan McKenzie's wife had died during childbirth, so his aunt, Priscilla Sykes, had raised him.

'Eliza says you were with Jake this afternoon on the way home from school, Horace,' said Mrs Garret.

Eliza tried not to catch Horace's eye, or her mother's, or his aunt's.

'So?' asked Horace.

'Was he all right?' asked Mrs Garret, an edge creeping into her voice.

'I didn't do nothing,' said Horace.

'How many times do I have to tell you,' said his aunt, '"I didn't do *any*thing."'

'Well, I didn't,' said Horace.

'I'm sorry, Mrs Garret,' said Horace's aunt, 'but Horace came home, alone, right about his usual time.'

'You didn't see which way he went?' Mrs Garret asked Horace.

'Left him right by the rhododendrons,' said Horace. 'Can I go now?'

'Go wash your hands ready for supper,' said his aunt, 'and mind your manners in front of people.'

On the way back to the forge, Eliza wanted to tell her mother what had really happened. She knew just how much trouble she'd be in, even though she hadn't really lied, not properly. Horace was horrible, but he wouldn't really hurt Jake, surely?

Eventually, the Garrets sat down to supper, but none of them ate very much, except the twins. Eight-year-old boys' appetites aren't spoilt by anything, and David and Michael tucked into the meal with gusto.

Later, when Mrs Garret was clearing supper away, she noticed that the bread was missing and the ham had disappeared off the dresser. The Garrets searched the rest of the house frantically and found that the spare blanket had gone, and a knife and compass, as well as one of Garret's old jackets.

'He'll be warm and fed at least,' said Mrs Garret.

'He's not the sort to run away,' said Garret.

'I don't see what else he can have done,' said Mrs Garret.

'It's going to be cold out tonight,' said Garret, 'and he hasn't taken a tinderbox. A boy won't survive out on his own for long at this time of year, and if the weather turns . . .'

'Jake's got his wits about him,' said Mrs Garret, 'and your jacket and the good blanket. He'll be safe until we find him.'

'First thing in the morning, I'll round up some help and we'll get looking for him,' said Garret.

'I won't sleep a wink,' said Mrs Garret.

'None of us will,' said Garret, 'but there's nothing else for it.'

Eliza Garret felt about as wretched as she had ever felt in her whole life. She had been taught to say her prayers every night, and most nights she said the same old thing without even thinking. That night, Eliza thought hard about what she'd done to Jake and asked the good Lord to protect him and to forgive her part in his disappearance. It did not make her guilt go away.

Eliza tossed and turned, until she decided to confess to her father first thing in the morning. She would accept any punishment, if only Jake could be found safe and well.

21

Jake fell into the deep sleep of the exhausted, but, as dawn broke, his mind filled with dreams, just like the ones he'd dreamed at the Native settlement.

Jake saw clearly, in his mind's eye, the lie of the land. He saw the shapes of the indigo mountains on the eastern horizon. He saw the meandering curves of the river below the high plateau where the Natives made their home, and he saw the height of the cliff. He saw the shape of the treeline and the angle of the sun. He even saw the configuration and colours of the rocks on the path Yellow Cloud's horse had taken when he'd been slung over its back. He saw thunder and lightning in his dream, against a milky sky the colour of moonstones, and he thought of White Thunder.

He was thinking of her when he began to wake. He rolled over in his blanket, forgetting that he was in the forest and not in Eliza's bed at the forge house. Then he woke up enough to remember where he was, and, despite the cold, despite the fact that the sun was only just rising, and despite his little fire going out in the night, Jake smiled.

He suddenly knew what he was looking for. All the clues were in his dreams, and all he had to do was find them and follow them. For the first time since he'd left McKenzie's Prospect, Jake honestly believed that he'd find the Natives and that all his questions would be answered.

He kicked over his fire and picked up the ham and bread. He dropped them again suddenly when he saw they were covered in insects. It looked like various rodents had eaten most of the meat in the night, and the bread was soggy and dirty. It was at least twelve hours since Jake had eaten and he was more than ready for a hearty breakfast.

He wrapped his blanket around his shoulders, stuffed his clothes into the front of his jacket and checked the other things were in his pockets. Jake knew he needed to travel west, so he stood with his back to the rising sun. He also needed to head for high ground, since the Native settlement stood on a plateau above the valley.

Jake wove a path between the trees. The ground underfoot was mulchy and slippery with fallen leaves and dew, and a low, heavy mist cut down on visibility. His initial confidence began to subside, and Jake found himself humming his mother's favourite hymn as he picked his way through the forest. More than once, he found himself ankle-deep in squelchy mud, and, several times, he tripped over exposed tree roots. He had been walking for half an hour and had covered only a few hundred yards, but he had already scraped his legs and scratched the back of his right hand falling into something that felt like a bramble, and he was cross and fearful.

Jake clutched at saplings as he clambered up a slippery slope. He had almost reached the top with its mass of rhododendrons, when his left foot slipped out from under him. He thrust out a hand for something to cling to, but found nothing but fresh air.

Suddenly, he was falling.

This wasn't the same as slipping and sliding up the slope; this was actually falling through the air at an alarming speed.

The ground had crumbled under Jake's feet and, surrounded by trees and mist, he had not realized that he was on the edge of a precipice. He finally grabbed a tree trunk. The top of the slope fell away abruptly to a depth of ten or twelve yards, and Jake's feet were dangling out over the escarpment. He could see a broad, slow-moving river that glinted in the warm, grey morning light, and the low, boulder-covered bank that trickled down to it. It would have been a beautiful scene, like an illustration in an H. N. Matchstruck novel, if it wasn't for the fact that Jake was clinging on for dear life.

He kicked his feet, trying to find some solid ground to stand on. He quickly realized that was impossible, and he twisted his body so that his right side was against the slope. Unable to hang on any longer, he let go of the tree, turning his body so that he could grasp at handholds on the way down. When he realized there were none, he turned so that his face was out of the wet mud and leaned his back into the slope.

Jake's feet finally hit firm ground, his knees buckled, and he stopped. He was covered in filth, and his blanket had been pulled from his shoulders and was clinging to the muddy slope. He checked that he hadn't hurt himself and then pulled at the muddy blanket, which came down on top of him. Once he had untangled himself, Jake folded the dirty blanket and tucked it into a hollow at the bottom of the slope where he'd be able to find it again.

The rising sun still hung low, casting flashing white lights across the water in front of him. A twist of curling smoke rose grey-white against the blue and orange sky away to Jake's right. Then he noticed a small camp with a fire and a tent. Keeping close to the slope, Jake tiptoed towards the tent, and, before long, he caught a whiff of coffee and frying bacon on the air.

Jake's mouth watered, but the campfire must belong to someone, and the tent, the coffee and the bacon too. He didn't like to steal, but, from the size of the pan and the strong smell in the air, Jake was sure that a lot of bacon was being cooked. Surely one slice wouldn't be missed.

Jake could see no one in the camp, and the tent was only big enough for two people at most. Beyond the fire and the tent, he caught sight of a mule tethered to a shrub that was growing at an angle out of the slope.

As well as the fire with its skillet of bacon and coffee pot, there was a tin bowl full of gently steaming soapy water and a shaving brush and mirror. A pair of good boots stood a few yards away, the sort that came all the way up to the knee, like a military man might wear.

With no one in sight, Jake edged out around the boulder that separated him from the camp and took the two paces to the fire. He snatched up a piece of bacon and tossed it from hand to hand so it wouldn't burn his fingers.

'Can I help you, young man?' asked a voice, just as Jake was stuffing the bacon into his mouth.

Jake forgot for a moment that it wasn't a good idea to breathe and swallow at the same time. He found himself choking on the bacon and turned to the stranger, pointing to his reddening face.

'Righto,' said the stranger, turning Jake squarely by the shoulders and pounding him on his back. The half-chewed piece of bacon leapt out of Jake's throat and landed in the fire, where it spat and sizzled as it burned to a crisp.

'Thank you,' said Jake, gasping for air.

'For the bacon?' asked the stranger. 'Or for saving your life? I should think you might thank me for both, given the circumstances. Heh?'

Then the stranger thrust out his hand and said, 'Masefield Haskell, geologist and surveyor, at your service.'

Jake looked down at his hands and then showed them to Masefield Haskell. Haskell looked at them and said, 'You might wipe them down your . . .' By this time, the boy and the man were both looking up and down Jake's very dirty body. It seemed to have no clean spot on it where he might wipe his hands before shaking with Mr Haskell.

'Perhaps not,' said Mr Haskell.

Jake wasn't sure what a surveyor was, but he knew that a geologist was a kind of scientist who knew about rocks and things. Jake thought that if he'd ever had to guess what a geologist looked like, it would be nothing like Mr Masefield Haskell. Mr Haskell looked more like a poet to Jake.

Haskell was wearing trousers, rolled up, and his feet were bare. His jacket matched his trousers, and they were sewn from very fine, checked cloth that looked like the sort of tweed that came from England

and was sold in the smartest shops in St Louis. He was also wearing a linen shirt that was as clean as a new pin. His hair was thick and curly and flopped about all over his head. He had a pair of field glasses hanging around his neck, the likes of which Jake had never seen before, and he was holding a sketchbook and pencil. His face still had patches of soap on it where he had not finished shaving.

'I'll tell you what,' said Masefield Haskell, 'you can wash in my water when I've finished shaving. Then you can tell me all about whatever it is, over breakfast.'

Listening to Haskell, Jake thought that the cloth for his suit wasn't the only thing that had come from England. He'd only heard an English accent once before, but he was sure it was the same.

Mr Haskell threw the sketchbook and pencil down and took up his razor. 'You might wonder what a geologist is doing out west,' he said as he shaved. 'Working for Nathan McKenzie, out of McKenzie's Prospect, that's what. Heard of him?'

Jake nodded, but Haskell was too preoccupied with shaving his neck and had his head tipped back.

'He thinks there's gold in those hills, or gems anyway,' he went on, gesturing with the blade of his razor, which glinted alarmingly in the sun. 'Of course, in a year or two, we'll all be working on the land survey for the railroad companies. Imagine it, from sea to shining sea, or ocean anyway, from north to south and back again, a railroad, the envy of the world.'

'Not birds then?' asked Jake when Haskell was at work on his moustache and couldn't talk lest he cut himself. Jake was looking at the sketchbook where it had fallen open at a page with a rather good drawing of a bird of prey.

'Hobby,' said Haskell, flicking the soap off his razor. 'I saw a goshawk,' he said, waving the razor again as the last of the soap slid off it. 'I had to draw it before it flew away and hence halfway through a shave.'

He wiped his face and pointed at the bowl of water to indicate that it was Jake's turn. Once they were both cleaned up, they sat on either side of the skillet of bacon and ate from it. Haskell fed himself from a penknife, having given Jake his fork. 'Your turn,' he said. 'What brings you out into this wild country?'

So, while they ate, Jake told Haskell his story. He watched the scientist's face for signs of wonder, but it remained mostly calm, although he was clearly fascinated by the dragons. Jake was confident about calling them dragons, and he didn't stint on his descriptions of the beasts. He even showed Haskell his tattoo, to verify his story, even though Haskell seemed to believe him.

'That settles it,' said Haskell when the skillet was empty and the story told. 'We'll have to get you back to McKenzie's Prospect at once.'

It was the last thing that Jake wanted to hear, and he tried to protest, but Haskell was adamant.

'The blacksmith and his wife . . . the Garrets, is it?' he asked. 'It sounds like they've had enough sadness in their lives without you running away and causing more upset.'

'But –' began Jake.

'But me no buts,' said Haskell, 'as my mother, Mrs Haskell, would say to me when I was a boy your age. But me no buts. I wouldn't be a responsible sort of chap if I didn't take you home. It's far too dangerous for a young man out alone in these parts, especially if your stories are to be believed. They are very, very good stories.'

'Thank you,' said Jake.

'For taking you home or for the compliment?' asked Haskell. 'I should think you might thank me for both.'

'I should think I might not,' said Jake.

Haskell glared at Jake and the boy sat heavily back down, apparently resigned to his fate.

'Have you any luggage?' asked Haskell. 'No, I suppose not.'

'I stuffed Mrs Garret's blanket . . .' Jake began to say, and then thought better of it. He might need it if he got a chance to slip away from the geologist.

'What?' asked Haskell.

'No,' said Jake. 'No luggage.'

'Give me a hand to load Jenny then, and we'll be on our way,' said Haskell. Jake assumed that the mule must be called Jenny.

Jake helped to load the mule after Haskell stowed his belongings in various canvas bags, which all bore his initials in dark, glossy ink: M. N. H.

When Jenny was ready to go, Haskell straightened his jacket, pulled on a hat and kicked over the traces of the fire on which he'd cooked the bacon. While he was busy, Jake planted a good hard slap on Jenny's rump, and the mule began to trot merrily off along the river path. Jake darted back along the slope and ducked behind the boulders, collecting Mrs Garret's blanket on the way. Two minutes later, Jenny brayed, and Haskell looked up to see that she was a hundred yards away and picking up speed. Waving his hat at her, Haskell chased after the mule, without a second thought for the boy. He eventually caught up with the mule, but, by the time he'd led her back to the campsite, Jake was long gone.

Haskell looked for the boy for a few minutes and then sighed at his unhappy fate. Jenny was loaded, however, so he made the decision to go back to McKenzie's Prospect. The boy needed help, and Haskell would make sure that he got it.

22

As usual, Pius Garret awoke before the first cock crowed. The sun would soon be up, and the blacksmith wanted to waste no time hunting for Jake.

As he and his wife walked around McKenzie's Prospect, Garret decided they'd need a much broader search to find the boy. If Jake had got lost in the forest, he could be in all kinds of trouble.

Everything that mattered in McKenzie's Prospect happened at the mercantile. That's where people went when they needed help with just about anything. So the Garrets packed the children off to school and headed straight there. When they stepped into the emporium, they were surprised to find Nathan McKenzie standing at the counter with his sister and Horace, and Trapper Watkiss. Lem stood quietly behind the counter.

'We've been waiting for you, Garret,' said Nathan McKenzie.

'Waiting for us?' asked Mrs Garret. 'Why?'

'Horace has got something to say,' said McKenzie,

shoving Horace forward. The boy's head was down and he was clutching his hands together so that his knuckles were white.

'Speak up,' said his father. 'It takes a man to 'fess up and take the beating he deserves.'

Mrs Garret put a gentle hand on Horace's arm.

'If you could help us find Jacob, we'd be very grateful,' she said. '"To err is human", Horace, "to forgive divine", and I plan to do a whole lot of forgiving today.'

'He thought there were dragons,' said Horace. 'He was as mad as a ferret, and he made me as mad as a bear.'

'Just tell what happened,' said Horace's aunt.

'I didn't like getting beat at the spelling bee by a boy who wasn't in his right mind, so I got mad and I beat him back,' said Horace.

'There's nothing wrong with Jake's mind,' said Mrs Garret. 'He just lost his family.'

'We thought he was crazy,' said Horace.

'Where did you beat him?' asked Garret.

'On Drum Hill, down by the rhododendrons,' said Horace.

'Tell me exactly what happened,' said Garret. Horace was an inch taller than Garret and thirty pounds heavier, but that didn't stop him being afraid of the blacksmith. He soon told the whole story.

'Which is where Trapper comes in,' said McKenzie

as soon as Horace had finished. 'He can track the boy and find him in no time flat.'

'Know them forests like the back of my hand,' said Trapper Watkiss, keen to go after the boy.

'I'll go with you,' said Garret.

'You'll slow me down,' said Trapper. 'Besides, I need a clear head to follow a trail. I don't want the worry of a civilian getting in my way.'

McKenzie put his hand on Garret's shoulder, partly to reassure him, but mostly to control him.

'He'll have the boy home by tomorrow, just you wait and see,' he said. Garret looked hard at McKenzie's hand on his shoulder, and McKenzie took it away.

'Mind that you find him safe, and mind that you do it quickly,' said Garret.

23

Eliza Garret took her brothers to school. She explained to Miss Ballantine that Jake was missing and that she was helping with the search. Even though she'd promised her parents she'd look after the twins and stay out of trouble, Eliza was determined to help find Jake. It was her fault that he was missing, and she was eaten up inside with guilt. Her belly felt odd and she hadn't slept, thinking about telling her father what she had done. She couldn't concentrate properly, and she knew that the only cure for her troubles was to find Jake and bring him home. She'd never forgive herself if she didn't.

'That's three of my class missing today,' said Miss Ballantine.

'Three?' asked Eliza.

'Jake and you,' said Miss Ballantine, 'and there's no sign of Horace McKenzie.'

Eliza wondered if Horace had come down with an attack of guilt too. If he felt anything like as miserable as she did, it served him right.

Walking away from the schoolhouse, Eliza reasoned that, if Horace had felt guilty, he might have talked to his father. Since she had no other leads, she made her way back to the mercantile in search of Horace McKenzie. She kept to the backs of the buildings and then crept around the side of the mercantile to see what she could see.

There was a small window behind the counter, and, standing on her tiptoes, Eliza could just peek over the window ledge and into the store. She couldn't hear what anyone was saying, but it was clear that Horace had told his story and that a search party was being sent out to look for Jake.

Eliza made a dash for home. She wondered how much Horace had said and whether he had shared her part in Jake's disappearance. After all, if she hadn't told him about Jake's fever and about the dragons, Horace might not have thought him a madman in the first place.

Would the guilt never end?

Eliza arrived at the forge house, and took an extra sweater and her father's second-best winter jacket out of the blanket box. She also found the hat that Daniel had worn when he'd gone shooting. She tied her braids on top of her head and pushed the hat down over them. Then she took her gun from behind her bed and shoved a box of home-made cartridges in her pocket. Lastly, she took a pencil and paper out of her mother's dresser and wrote a note. She placed it on her pillow, where her mother would find it, but hoped that it would be long after she was gone.

Eliza took the road west from the forge. She thought that Jake might head back to the forest, back to the Natives. Besides, east of McKenzie's Prospect was mostly farmland, and Jake didn't know anyone from the rural community.

Eliza reached the edge of town and tucked herself behind the Murphys' outhouse. She had a good view of the road from there. Less than half an hour later, Eliza watched Trapper Watkiss and his mule walk down the road. Trapper looked this way and that, sniffed the air and held a finger up every so often. Eliza assumed that it all had something to do with tracking Jake. She waited for Trapper to reach the nearest bend in the path and then began to follow him.

24

Jake's first thought when he'd got rid of Mr Haskell was to get away as quickly as possible. His second thought was to wonder how to scale the steep incline that he'd ridden down on his back an hour earlier.

It was impossible.

The sun was rising in a clear blue sky, and Jake believed that a sunny day would follow. It didn't make the slope any less steep or any less slippery. Just as there had been no handholds on the way down, Jake could see none to help him climb back up.

He was sure he needed to travel uphill and even surer that he needed to travel through the forest. All he could do was follow the base of the slope and hope that the gradient would ease off enough for him to be able to walk up the slope, back to where he wanted to be.

The river was wide and the views across it were good. It wouldn't be difficult for someone to spot Jake from quite a distance, and he didn't want to be spotted at all. As he hurried along, Jake kept his eyes glued to the slope. Once or twice, he used a tree or rock to try to climb it, but his attempts ended in failure. By mid-morning, he was becoming increasingly fearful that he would be seen. The sun was high, and the mist had drifted away.

Then Jake had to avoid a boulder that appeared to be leaning against the bottom of the slope. The rock had a deep notch in the side nearest to him, and the top was flat. Somehow, it didn't look as if it belonged there, and there was no other boulder so large or so close to the slope.

Jake stood next to the boulder. He wrapped his blanket around his shoulders so that he didn't have to carry it and put the toe of his right foot into the notch in the rock. It was a perfect fit. He then hoisted himself on to the top of the rock, which was exactly the right size for two adult feet to stand on, facing to the left. Looking up the slope, he saw a clump of grass just above his head. He reached his hand up and realized that the grass was growing out of a scooped hole in the side of the slope. His hand fitted easily inside, and he guessed that he could use it as a foothold if he could just find another somewhere in between.

Jake scanned the area around waist-level and found a tree root that had woven its way out of the soil and then turned and entered the earth again. It looked just like the rung of a ladder. Jake put his toe on it and lifted himself up, placing his hand firmly in the handhold. Then he began to see more places he could use to pull himself up. He would never have seen them from the ground, but, the more he climbed, the more he saw a way up the slope.

When Jake reached the top, he spread the blanket on the ground and flopped on to it. The climb had only been thirty feet, but it was a long way to fall without a safety net. Reaching the top had been hard work, but if Jake had been as tall as an adult man he would have found the ladder much less tricky.

Then it dawned on Jake that the ladder might not be natural, that the spacing was too regular, too convenient. Perhaps the ladder had been built on purpose. He felt a thrill of excitement. Perhaps Natives had built the path; perhaps he was finally on the right track.

He began to work his way uphill. Everything seemed familiar. He recognized the patterns of light as the sun penetrated the heavy canopy and fell in patches on the forest floor. The shapes of the moss on the north sides of the trees seemed familiar. The height and spacing of the shrubs and undergrowth that Jake worked his way through were not new to him, and, when they came into view, the lumps and bumps of the horizon were just as he remembered them.

There were sounds too. Jake didn't jump at the

calls of birds or at the barks and howls of the dogs that inhabited the forest. He had no trouble estimating distances and directions, and he managed to avoid the larger animals. Besides, he wasn't afraid of them any more.

Then Jake's left arm began to itch. He was still wearing both jackets, and, as well as his arm itching, he was getting hot. He wound the blanket from around his shoulders and folded it carefully before putting it on the ground to sit on. Then he took off Garret's jacket. He wasn't sure about scratching his arm, so he gently rubbed it through the other jacket. Then Jake carefully took off that jacket, right sleeve first. There was no sign of anything unusual, and he breathed a sigh of relief. It took him another three minutes to pluck up the courage to take the left sleeve off.

Jake had seen his arm for the first time during the fight with Horace and his cronies, and he'd shown his tattoo to Mr Haskell only a few hours ago. That first time he'd seen it, Jake had looked at the tattoo in fear and wonder, not sure whether to be impressed or horrified. When he'd taken Daniel's jacket off to try to stitch the sleeve back on, he'd wrapped the blanket around his body to keep warm and had concentrated so hard that he hadn't really looked at the tattoo.

Jake idly picked at the string stitches at the top of

the sleeve and then stopped. He didn't want to have to sew the sleeve back on again because sewing wasn't as easy as it looked. Finally, he closed his eyes tight and pulled the jacket off in one swift motion. Then he placed his right hand gently over his left wrist to see if he could feel anything.

The skin felt smooth, almost glossy in places, and puckered in others. It was not sore or swollen, but the itching hadn't gone away. After another minute, feeling faintly ridiculous, Jake opened one eye and looked at his arm. The tattoo wove around his wrist and up his arm, past the elbow and right up to his shoulder. The fine outlines were beautifully etched into his flesh around the areas of new skin where he had been burned. The wing that spread the length of his arm appeared to be made up of dozens of interlocking shapes, like great feathers. *No, more like flames*, Jake thought.

Some of the skin was yellow and some pink, but it was all healthy. The tattoo was pristine. Jake touched the edge of one of the flames with the tip of his forefinger. Where the tattoo had been inked in place, the skin was totally smooth, even though he'd expected to feel a groove in the skin or a raised area. All of the texture was in the areas of his skin that had been burned. There were no blisters or scabs, no rashes and no signs of broken skin or infection.

Jake looked more closely at the skin and then placed his hand firmly around his forearm, over the wing shapes. He detected the faintest throb and a little heat, which might account for the itching, but nothing else. He decided that he really was much more impressed by his tattoo than horrified.

He thought about looking at his hand too, but changed his mind. It was sore, and he was sure it was still healing.

Satisfied that all was well, Jake prepared for the next stage of his journey. First, he shook out the blanket. Most of the mud had dried, and a lot of it flew off easily. So, by the time he was finished, it was fairly clean. Daniel's old jacket, despite the badly sewn sleeve, was the cleanest, so Jake folded it into the blanket to protect it and put Garret's jacket back on. He tucked the blanket under his arm and continued walking uphill, through the forest, always aware of the pictures of the landmarks in his head.

An hour later, Jake could see the horizon and a long escarpment leading towards it. He could not judge the distance, but he knew that he was heading for a spot on that ridge. The itch in his arm had grown more persistent, and Jake rubbed it, as he had done every ten minutes since he'd stopped.

Some time after that, Jake removed his jacket. The view hadn't changed much, but his arm had begun to itch more and more, and he brought it up to his face to get another good look at his tattoo. It looked as if the skin up and down his arm was changing colour where the wing was drawn. The tattooed lines seemed darker and even more intense, and the skin tingled and throbbed.

Jake was convinced that he was heading in the right direction. Everything looked exactly the way it had in his dream, and even his tattoo was reassuring him that he was on the right course.

25

Eliza watched Trapper Watkiss, not very carefully or very closely, but she certainly watched him.

To begin with, she wasn't very impressed with his progress. He was simply wandering about, apparently directionless, and taking a long time over it.

She was bored, and she still felt guilty, and she wanted Trapper and his mule to go faster, so Eliza decided to get closer to the old man and actually watch him. There were plenty of rocks and trees to hide behind, and shadows too. After an hour, before they'd even covered the first mile, Eliza suddenly realized that the old man never once looked back.

Trapper Watkiss knew, as every good tracker knows, that once an area has been covered it's better not to turn back. Turning back causes confusion. Trapper Watkiss also knew that the most important thing was to get the lay of the land, to judge how firm the ground is, how deep any tracks might be and how long they might remain on the surface. Trapper Watkiss spent the first hour looking for signs of anyone on the road, and then he spent more time working out how long ago each person might have passed by. He knew how tall and heavy the boy was and that his prints would disappear long before a big man's prints would be lost. He also knew that Jake's prints would remain long after dog prints were gone.

Scents were another thing. Scent didn't last long in the air, but a deer could pick it up. It could see a man and stay calm, but if it caught one whiff of a man you'd never know it had been there.

Every living thing on earth had to eat, sleep and relieve itself. Every time a man or a beast did any of those things, he left a scent behind. If a man or beast relieved himself, he left his scent for a *long* time. It was easy to learn the differences between the smells of a dog, a deer, a bear or a man, but to tell the scent of one man from another was a gift, especially if the smell was old.

Two or three miles further on, Trapper Watkiss stopped for several minutes, examining a narrow path that veered off into the woods. Eliza drew up close behind him, keeping to the shadows, and was surprised to hear the old man talking.

'Got him good and proper, Sarah old girl,' he said.

Eliza jumped, convinced for a moment that Trapper had spoken her name.

'You and me, old thing,' said Watkiss, patting his mule's flanks. 'We'll track this pup down in no time.'

Eliza breathed a sigh of relief and then giggled. She could hardly believe that the gruff, scary old man would talk to his animals. Some people spoke to their dogs or horses, and Eliza believed that old ladies sometimes kept cats for their laps rather than for catching mice. Even so, she thought it very peculiar that Trapper would name his mule, let alone talk to it.

'We're sure of his footfalls now,' said Trapper, 'but this is the thing!'

Eliza watched as the old man leaned over and sniffed the edge of the path, between two trees that stood close together.

'Let's see how often he makes water, shall we, Sarah?' Watkiss asked the mule. 'A young man answered a call of nature right here and no mistake.'

Eliza clapped her hand over her mouth so as not to laugh out loud. Not only was Trapper talking to a mule, he was talking to her about Jake's outhouse habits. Eliza very nearly choked on the back of her hand trying to stifle her glee. When this was all over, she would have a splendid story to tell. Then the very idea that she would tell stories about Trapper made Eliza suddenly very serious. The last time she'd told stories it had ended badly, and she promised herself that she wouldn't start any more gossip.

Once they were on the woodland path, Trapper

began to move much faster. The earth was wetter and held tracks for longer, and Trapper had no problem following Jake's progress.

'Like a rampaging bull,' Trapper told Sarah as he examined a broken twig close to the path. 'That boy might as well have left a trail of little stones, like what's-'is-name from Hansel and Gretel. That boy'll be Hansel to us forever more.'

Eliza was surprised that Trapper knew a children's fairy story, but was quite entranced by his conversation with the mule, so she stayed close. Being near the old man also made her feel safe. She had been in the forest with her father, for shooting practice, but not too far or for too long.

'Once upon a time, a man could expect tracking to be a real task, old girl,' said Trapper. 'I knew men who could walk ten miles a day and never leave a twig snapped nor a leaf stirred, nor a single footprint neither. I've followed men who could move without a sound, and, if they had to make a sound, could imitate any bird or beast. I knew a man who could sound like a fast-running stream or a broad, slow river. French he was, fur trapper in British Columbia. Those were the days, when men was men. Woodland runners we called them. Worked with them too, when I had half the years I've got now.'

Eliza had no idea that Trapper Watkiss had lived

such an interesting pioneering life. His stories might not be true, of course, but who on earth would lie to a mule?

'Called me "Rousse", the Frenchies, on account of the red beard,' he went on. 'Only found out what it meant when the Injuns started calling me "Flame Beard". Frenchies laughed at that for months. Different you see, old girl, but then the same.'

In the middle of the afternoon, Trapper Watkiss stopped at the place where Jake had made camp the night before. It wasn't difficult to find the fire or the ham bone that had been dragged about and dumped by the last rodent to get a bite of meat off it. Trapper tethered Sarah and walked around the site, tutting. Eliza waited three or four yards away, relying on a tree for cover.

After he'd kicked over the fire, Trapper rummaged about in one of Sarah's leather panniers.

'The boy lit a fire and ate too. Now, let's see how he got that fire going without a tinderbox.' Trapper began to dig in the scorched earth. 'Cleared a patch. Stones might've been better.'

The old man thrust his hand into the mulch of dead leaves and then looked into the canopy above. The setting sun was casting light through it at an angle.

'Without a tinderbox, where'd he find good kindling? Clever.'

Eliza watched.

'Well, would you credit it?' Trapper asked Sarah. He held something between his thumb and forefinger, and waggled it at the mule. Then Trapper brought his hand up to his face, as if he was struggling to focus on the thing he held there.

'Ha! Cotton rags!' he said. 'The boy tore the shirt off his back for a bit of tinder. The fire'd keep him warmer than a rag shirt. Ain't that right, old girl?'

Eliza couldn't imagine Jake tearing up a borrowed shirt, and then she thought about how carefully her mother had bandaged his left hand to keep his wound clean and free of infection. A cold chill ran down Eliza's back, and she had visions of Jake suffering from the terrible fever. If he came down with it, in the woods, he'd surely die.

Trapper used a little spade to bury the ham bone, so he wouldn't be plagued by rodents. Then he made another circuit of the campsite, sniffing around the trees. He stopped when he found what he was looking for.

'That's him making water again,' he said, 'as sure as I'm standing here.'

Trapper took some more things out of Sarah's panniers and carried them over to the fallen tree, where he sat down.

'Even found a place he could sit without getting the damp and cold in his trousers,' he said. 'It's good enough for me, old girl.' He set down his things and put his tinderbox in his pocket while he collected wood for a fire.

Eliza had thought that Trapper Watkiss would keep tracking until dusk, but he clearly had other ideas. He lit a fire, unpacked some food from his panniers and settled down to supper. She couldn't quite believe the number of things that he could pack into a pannier. There was cooking equipment, various knives, an axe, spare clothes and his bedroll. She saw a towel too and hoped there might be soap, but, if there was, she never saw it. Eliza wished she was half so well-equipped, and she began to think that the night would stretch on forever without enough to eat, and with nothing at all to do. Besides, she'd been watching and listening to Trapper for long enough to know that he was very good at what he did. She only hoped that she could stay hidden until after he'd found Jake.

26

Jake kept walking for as long as the sun was up. He'd thought he'd get to the Native settlement sooner, but the long view in front of him never seemed to change, and he wasn't sure exactly where on the escarpment he was heading for.

By dusk, Jake was tired and his arm was throbbing constantly. He had become used to the sensation as the day wore on. It was almost reassuring, but it was also wearying, and he needed to rest. He hadn't eaten since the bacon at breakfast. He'd been very hungry and had taken as much as he thought was polite, but that was eight or ten hours ago, and he'd been on his feet all day. He needed to rest, and he needed food.

Jake found a small deadfall of trees, covered in ferns, and planned to make camp. The ground was harder at the higher altitudes, and the mulch of leaves was drier than the muddy undergrowth lower down. Some of the plants and trees also looked familiar. He began to recognize some of the leafy plants that the Natives ate in the settlement. Then he spotted berries on a shrub and recognized them too. He began to gather food, including tubers from below the ground to bake in the bottom of his fire, and he took water from a wellspring. Then he lit a fire, using the knife and a stone and the dry leaves as tinder. He was soon comfortable.

Jake wondered where he'd learned the skills to forage for food and how he knew to smell the plants to make sure they were edible before he cooked them. He banked up his fire so that it would be safe to burn overnight and wrapped himself in layers of clothes and the blanket. Then he settled down to get a good night's sleep.

Jake awoke with a start in the night. He was up and had the knife in his hand before he even realized that he was awake, his heart pounding in his chest. He heard a snuffling sound and cast his eyes around. The fire was low and the darkness was all-consuming. He could see almost nothing. Something flashed between the trees, three or four yards away. Then there were two more flashes. Whatever was out there had eyes. There was another grunt and a snuffle and then the flashing again. Then reflected firelight glinted off large white teeth.

Jake's fear subsided as he watched the bear lumbering past his campsite. If the fire had gone out, he might not have been so lucky. When he could no longer hear the snuffling growl and the shuffling gait, Jake built his fire up so that it would burn until dawn and settled back down in his blanket.

27

Eliza was not nearly as comfortable as Trapper Watkiss. She decided discomfort was a fair punishment for being so mean about Jake.

She ate an apple and the cornbread that nobody had finished the day before, and she began to wonder why she didn't like Jake, except for the fact that everybody else did. She decided that she owed it to herself to give him another chance.

Eliza had chosen a spot behind a tree, hidden from Trapper Watkiss's view, but, at the same time, she could take a peek at him whenever she needed reassurance. She also liked watching him and listening to him talking to Sarah.

It crossed Eliza's mind that she hadn't heard the old man talking for some time, and she wondered if he was asleep. She listened for a moment, and, hearing nothing, she looked around the tree trunk. Trapper Watkiss wasn't sitting by the fire. Eliza cast her eyes around the campsite. He wasn't looking after Sarah, who was munching at the lower branches of one of the trees, and he wasn't sorting his pile of luggage.

Eliza was suddenly worried. She stood up and, with most of her body still behind the tree, took another good look. She was a couple of feet taller standing, so she had a better view of the campsite.

Trapper Watkiss wasn't there.

Eliza thought about walking into the camp, but didn't dare. Then she thought about making an animal noise to see if he would appear, but she wasn't sure how good her impersonations of animals were.

After two or three minutes of looking into the camp, which was getting darker all the time, Eliza decided on a course of action. She bent down to look for something she could throw. Maybe, if she made Sarah bray, she could catch Watkiss's attention, wherever he was. The stone had to be big enough to make the mule cry out, but small enough not to hurt her.

Eliza felt around until she found the perfect stone, and then she stood up. She gasped and almost fell straight back down again.

There was the smell to begin with, the sudden sharp tang of dirt and stale food grease, and the sour smell of old sweat. Then there was the grubby red beard and that breath. Eliza took a step backwards, almost tripping over, and she very nearly screamed.

'What d'you think you're doing, boy?' growled Trapper Watkiss.

Eliza looked down and saw that Trapper had a knife in his hand, which made her gasp again. The old man had been amusing from a distance, but she'd always been afraid of him, and now she was as terrified as she'd ever been.

'You gonna tell me why you been following me all day, boy?' asked Trapper, bringing his knife hand up to Eliza's chest.

'I . . . I . . .' she began, in a voice that sounded ridiculously high, even for a girl. She swallowed. Her clothes weren't meant as a disguise, but if Trapper Watkiss thought she was a boy maybe it would be simpler if she went along with it.

Trapper looked right into her eyes and must have been able to see her fear. Surely the old man wouldn't actually kill her?

'You fixing to rob me?' he asked.

'I'm . . . I'm a f-friend of J-Jacob Polson,' Eliza finally managed to stammer out. 'I only wanted to h-help.'

'Don't know you, do I?' asked Trapper, peering at Eliza.

'No,' said Eliza. 'I'm new. I'm E-Elijah.' She was beginning to calm down, and Trapper didn't look like he wanted to kill anyone, not unless he had to.

'Should give you a good hiding, boy, and run you back home.'

Eliza looked crestfallen.

'Ain't got the time. Got that clever boy to find, so you'll be travelling alongside me. Slow me down, just once, and I'll leave you out here to fend for yourself.'

'And when we find him?' asked Eliza.

'When we find him, you'd better make him do as I say,' said Trapper Watkiss. 'Or I'll do for you.'

Eliza didn't have to think twice about Trapper Watkiss's threat.

The knife still in his hand, he gestured towards the campfire, indicating that Eliza should join him. She shrugged, picked up her things and stepped into the clearing. She figured she had no choice in the matter.

28

The Garrets didn't find out that Eliza had left McKenzie's Prospect until David and Michael arrived home from school that afternoon.

Pius Garret was in the forge. He hadn't planned to work until Jake was found, but, when it was clear that Trapper Watkiss was going to search for Jake on his own, he had gone back to his anvil. He'd been toiling like ten men all afternoon. He felt totally powerless to help, so he threw all his energy into his work.

Elizabeth Garret had spent most of the day tending the garden, collecting fruit and vegetables and preparing them for storage in the root cellar. Like her husband, all she could do was keep busy while she waited for Jake's return.

David and Michael walked into the kitchen where their mother poured them tall beakers of milk and put a plate of cookies on the kitchen table.

'Where's Eliza?' she asked.

'Here,' said David, spitting crumbs. Michael laughed, causing him to spit crumbs too.

'Here, where?' asked their mother, cutting through their mirth.

'Here, at home, here,' said Michael.

'She didn't come in with you,' said Mrs Garret.

'Because she was already here,' said David.

'Boys,' said Mrs Garret in her serious voice, 'would you please tell me where Eliza is?'

'Why should we know where Eliza is?' asked Michael.

The colour started to drain from Mrs Garret's face.

'Eliza was supposed to be at school with you today,' she said. 'She was supposed to walk you home afterwards.'

'She wasn't,' said Michael.

'She didn't,' added David.

'Pius!' called Mrs Garret, her face as white as a sheet. She began to clear the kitchen table, and the boys wondered why she was taking away their half-finished milk and, worse still, the plate of cookies.

'Pius!' called Mrs Garret again, scurrying into the forge.

Pius Garret had heard his wife the first time. He'd dropped the horseshoe into the quenching bucket and was taking off his leather apron when she surged into the forge like a whirlwind.

'Slow down, Elizabeth,' said Pius, 'and tell me all about it.'

'Eliza's gone!' said Mrs Garret.

Pius took his wife in his arms and made her tell him everything she knew, which wasn't much.

'Go see if she took anything with her,' said Garret as soon as Elizabeth was a little calmer.

Mrs Garret only needed a minute or two in the loft to know what had happened to Eliza. First, she checked the blanket box, and then she saw the note on her daughter's pillow.

She read it quickly and took it downstairs for Pius to see.

Dear Mama, Papa and boys,

Please don't hate me. It's my fault that Jake left. I told stories about him and the dragons, and set Horace after him. I wish I hadn't done it. I want to make things right, so I've gone to help Trapper Watkiss find him. I'll bring Jake back, I promise.

Love from,
Eliza

'Oh no!' said Pius. 'I don't think I could bear to lose another child.'

'You must get a search party together,' said Mrs

Garret. 'There's a couple of hours before it gets dark. McKenzie will help you . . . He must help you.'

'Promise you'll stay with the boys,' said Pius, jumping up and pulling on his jacket. He got his hat and took the gun off its hook by the door.

'Can't we help?' asked David and Michael.

'Yes,' said their mother. 'You can help by staying home safe with me and doing your chores and your homework and eating all your supper.'

'That's not helping,' said Michael.

'That's all the helping you get to do,' said their father.

With that, Pius Garret went in search of his daughter and of the boy who had begun to plug the hole in his heart caused by the death of his eldest son.

29

On his way to Main Street, Pius Garret knocked on the doors of his neighbours' and friends' homes and soon had a dozen volunteers for a search party.

Lem Sykes was locking up the mercantile as Garret entered.

'Where's Mr McKenzie, Lem?' asked Garret.

Lem noticed the pack on Garret's shoulders and the gun in his hand.

'I'm to meet him in the saloon,' said Lem. 'Can I help you with something, Mr Garret?'

'I'm getting up a search party to help Trapper Watkiss find Jake and Eliza,' said Garret. 'Don't you worry, Lem, I'll find your uncle.'

'You wouldn't know where he is, would you?' someone asked from behind Garret.

'Mr Haskell,' said Lem. 'Uncle Nathan's headed over to the saloon.'

'Not to worry,' said Mr Haskell. 'Your business seems more urgent than mine, although "sooner is better" as my mother, Mrs Haskell, would say to me. "Sooner is better."'

'Why don't we all walk over?' asked Garret.

'You might want to bring all those wonderfully equipped men with you,' said Mr Haskell. 'I'm sure Mr McKenzie will send out a search party when he hears what I have to say.'

On the walk over to the saloon, Haskell told Garret all about his encounter with Jake.

'I'm sorry it took me so long to get back to town,' said Masefield Haskell. 'I stopped when I saw that goshawk the second time. It took a quarter of an hour to make a sketch. Sadly, it took me a further two hours to find Jenny at her biscuit-root.'

'Was Jake hurt?' asked Garret.

'It was hard to tell until he washed in my shaving water. I noticed his left hand was wrapped up, but he hightailed it away from me without any trouble.'

'Good. Thank you,' said Garret.

'Are you thanking me for letting him wash or for noticing his condition?' asked Haskell. 'I should think you might thank me for both, given the circumstances.'

Garret thanked him again.

Nathan McKenzie was none too pleased to see Garret walk into the saloon with Haskell. He paid the surveyor to dig for gem-mining sites, not to mix with the townsfolk. Nathan McKenzie's only ambition was to be the rich founder of a prosperous town and to control the interests in it. To that end, he wanted to buy his way out of the Hudson's Bay Company, and that took money.

For years, Trapper Watkiss had made claims about gold and gems in the mountains and how the 'Injuns' kept the good stuff for themselves. Nathan McKenzie had always thought that Trapper Watkiss was partly right, even if he was mostly crazy. That's where Haskell came in, with his fancy geology degree from a fancy English university. Nathan McKenzie believed that Trapper Watkiss and Professor Haskell would make him rich.

Then Horace had told his father Jake's dragon stories, and he'd got a swift clip around the ear for his efforts. Nathan couldn't let a story like that ruin his chances by driving away the prospectors that would bring new wealth and prosperity to his town. There were riches to be had in the forests and mountains where the Natives lived, and Jake might be able to lead Trapper right to them.

When he'd sat down on his stool in the saloon that afternoon, the last thing Nathan McKenzie had wanted or expected to see was Haskell and Garret standing together with a search party right behind them.

'That's all very well,' Nathan McKenzie said when

Garret and Haskell had finished talking, 'but soon there'll be no light to see by.'

'There are enough of us to shed a good amount of torchlight,' said Garret, 'and with Eliza gone too, I need to do something useful.'

'Trapper's probably halfway back to town by now,' said McKenzie, 'and, if Professor Haskell's right, the boy walked around in circles. That bend in the river isn't half a dozen miles from here.'

'Thank you,' said Haskell, 'but I'm not a professor.'

Garret and McKenzie looked at the geologist. No one cared whether he was a professor or not.

'Mr Haskell has been in the forest for the better part of a week,' said McKenzie. 'I'm sure he needs a good supper and a soft mattress before you drag him back out there.'

'It's no trouble,' said Mr Haskell, but McKenzie was determined not to let him intercede.

'I'm paying your wages, Mr Haskell, and I say you've worked hard enough. You'll get further leaving at dawn than fighting your way through the dusk.'

Some of the men in the search party murmured their agreement. If the boy had survived one night in the forest, he'd manage a second. Garret was clearly outnumbered.

'Have a drink with me, blacksmith,' said McKenzie, clapping Garret on the shoulder in his oddly grasping way.

'I won't, thank you all the same,' said Garret, and he turned to leave.

The men lined up to take a drink at the founder's expense, and Nathan McKenzie called out over their heads, 'Back here before the cock crows. You too, Professor.'

30

Jake struck camp early, after a good night's sleep, despite being woken by a bear. The sun had not yet penetrated the canopy and was barely visible through the mist that shrouded the forest.

Filled with confidence, he packed his belongings and set out on his uphill climb. He could hardly see a hand in front of his face, but he had faith in the tingle in his arm, and he was no longer fearful of the forest.

Jake travelled for two or three hours, and the mist still did not lift. Then he felt a twinge of recognition. He retraced his steps and stopped. Everything suddenly felt terribly familiar. Jake had been here before. He had been here only an hour or two ago.

He put down his bundle and pulled up his left sleeve. He placed his right hand around his left wrist and felt for the throb, the heat, the itch that had plagued him. The sensation that he had begun to take for granted had subsided. There was a tingle, but not the itch or throb that he had grown used to.

Jake shook involuntarily, but he wasn't cold. He had been so sure about finding the dragons and about the Natives being the key to finding his family. He'd been so sure he was on the right track that he hadn't given his route another thought, and now his confidence was deserting him.

Jake touched a tree. There was a prominent knot in the bark beneath his hand and a small broken-off branch protruding. He blinked and looked at the trunk. He stepped back suddenly and brought his hand up to his mouth as if to stifle a scream. The knots and swirls in the branch looked like staring eyes and a gaping mouth, and the broken branch looked like a gnarled, stubby nose. The tree appeared to be laughing at Jake, and he didn't like it at all.

Jake was determined to take a different path, until he realized that there was only one path into this patch of forest and only one path out. The undergrowth was dense and thorny, and it came up to his waist. He had to go back along the path he had walked before. He had become so intent on finding his way that he forgot to breathe, and everything began to swim before his eyes. The mist swirled and collected into the shapes of laughing faces, of horses and rag dolls, and of dragons. Jake could see sinuous tails and cavernous flaring nostrils exhaling bright streams of smoke.

All the trees suddenly wore mocking, leering

faces, frightening Jake almost out of his wits. He felt a throb, but it was not his arm. Jake's entire body throbbed with the pounding heartbeat that he thought could be heard for miles. He clutched the blanket tightly to his chest and ran as fast as he could, as far as he could from the mist-creatures. He didn't care that his legs were getting scratched by the undergrowth. He didn't care that he had no idea where he was heading. He just wanted to get away.

When he could run no further, Jake slumped down at the mossy base of an old tree and held his head in his hands. Gasping for breath, his head between his knees, he began to feel a little better. He told himself that his mind had been playing tricks and that he'd been too confident for his own good.

Then Jake heard something. He heard a low, rumbling sound, like a sonorous, continuous roar. He thought it might be the dragons from his mind's eye. He thought it might be the sound of dozens, even hundreds, of pairs of great scaled wings, beating an overlapping rhythm, shifting and bending the air into strange sound-waves.

He felt an urge to follow it, but, at the same time, dreaded coming face to face with the creatures of his imagination. He felt a tug, but he didn't know whether to run towards or away from it. He had followed the throb and itch in his arm, certain that they would lead him to his destination, but they had not.

Jake took a deep breath and ran as hard as the uneven forest floor would allow, through the trees and the mist, locking his eyes on a spot in the distance. He didn't follow the sound, and yet it seemed to surround him, thrumming and booming, becoming louder and more continuous. There was no rhythm to it any more; it was simply a fathomless roar.

Jake came suddenly out into the light. The trees of the forest were behind and below him, and he felt like he had climbed to the roof of the world. All he could see was a great open space with the bright blue sky as much below him as it was above him. The rainbow that arced into the endless distance seemed to terminate in a cloud several hundred feet below where he stood.

Everything was shades of blue and white and grey. The glistening grey rocks caught every spark of light that fell on their slick surfaces. The frothing white water crashed off those rocks, travelling at unimaginable speeds. Then it fell into the glistening turquoise expanse of the lagoon below. The endless drifts of mist that cut across everything were a milky, bluish white, backlit and coloured by the endless purple edge of the rainbow. Jake thought that if the booming roar of millions of gallons of water could be a colour, then that colour would also be blue.

The thundering water had cut a gorge in the rock so vast and so deep that Jake felt as if he was standing on top of the world. He looked out into the sky, his senses filled with the sound and sight and smell of water. He could even feel it on his skin in the spray of millions of droplets in the fresh mist. It quickly drenched his hair and face and clothes, and even the bandage on his hand.

Jake opened his mouth. He felt a myriad tiny pinpricks as droplets of water, flung through the air, struck the flesh of his tongue. The water tasted blue and white, and as clean and fresh as it could be.

Jake didn't need to think. He knew, as if he had known it always, that this waterfall was the key to finding the Native settlement. He was on his way.

Suddenly, a hand fell heavily on the drenched shoulder of Garret's jacket, bringing Jake back down to earth.

He heard a voice and felt warm breath very close to his ear.

31

'Injuns call it Smoke Mountain,' said Trapper Watkiss, right in Jake's ear.

The force of falling water was so great that it filled all the senses, including making the ground vibrate underfoot, and Trapper didn't know if Jake had heard him. He held firmly on to the boy's shoulder, turned him and walked him slowly away from the edge of the cataract.

By the time the mist had cleared from his eyes, and Jake had returned to his senses, he was standing a couple of hundred yards from the waterfall, face to face with Pa Watkiss's strange brother.

'Injuns call it Smoke Mountain,' repeated Trapper. Jake stared at the old man, but he said nothing.

Trapper backed away from Jake, afraid that he might have spooked him, and looked around for the boy Elijah.

Eliza was struggling up the steep path behind Trapper when she spotted Jake. She ducked her head so that he couldn't see her face and stayed behind Trapper.

'It's all right, lad,' said Trapper. 'Your folks were worried. Sent me to track you down.'

Jake still said nothing. He brought a hand up to the long lock of hair that clung, wetly, to his forehead and swept it away.

Trapper Watkiss gestured wildly at Eliza while keeping his eyes firmly on his prize.

'Brought your old wheel-horse for company. Elijah,' he said. Jake frowned and tried to see who was standing behind the old man.

'Elijah?' asked Jake.

'Your old buddy,' said Watkiss, still waving at Eliza. There was a long silence, and then Eliza stepped up beside Trapper. She looked at Jake from under the brim of Daniel's old hat.

'ELIZA!' Jake blurted with surprise.

'I'm sorry, Jake,' she said. 'Please forgive me.'

There was another long pause while Eliza waited for Jake's reaction.

'*Elijah?*' asked Jake, beginning to smile.

'He thought I was a boy,' said Eliza, pointing at Trapper. She pulled off her hat and scratched her head, letting her braids fall down. Her hair was ratty and had made her head hot, and she had a line of sweat across her forehead from her hat. Then she hurried to Jake's side, as if it was two against one.

'Darn and blast it all to blue blazes,' said Trapper Watkiss, locating a hump in the grass to sit on to wear out his anger at being tricked by the slip of a girl.

Eliza took Jake's hand and led him over to Sarah. She began to unpack one of the panniers, pulling out Trapper's threadbare linen towel and giving it to Jake.

'Take off that wet jacket,' she said. 'I'm sure there's something dry in here. It might not be clean, though.'

'Why are you doing this?' asked Jake, towelling his hair.

'Because I was wrong to treat you badly and be jealous,' said Eliza. 'I know Mama and Papa have got enough love to go around, even if you aren't my actual brother, and I said some awful things about you to Horace and the others.'

Jake blushed, thrust the towel back into Eliza's hands and walked away. She had told Horace and the others about his dreams. She had told them that he was crazy, that he believed in dragons. All the old humiliations welled up in Jake, and he vowed that he wouldn't go back to McKenzie's Prospect with Eliza. Besides, he was so close to finding the Natives and the dragons, and, once he found them, he would learn what had happened to his own family.

Jake slumped down on the grass near Trapper and began to take his jacket off. It was clinging to him, making him colder instead of warmer. The blanket was wet, and he hoped that Daniel's old jacket might still be dry.

Eliza messed about with Sarah's panniers, playing for time, deciding what to say to Jake. Then she started walking towards him.

'Papa treated you the same as Dan. I should've known he'd treat anyone like that, but I was sad and jealous. You were sick, and it wasn't your fault. I should never have told Horace that you believed you'd seen a dragon . . . It was stupid.'

'Dragons,' said Trapper Watkiss, almost to himself. 'Saw one mesself a long time ago. Not much chance of seeing one again, I s'pose.'

'What did you say?' asked Eliza.

Jake rubbed his damp arms with the linen towel, blotting the sheen of cold water from his tattoo.

'Did you say something about dragons, old man?' asked Eliza.

Trapper looked past Eliza at Jake. 'What do you think that is, then?' he asked.

'What?' asked Eliza, turning to look at Jake.

Trapper Watkiss got up and walked towards the boy. He took hold of Jake's arm and held it at an angle for Eliza to see.

'What do you think this is?'

'I don't know,' she said, looking from Jake's arm to his face. 'What is that?'

'Sign of the Thunderbird. That's what the Natives call 'em,' said Trapper Watkiss. 'They all have the tattoos and the burns. Fire-breathing beasts mark their own.'

'I don't understand,' said Jake.

'You belong to the dragon-kind now, boy,' said Trapper. 'They've marked you.'

'That can't be true,' said Eliza, her fingers hovering close to Jake's tattoo.

Trapper Watkiss let Jake's arm fall and pushed his right hand up his own sleeve, feeling around for something. He found it and pulled his hand out, bringing with it a leather thong threaded with smooth, glassy green and blue beads, some cloudy, some clear, but all quite beautiful.

'They've all got one of those,' said Trapper, nodding towards Jake's tattoo. Then he pulled at the thong, so the beads rattled together, and said, 'And they've all got one of these.'

'Take it off,' said Jake, the colour rising in his cheeks, his voice urgent.

'Won't,' said Trapper, tucking the bracelet back under his cuff.

'How could you possibly know that dragons exist?' asked Eliza.

'Seen 'em,' said Trapper Watkiss. 'Got stuck on the mountain, years ago. Got sick, and the Injuns found me. I lived with them in a settlement, high up on a plateau, overlooking a valley. Never did find it again.'

'They had teepees painted with dragons,' said Jake. 'They had a corral for their horses and another for the dragons. They fed them fish from beautiful baskets –'

'Dragons on them baskets too,' said Trapper Watkiss.

'They covered their burns with tattoos,' Jake said, 'drawn on by the medicine man.'

'Seen it done,' said Trapper. 'Never caught the fancy of a dragon, though, not like you.'

'Show me the bracelet again,' said Jake.

'Only if you know where we can get more like it,' said Trapper Watkiss. 'They're real gems. Old man McKenzie wants prospectors mining for gems. I'm supposed to help.'

'You told me Mr McKenzie sent you to find Jake and bring him home,' said Eliza.

'Mr McKenzie sent me to follow Jake to the Native settlement,' said Trapper Watkiss.

What Mr McKenzie wanted didn't matter to Jake, and he wasn't afraid of Trapper Watkiss. Jake had got this far on his own, but the old man might hold the key to getting him where he really needed to be.

'Give me the bracelet,' said Jake, 'and I'll try to find the settlement.'

32

When Trapper Watkiss dropped the bead bracelet into Jake's left hand, the boy felt a bolt of lightning searing through his left arm. He clutched his left wrist and gasped. Then his arm warmed and tingled with a strange sensation of lightness and of power. Jake felt that, if he only tried, he could lift a boulder as big as a house.

He looked at the bead bracelet. Then he took hold of it by one end, in his left hand, and he raised his arm in the air. A smile spread across his face, and he started to swing the beads in small fast circles. He kept his arm straight and steady, and rotated at the wrist, just as he had seen Yellow Cloud do in his dreams. He guessed the bracelet would act as a whistle when air was pushed through the beads, piping a high clean note into the air.

Nothing happened.

Jake let his arm drop. He had wanted nothing more than to reach the Native settlement, to find out what had happened the night the wagon train caught fire, and to prove that dragons were real. He was terrified, but he was also desperate to look a dragon deep in the eyes and see what dwelt in its mind.

'We should go home,' said Eliza, breaking through Jake's thoughts.

'You can go,' he replied. 'I'm going to meet a dragon.'

'Don't be ridiculous,' said Eliza. 'Can't you see the old man's mad? And if I know anything it's that Nathan McKenzie is not to be trusted.'

'That's the pot calling the kettle black,' said Jake. He was cross and felt foolish that swinging the bracelet had not worked for him as it had for Yellow Cloud.

'I'm going back,' said Eliza, striding deliberately away.

'Foolish girl! You'll lose yourself and I'll be blamed,' shouted Trapper Watkiss, stomping off after Eliza. When he reached Sarah, he called out again, 'When I catch up to you, I'll tan your hide, girl or not.'

He pulled a pack out of Sarah's pannier and disappeared into the forest. When he caught up with Eliza, she was examining a curved notch, carved into a tree trunk.

'Is this one of yours?' she asked as Trapper Watkiss appeared.

'Yes,' said Trapper. 'Is your gun loaded?' he asked, pointing at it. 'And do you know how to use it?'

'Yes, and yes again,' said Eliza.

'Good,' said Trapper. 'Look for straight trees a foot across, and, when you find one, look for my mark.'

'Like Gretel,' said Eliza, 'I can find my way home.'

Trapper Watkiss looked at Eliza, and she smiled at him. He was a little surprised to realize that he was smiling back. He stopped, not wanting to make a habit of it.

'Take this,' said Trapper. 'Emergency pack. Food mostly, tinderbox, knife.'

Eliza took the pack. 'At least this way, Mama and Papa will know Jake's safe,' she said. 'You will bring him back, won't you?'

'Yes,' said Trapper, 'after I've done Mr McKenzie's work. He's good to me, and I won't let him down.'

Eliza thought she might kiss the old man on the cheek. She looked at his hairy face, remembered his smell and decided against it.

'Thanks,' she said, and walked away through the undergrowth, looking at the trees as she went.

Trapper Watkiss was making his way back to Jake when he heard a sound. The waterfall continued to rumble away in the background and could be heard a mile away, but this was different. He picked up the pace and was soon back at Sarah's side. He reached for the Hawken rifle he kept strapped to her back and made sure it was loaded and ready to shoot.

33

Jake stood alone on a stretch of open ground between the treeline and the waterfall a couple of hundred yards away. All he could hear was the rolling throb of the water cascading into the lagoon.

He held the bead bracelet in the palm of his left hand and looked at it. He had been sure it was like the one that Yellow Cloud had used to whistle at the dragons, except the beads were green or blue, and there was not a single red gem among them.

Jake shoved the bracelet into his pocket. The way things were going, with no sign of the Natives' settlement, he was sure he'd have to spend another night in the open. He bundled Trapper Watkiss's towel into the blanket with everything else and shrugged on the drier jacket. He was just about ready to leave when he heard a rhythmic slap, like the sound a wagon canopy made when it came loose and flapped back against itself. Then Jake felt the tingle in his arm, his head was suddenly hot, and he felt sick to his stomach.

He thought he caught a glimpse of something rising beyond the waterfall. He blinked and stared, and the slapping noise grew louder, until it was clearly audible over the water. Jake could hardly believe his eyes when the head and neck of the beast appeared through a mist of water droplets. The huge head was quickly followed by the great body and wings of the dragon, and Jake could clearly see Yellow Cloud riding the extraordinary beast.

He finally knew that what he'd seen when the wagon train was attacked was real. He had seen a dragon and they weren't just mythical creatures in storybooks. Jake was in awe of the animal before him, but he was also horrified, for he believed that a dragon had set fire to the wagon train and tried to kill his parents and his sister.

He had spun the bracelet because he wanted to meet a dragon, to prove he was telling the truth. Now, face to face with one, he wanted nothing more than to destroy it. The mists began to clear and Jake saw Yellow Cloud gesturing to him.

From behind, he heard Trapper's voice.

'Don't you dare move.'

Jake didn't know whether the old man was talking to him or to the Native. The dragon in front of him hovered as if on a thermal wind, and the spell was broken. Jake turned to find Trapper Watkiss levelling his rifle at the dragon's head. There was nothing for it. He rolled his body heavily into Trapper's side, knocking the old man off balance and bowling him over into the long grass. The rifle fired, a sharp crack against the thrum of the falling water. Jake heard the slow beat of the dragon's wings. Then he jumped to his feet as the echo of the gunshot rolled through the air. The dragon lifted its wings and dropped at a steep angle to the ground, flattening the long grass in its downdraught.

Trapper, terrified, scrambled to his feet. For twenty years, he'd been telling anyone who would listen that dragons existed, but no one had ever believed him. He'd never truly expected to see a dragon, and, now that he was staring one in the face, he could think of nothing better to do than run away. Trapper grabbed Sarah's rope, and he and the mule were soon lost beyond the treeline.

Jake, however, was glued to the spot as the dragon landed in a billowing gust of wind. It nestled close to the ground and folded its wings, and Jake breathed an almighty gulp of air. Then he looked into the dragon's huge red eyes. He didn't notice Yellow Cloud slide off the dragon's back and walk over to him, until he was standing beside him.

'Come,' said Yellow Cloud. 'Do not be afraid.'

'I don't think I am afraid,' said Jake, pulling his gaze away from the dragon's eyes and looking at the Native, 'but how do I know I can trust you?'

Yellow Cloud looked steadily at Jake. 'You cannot know,' he said, 'but you have my word.'

Jake scowled hard at the Native for a long moment, still unsure of the man. He was only sure that if he didn't go with Yellow Cloud there was no hope of having his questions answered. So, finally, Jake allowed the Native to help him on to the dragon's neck. He pushed his hands into the ruff of feathers and hung on. He noticed, for the first time, that dragons really were like birds, with ruffs and frills of coloured feathers around their feet, the backs of their necks and their wing joints. They were the same feathers that adorned the jewels and headdresses that the Nimi'ipuu people wore.

Yellow Cloud climbed up behind Jake, and soon they were being swept up into the air. The ground fell away beneath them, and Jake remembered the feeling of flight, despite being unconscious when he'd flown to McKenzie's Prospect a few short weeks before.

Jake felt entirely at home on the creature's back, soaring out over the forest. Yellow Cloud had his arms around Jake's sides, holding him in place, and his hands were woven into the feathers on the dragon's neck. The dragon's back rose and arched with the beat of its wings, and Jake imagined that it felt just like riding in a boat on the ocean.

The crack of another rifle shot split the air, and

Jake felt the dragon beneath him suddenly dip closer to the tree canopy. He looked down at the spread of trees and the swirling mists that surrounded them. Eliza and Trapper Watkiss were standing in a clearing below them. Eliza was transfixed, staring between the trees at the dragon, a look of terror in her eyes.

Trapper tried to reload his gun. Then a second huge looming shadow fell across the clearing. Jake looked to left and right and realized that his dragon was flanked by two others, both with riders on their backs. One of the dragons dropped suddenly and landed heavily in the broad branches of a tree, which lurched under the weight of the great beast.

Eliza fell to the ground as the dragon descended, partly because of the force of its downdraught and partly because her legs had turned to jelly and would no longer hold her up.

Trapper Watkiss stopped trying to load his rifle and drew the Colt revolver that he wore in a belt, below the bulge of his belly.

The Native, who had been riding the dragon that had landed in the tree, slid down the trunk into the clearing and ran over to where Eliza was lying on the ground.

Trapper Watkiss turned his gun on the Native and then pointed it back at the dragon that was hovering above him. He didn't know who was in more danger:

Eliza or himself. He turned back and forth twice more.

'Drop the gun, Mr Watkiss,' Jake shouted. 'Don't shoot.'

Trapper levelled the gun at the Native again and then turned back to aim at Jake's dragon. He pulled the trigger, and there was a bright, hard sound in the air as the bullet sailed past its head.

Jake's ride dropped and began to fold its wings. He couldn't believe the beast was going to land in the tiny clearing. Then the muscles in the dragon's back extended, and two huge claws stretched out below the curve of its chest. The dragon picked Trapper Watkiss up by the shoulders of his jacket and lifted him into the canopy. Jake gasped in surprise, and then smiled. *Serves the old man right*, he thought.

Trapper got off another shot, but the jerk of his shoulder as the dragon grasped his jacket sent it high and wide, and the distinct crack of the bullet was drowned out by the harsh, bellowing shriek that escaped Trapper's mouth as he was hoisted away.

34

Eliza lay in the arms of the Native who had come to her aid. He was reassuring her gently, in his broken English, that everything would be all right.

At first, she could not speak; she could only stare up at the dragon, her mouth half-open. She let out an odd squeak when the dragon sitting high in the branches above her adjusted its position, making the tree dip and sway. The Native lifted his left arm and swung his bracelet in the air. It emitted a high-pitched whistle that cut across the sound of the waterfall and the rumbling, slow beat of the dragon's wings.

The beast that was perched in the tree elongated its neck as if to listen. Then, spreading its wings carefully, it lifted itself out of the tree. The tree trunk, like some great spring, flew back and oscillated before settling to its original position.

Trapper Watkiss hung limply from the dragon's strong claws, but Jake didn't think he was hurt. He had merely fainted and dropped his revolver. Jake felt the flex of the beast's shoulders once more, as it lifted them all up into the sky and away.

They flew back to the grassland at the edge of the forest, where the dragon hovered low to the ground. When it let go of Trapper Watkiss, the man's body was already half-sitting on the ground, and he fell sideways on to his left shoulder in the long grass. The dragon landed to a cacophony of manic braying from Trapper's mule, Sarah, who trotted around and around on the spot. Yellow Cloud dismounted from the dragon, and Jake jumped down, his brow furrowed with anger that had been building up ever since he had first laid eyes on Yellow Cloud. Before he even realized what he was doing, Jake put his head down and lunged at Yellow Cloud, driving him over on to his back.

'Was it you?' Jake shouted at Yellow Cloud, standing over him. 'Was it that?' he asked, pointing to the dragon sitting on the ground behind him. 'Did you kill them?'

Yellow Cloud said nothing.

'Where is my family?' Jake yelled again. 'You know what happened to them, and I'm not leaving until you tell me.'

Yellow Cloud got up and shook the dust from his trousers. He glared at Jake, but said nothing. He strode over to Trapper Watkiss, still lying unconscious, and checked that the old man was breathing.

'He is unhurt,' Yellow Cloud said. Then he laid the man on his side in a more comfortable position.

Hearing a rustling sound coming from the treeline, Yellow Cloud and Jake watched as the other Native walked into the open, carrying Eliza. She was pale but conscious, her arms wrapped tightly around the neck of her saviour.

His dragon, which was a darker, richer blue than Yellow Cloud's beast, landed on the ground close by, flattening the tall grass. The third dragon, paler and yellower, sat a dozen yards away, its rider still on its back, as if performing some sort of sentry duty.

Sarah began braying again, and Eliza instantly became more alert, craning her neck to see the little mule.

'Poor Sarah,' she said.

The Native who was carrying her put Eliza down beside Jake and walked over to the mule, clucking and tutting at it gently. He was soon able to take hold of the rope around her neck and ease her head down into his arms. He stroked the mule's nose and whispered in its ear. Then he set Sarah loose from her tether and patted her gently on the rump. The mule trotted off beyond the treeline and was quickly lost to view.

'We must leave,' said Yellow Cloud.

'Not until you answer me,' said Jake.

'And please not on those,' said Eliza, nodding

towards the dragons. Her face was losing its colour again, and her knuckles showed white as she clung to Jake's arm, standing half-behind him.

'We will talk at the settlement. Bear Paw will take your friend,' said Yellow Cloud, nodding towards the Native who had carried Eliza out of the clearing. 'There is much to say.'

'I've got plenty to say too,' said Jake, trying to sound brave.

Bear Paw bent over Trapper Watkiss, and, with a graceful rock of his knees and back, he lifted the old man over his shoulder. He put an arm around Trapper to make sure that he didn't fall and carried him over to the third dragon. He arranged the old man over the beast's neck, and the rider lashed him in place with a plaited leather cord.

Eliza shook as Bear Paw returned, but Jake gave her a reassuring nod. He'd known, all along, that he wouldn't get any answers unless they returned to the settlement. Bear Paw lifted her and sat her gently on his dragon's neck, placing her hands close together in the feathers in front of her.

'If I close my eyes, I can bear it,' she said to no one in particular, and she took another deep breath.

Despite his anger, Jake needed no persuading to mount Yellow Cloud's dragon. He perched on the beast's neck, instinctively holding the feathers in the correct manner. Yellow Cloud climbed up behind

Jake, and the three dragons spread their leathery, scaled wings. Then they lifted their great bodies effortlessly into the sky. Yellow Cloud took the lead, and the dragon carrying Trapper Watkiss brought up the rear.

Jake had a mesmerizing view. As they rose, he could see the treeline and the extent of the forest beyond as it staggered down the long rise that formed the backbone of the mountain ridge. The waterfall boomed as it cascaded away below and Jake felt a fine mist on his skin as the dragons followed its crest.

Once they had cleared the waterfall, they flew into a broad, blue sky, high above a great grey blanket of clouds and fog beneath them. Jake remembered Trapper's voice, telling him that the Natives called this Smoke Mountain, and the clouds beneath them looked exactly like a great bank of swirling grey smoke. Jake knew that he would never have been able to navigate through the fog at ground level, just as Trapper Watkiss had never been able to find the Native settlement again once he had left it. Viewed from above, it was obvious why it was so well hidden. The fog was no impediment to the Natives. They could navigate the clear skies above the great grey pall from the backs of their Thunderbird dragons.

35

A broad ridge of land broke through the cloud below them, spreading into a wide green plateau. From above, the collection of teepees reminded Jake of the circle his mother's skirts had made, spread across the water of the river. The people milling around looked like tiny figures whittled from glossy twigs.

The dragons circled the settlement twice and Jake got an idea of the size of the place. There must be almost as many dwellings here as there were in McKenzie's Prospect. Everyone seemed to be doing some sort of work: cooking at fires, preparing skins, tending to the animals.

As they made a second broad circle, lower than the first, Jake saw the corral of dragons. He had been so in awe of the beasts that he realized he hadn't taken a proper look at them.

The dragons came in various sizes and colours. Some were the size of a horse, and Jake supposed they must be infants. Others, like the one he was riding, were two or three times the size of an

Appaloosa, and one or two were perhaps double that size. They ranged in colour from a buttery yellow, to green, and on through the spectrum to dark, rich blues. Their iridescent scales were not uniform, but came in vivid, irregular patches, much like the random colour patterns of the Appaloosas.

The beast Jake sat astride was a rich, deep, emerald green, with brighter, lighter patches, the colour of fresh young grass.

As the dragon swept around, Jake could see more details. The Natives wore feathers in their hair and clothes, and in the jewellery that adorned their necks, wrists and ankles. They wore soft buckskin trousers and shoes, and their long hair was glossy and dark and impossibly straight.

The settlement was calm and industrious, and Jake felt reassured by the familiarity of everything. He needed to remain cautious until he found out what had happened to his family, but he was also reminded of how well he had been cared for the last time he was there. As they landed, Jake looked for White Thunder and Tall Elk.

Trapper Watkiss was still unconscious when his dragon landed, and he was carried to a teepee in the same manner that he had been carried to his transport, slung over the shoulder of one of the Natives.

Eliza's dragon landed last. Bear Paw dismounted

and then lifted Eliza down. She looked pale, her shoulders were hunched and her hands trembled. Bear Paw put her down gently, but Eliza's legs buckled beneath her and she vomited copiously at the man's feet. He lifted her swiftly back into his arms and strode towards the teepee that Trapper Watkiss had been taken to.

'Hey, where are you going with her?' Jake asked. He knew that Eliza was scared, so he followed Bear Paw. He trusted the Natives to care for Eliza as they had for him, but he wanted to make sure she was all right.

The teepee was cool and comfortable, with matting, blankets and skins on the floor. Bear Paw lowered Eliza to the ground, as Jake poured her some water from the provisions laid out on a low table.

'Are you all right?' Jake asked her.

'Sick,' said Eliza, 'and scared.'

'You're perfectly safe with me,' said Jake. 'The Natives could have let me die, and they brought me here instead. They looked after me as well as they could and I'll make sure they look after you too.'

Eliza shook her head and said, 'It's silly, I know.'

'It isn't silly to be scared,' said Jake.

'But it's crazy to think that dragons exist,' she said, unable to meet his gaze.

'This time, we both saw them with our own eyes,'

said Jake, smiling at the girl, who looked very small dressed in her borrowed clothes.

'How will we get back?' asked Eliza. 'How will they find us?'

'The Natives know how to find McKenzie's Prospect, even if the people there don't know how to find this settlement,' said Jake. 'Don't worry.'

'What about him?' asked Eliza, gesturing towards Trapper Watkiss. 'He tried to shoot them.'

'He won't do it again,' said Jake. 'They won't let him, and, besides, he dropped his guns.'

Whether Trapper had heard them talking or whether he was coming around naturally, the old man groaned and rolled over. Eliza jumped slightly, but she relaxed again when she realized that he wasn't quite ready to wake up, after all.

The fold of skin that covered the opening of the teepee had been dropped into place after they had entered. Jake pulled it back to look outside.

'What are they doing?' asked Eliza.

'I don't know,' said Jake.

Yellow Cloud, Bear Paw and the other rider were standing in a little group too far away for Jake to be able to hear them, and, even if he could, he wouldn't have been able to understand the language.

Beyond them, Yellow Cloud's dragon was back in the corral, being fed fish from a large basket. Jake was watching intently when something cut across his field of view. When he looked again, the dragon was rubbing necks with one of the brighter, yellower beasts. He dropped the skin back into place, deciding to stay in the teepee until someone was ready to speak to them.

They didn't have long to wait. Soon, the flap was drawn back, and White Thunder walked in, smiling and carrying a basket of fruit.

'Hello,' said Jake, not sure if he should acknowledge their previous meeting.

'Hello,' said White Thunder. There was silence for a moment, and then Eliza thrust her hand out at the girl.

'Sorry,' said Jake. 'White Thunder, this is Eliza.'

'Are you quite well?' asked White Thunder, looking at Eliza with concern.

'Fine,' said Eliza. 'Just . . . I'm all right really. I just never flew before.'

White Thunder laughed.

'Truly, it is not natural for us to do this,' she said. Then her forehead wrinkled and she looked serious again. 'Eat,' she said, putting the basket of fruit on the table. 'I cannot stay.'

As she turned to leave, Jake took hold of her wrist gently.

'What will they do?' he asked her.

'I do not know,' said White Thunder. 'They must

speak to Tall Elk and then Chief Half Moon. This has not happened before.'

'What hasn't happened before?' asked Jake, as White Thunder lifted the door flap.

She shrugged.

'The Thunderbirds have not chosen a stranger before,' she said, and then she left before Jake could ask her what she meant.

36

They'd been in the teepee for half an hour, and Eliza had begun to feel very much better. They'd drunk some water and eaten some fruit, and were sitting talking quietly when Trapper Watkiss groaned and kicked and turned over. Then his head reared up between them, and Eliza yelped.

'Where am I?' he asked. 'What's going on? Where's them Injuns?'

'We're at the settlement,' said Eliza without thinking. Suddenly, Trapper staggered to his feet, looking around warily and checking his gun holster. He shook his belt, angry not to find a weapon there.

'The Injun settlement?' he asked, wide-eyed.

'Yes,' said Eliza, 'but you're perfectly safe. That's what Jake says anyway.'

'What does a boy know?' asked Trapper, turning this way and that, looking for a way out of the teepee.

He almost tripped, dashing across the floor, and pulled back a small section of the door flap. After a moment, he thrust the flap back into place and turned again. Then he reached into his left boot. Jake watched in horror as the old man pulled a long, slender knife from his boot, a hunting knife with a bone handle.

Trapper Watkiss held the knife in his right hand, away from his body, and turned around again to get his bearings. Jake thought he was going to hurt someone, he looked so fierce and determined.

'Dangerous beggars, if you ask me,' said Trapper. 'You'd best stay close, if you want to get out of here alive.'

'We're not going anywhere,' said Jake. 'These people could help me find out what happened to my family, and you said you always wanted to find a dragon.'

'Well, now I've found one,' said Trapper, 'and all I know is I need to get back to McKenzie's Prospect and get up a posse with Mr McKenzie. We'll run the Injuns out of here, and they can take their Thunder-birds with them.'

'Don't,' said Jake, raising his hands to show Trapper that he couldn't hurt him, and, what's more, he didn't want to get hurt.

'Out of my way, boy,' said Trapper, jerking the knife in Jake's direction. 'You'll follow me, if you know what's best for you.'

Trapper lunged for the skin of the teepee opposite the door flap and cut a long, vertical slit in it. He stuck his head out for a moment. Then he drew it back in again, holding the two sides of the slit together to keep it closed.

'Horses, dead ahead,' said Trapper, turning to Jake and Eliza. His eyes were big and glazed, and his mouth was set in a determined line. A moment later, he stepped through the slit in the teepee.

'What do we do?' asked Eliza.

'You stay here,' said Jake, 'while I go after the old fool and make sure he doesn't get into any trouble. He spent twenty years trying to find his way here, and I don't like his chances of finding his way out again.'

Jake disappeared through the slit after Trapper Watkiss. He squatted down close to the teepee. Then, when his eyes had adjusted to the bright sunshine, he spotted Trapper a dozen yards away behind a woodpile.

Eliza didn't want to stay in the teepee alone, mostly because she didn't want to have to explain to a stranger why Trapper Watkiss had cut a slit in one of their beautiful tents. She cursed under her breath and paced up and down for a few seconds. Then she too stepped through the slit in the teepee, into bright afternoon sunlight.

Jake was still behind the teepee. He stood and took Eliza's arm, pointing at Trapper Watkiss, who was trying to make it to the horse corral without being noticed. Jake and Eliza made a short dash to the woodpile that Trapper had been hiding behind a few minutes before.

'Mr Watkiss,' called Jake in a harsh whisper. 'Mr Watkiss.' Jake called the old man a word that his mother had told him never to use. Then the two of them watched in horror.

A young Native man was crossing from one of the teepees to the horses' corral with a basket of grain under his arm. Trapper was only a few yards away when the Native waved at the old man. Then he looked at Trapper Watkiss again and realized that he was a stranger.

Trapper realized that he had been spotted, and he panicked. He lunged at the young man with his knife, and the Native didn't even have time to cry out. He dropped his basket, spilling the grain, which made a sound like heavy rain as it fell in an arcing stream to the baked earth.

As the Native writhed on the ground in agony, blood seeping from a wound in his belly, Trapper cut the bracelet from the man's wrist and shoved it in his pocket.

'Mr Watkiss!' Jake yelled again, horrified. 'Mr Watkiss!'

Trapper Watkiss was already running when Jake cried out. He turned at the sound of his name, veering off course and stumbling.

Before he knew it, Trapper Watkiss was half-running

and half-staggering right into a cauldron of the sticky tree sap they called pitch. It had been set over a firepit and was draining off into a deep dish to one side.

In his haste, Trapper Watkiss kicked over the dish, and the pitch began to spill out in an oozing, tarry stream. The Native woman who had collected the new baskets, ready for them to be lined with pitch to make them waterproof, dropped her load. She brought her hands up to her face and shrieked as two or three of her baskets fell into the fire and caught alight. As Trapper cleared the area and ran on, fire began to spread from the smouldering baskets to the pitch. The flammable liquid burned fast and easily, and the flames were soon shoulder-high.

The horses in their corral began to neigh and whinny, and Natives appeared from all over the settlement to beat the flames with blankets. Despite their efforts, the fire soon spread to the nearest teepee. The skins burned with an acrid smell, and smoke began to drift across the plateau.

With the Natives busy fighting the fire, Jake grabbed Eliza's hand and dashed across the settlement, towards Trapper Watkiss and the horses. First, he wanted to check on the Native that Trapper had stabbed. Jake feared that the man must be dead, but he had to be sure. He felt responsible for everything, and the idea terrified him.

Then he heard the noise. It sent a shudder through

his body and made his hands break out in a clammy sweat. His veins were filled with ice. He squeezed Eliza's hand. He made himself keep running towards Trapper Watkiss, despite the fact that he felt like he was crawling along, his feet sinking into some sort of quicksand.

Then the sound came again, a rumbling shriek, the tone too low for a man or even the horses, but it was still a visceral scream.

Jake heard the splintering of planks and the thudding of fence-posts being uprooted and dropped on the dusty earth. They had been running towards the horse corral, but the sound was coming from Jake's right, from beyond the smoking blaze of the teepee, whose skeleton was now visible as the skins had burned away almost entirely.

The dragon, freed from the enclosure, sped towards Trapper Watkiss without seeming to touch the ground, and yet it was not flying. It was so elegantly in control of its movement that it seemed to glide effortlessly towards the old man. Then it reared, bringing its head up high, showing the magnificent claws of its forelegs and the extended length of its chest. Its head was twenty feet off the ground in this rampant position, and it loomed over Trapper. Its red eyes gleamed, and its maw was open, showing bright white teeth. Its nostrils were large and round as if it was breathing hard.

Events unfolded before Jake's eyes, as if in slow motion, and yet too fast for him to reach Trapper and prevent his next move.

The dragon was defensive, but in control. It was too easy to think that it was spooked. It was not. Trapper Watkiss was another story. He had been spooked in the clearing when he'd first seen the beasts. He'd been so spooked that he'd fainted and been unconscious for hours. Trapper had been so scared that he'd tried to kill the dragons, and he'd attacked a Native. Trapper was still panicking.

The old man's eyes were wide with fear, and the blade in his hand winked light back and forth as it trembled in his grasp. Trapper lunged at the beast with his long knife, thrusting as hard and as fast as he could. The knife was jerked out of Trapper's hand as the dragon pulled away, yelping in pain. Trapper had hit his target, and the knife stuck out between the talons of the dragon's paw. The beast tossed its head and roared, and then it lowered its maw and spat a spinning ball of flames at Trapper as he turned to run.

The dragon's aim was true, and the ball of flames thumped into Trapper Watkiss's back. At first, he didn't know what had hit him. Then he smelled the back of his jacket beginning to singe and felt the penetrating heat of the flames.

Trapper Watkiss flapped at his back with his hands, but only managed to make himself look demented. When his attempts to beat out the flames didn't work, the old man removed his jacket. Then he half-ran and half-hopped away from the dragon, dancing down the ridge of the plateau, beyond the settlement.

Jake and Eliza could only watch, appalled. They didn't know how to help the old man. They didn't know whether they could even get to him in time to help him. He was on the far side of the dragon, and there was no easy way around the creature.

Trapper hurtled into the mists that marked the upper lip of the waterfall until he was just a ghostly figure. The roar of the water drowned out the dragon's shriek of pain, and Trapper's cries of panic. He ran towards the edge of the plateau, slapping at his head with both hands, trying to beat out a flame that had caught in his hair. There was a trail of clothes behind him, including a skin jacket, a kerchief and his gun-belt.

The last Jake saw of him, the old man was staggering out of his boots to remove his breeches, which were smouldering behind. Then Trapper Watkiss was gone, swallowed by the mists.

Jake and Eliza could do nothing more for the old man, and, besides, they had very little sympathy for his foolishness.

The injured dragon continued to wail its low-pitched shriek and stamped the ground with its powerful back legs. Two Native handlers had been feeding the beasts when the animal had broken out. It had turned and was snapping at the other dragons in the corral, spitting small gobs of flame among them. One of the Natives ducked a ball of fire the size of his fist, but, in doing so, landed inside the dragon's range. The dragon pawed the ground with its back feet and brought its head down to look directly at the Native sprawled on his back on the ground. The young man rose on his hands and knees, still watching the dragon, and tried to scramble backwards, out of its line of fire.

Jake dropped Eliza's hand and dashed over to where the man was lying. He stepped over the Native's body, so that he had one foot on either side of the young man's waist. He waved at the dragon, both arms above his head, drawing the creature's attention away from the Native lying on his back, vulnerable to whatever the creature chose to do to him.

While the dragon's eyes fixed on Jake, the young Native managed to crawl out of the way behind the boy. The Native stood next to Eliza, and they both watched, dumbstruck, as Jake and the dragon went head to head.

37

Jake hardly knew what he was doing. He only knew that he must save the Native handler from the dragon.

He did not believe that the creature meant to do the Native or himself any harm. Without stopping to think, Jake stepped over the Native's body and began to wave his arms over his head to get the dragon's attention.

His left arm felt oddly light as it swept through the air. The tattoo was warm and throbbed slightly, but waving it was no effort at all. By comparison, his right arm felt heavy, and he had to move it with a purpose, while his left had a will of its own.

Jake did not notice that the Native had escaped from between his legs. His attention was directed only and entirely at the dragon. The dragon looked down at him from a very great height. Nevertheless, Jake locked eyes with the creature and gazed deeply into the gleaming red orbs. He longed to see in them what he had seen on the night of the fire, when he had looked deeply into that other huge eye.

As Jake began to see light and shadows in the dragon's eyes, the warm feeling in his left arm migrated to the rest of his body. He felt a flush in his face and chest, and he felt light and powerful. He took a deep breath and concentrated.

The dragon shrieked another wail of pain and anguish, but all the aggression had gone out of the sound, which seemed now to be a pathetic plea.

Holding the dragon's stare, Jake began to walk slowly backwards. He lowered his arms to shoulder-height, his palms facing his chest, as if he was beckoning.

Silence fell over the Native settlement. Black Feather, who had been stabbed by Trapper Watkiss, but not killed, was taken away for his wound to be dressed. The fire had been put out, but people were not bustling around to make good the damage it had caused. The Natives had stopped talking and moving around, and were simply standing, watching.

Eliza was the only one who seemed to notice the reverent silence that had fallen over the settlement. She began to move away from the Native, but he placed a gentle hand on her shoulder and she looked up at him. He was watching something intently, so Eliza followed his eyes, until her gaze fell, once more, on Jake. She could not believe what she was seeing.

As Jake stepped backwards, the dragon lowered its body until its right forepaw was resting on the ground. Its head dropped too, although its gaze was still fixed on Jake's eyes. Keeping its left foreleg off the ground, it offered its injured paw to Jake, the knife still stuck between two of the talons.

Eliza gasped and looked around again. The Natives were still and silent and very serious. Only days before, she had hated Jake and made a mockery of his belief in dragons. Now all she could do was watch him in pure and utter wonder.

Jake made a soft clucking sound as he stepped towards the dragon. He stood right in front of the beast and put his left hand gently on the dragon's foreleg. He took the handle of Trapper Watkiss's knife in his right hand, and, swiftly and steadily, he pulled the blade out.

The dragon lifted its head and torso off the ground, pawed at the air with its forelegs, directly over Jake's head, and unfurled its wings. The action of its wings opening and flexing caused dust to fly up around the dragon and Jake. Jake stepped back again, slowly and deliberately. The dragon dropped down on to its forelegs, resting them on the ground in front of it, and lowered its head, as if bowing to the boy.

Then the dragon lifted its head and turned to its fellow creatures standing in small groups in the corral. They had been still and silent since Jake had begun waving, taking their lead from the wounded creature. As he looked at them, one by one, they too dropped to the ground and lowered their heads.

Eliza gasped again.

Jake turned to the corral, looking from one dragon to another, and bowing his head, acknowledging their obeisance. The dragon at his side laid his head down on the ground before Jake, and Jake placed his left hand on the crown of its head.

Everything was still for a long moment. Then Eliza and the Native standing beside her turned to see Yellow Cloud and Tall Elk striding towards Jake and the dragon.

Suddenly, the settlement was bustling. The women and young men began to clear the site of the fire and put things back in order. The horse handlers tended to the horses, many of them nervous from the commotion, and the Thunderbird handlers gathered beside the corral where all of the dragons were lying, still and calm. The dragons didn't need them, so the men began to stack the broken planks and fence posts, ready for repair.

Someone had told Chief Half Moon about what was happening in the settlement, and he had come to stand in front of his teepee, with several of the elders. He was resplendent in his tall hat, adorned with dragon feathers. It was a silk top hat of the type a well-dressed Englishman might wear, but no less dignified for that.

Yellow Cloud and Tall Elk stood on either side of Jake, each with a hand on one of his shoulders. Jake looked up at their faces. Surely the Natives would take him seriously now and answer his questions honestly. After all, that was all he had ever wanted. Yellow Cloud smiled down at him, but Tall Elk looked very serious.

The spell was broken, and the dragon trotted back into the corral as if nothing had happened. The other dragons rose from the ground to greet him, and they spent some time neck-rubbing and snuffling at each other.

'You are truly one of us,' said Yellow Cloud, as he and Tall Elk walked Jake towards Chief Half Moon.

38

The search party mustered outside the mercantile as the sun began to find a slow path up over the horizon. The heavens were aflame with orange and pink bursts of colour streaking across the sky above the ridge of distant mountains.

Haskell was wearing another matching tweed suit with the tall military-style boots. He had decided to leave Jenny in McKenzie's Prospect, since so many men were eager to accompany him. There was very little risk the party would be away from town for more than one night, two at the most, so he carried everything he might need in a pack on his back.

Several of the locals joined the party, although fewer than the night before, when darkness and urgency had added to the excitement. Several of the men who'd carried torches and taken a drink at Nathan McKenzie's expense had decided to go to work that morning. There was one addition to the party, though, much to Nathan McKenzie's disgust.

Lem Sykes had left his apron under the counter at the mercantile, put on his winter jacket and hat, and armed himself with a rifle. When Nathan protested, Lem shrugged his shoulders.

'You can mind the store, Uncle Nathan,' he said. 'We won't do much business today.'

The little group of a dozen men left McKenzie's Prospect at dawn, since Nathan McKenzie could think of no good reason to keep them in town. By late morning, Haskell had led the party back to where he and Jake had breakfasted the previous day. The fire was still visible, and the geologist showed Garret where Jake had slid down the muddy slope.

The party spread out and looked for clues to Jake's next move. None of them were expert trackers, however, and they found no evidence of his journey. In the absence of a track, they decided to keep following the line of the cliff and the bend of the river, searching all the while for signs of the boy.

The twelve men were busy discussing the situation, and no one noticed the boulder that sat snugly at the bottom of the cliff. They did not see the strange phenomenon of the apparently natural ladder up the steep face of the cliff, nor did they try to climb it.

Several hours passed as the men walked along the gravel bank of the river. Sometimes travelling as a pack, sometimes single file, they quickly covered a good deal of ground, but there was no sign of Jake or Eliza anywhere along the route.

In the last of the afternoon light, the men gathered to eat and fill their flasks. They needed to take a decision sooner rather than later about continuing to look for the children. Some of them were keen to return home, believing that the search was hopeless and that night would soon fall. Garret would not hear of it and tried to persuade them to continue.

Masefield Haskell left the group arguing and walked a little further along the bank. He raised his field glasses to his eyes for the umpteenth time, thinking it might be his last opportunity to find any sign of the children, since it would soon be dark. He concentrated on the distant curve of the river and examined the shingle bank. He thought he saw something, but he could not make sense of it.

Haskell adjusted the focus on his field glasses and took another look. There was something lying at the apex of the curve, right at the edge of the water. Everything was shades of blue and grey: the rocks, the water and the distant vegetation, but Haskell could see something bright red. It was at ground level and it appeared not to be moving, but the geologist was sure it was a clue. He dropped his field glasses on to his chest and strode back to

Garret and Lem Sykes, who were trying to persuade the others to keep going. Two or three men were already walking away, about a hundred yards distant.

'There's something out there,' said Haskell, as he got closer to the remaining searchers. 'There's something by the water.'

Everyone turned to the geologist. Garret's face showed a combination of hope and fear.

'What have you found?' he asked.

'That's just it,' said Haskell. 'I don't know. There is something at the next curve of the river.' He turned and pointed to the cliff where it met the horizon. 'Whatever it is, I recommend that we treat it as a clue.'

'Thank you,' said Garret, clapping his strong hand on the young man's shoulder.

'Are you thanking me for finding the clue or for recognizing it as such?' asked Haskell. 'I should think you might thank me for both, given the circumstances.'

'I should, and I do,' said Garret. 'Thank you for both.'

'Good then,' said Haskell.

The remaining men picked up their packs and weapons, and began to follow Haskell and Garret along the bank of the river with renewed enthusiasm. The distance was difficult to judge with only the sky, the water and the cliff for reference, and, for the first hour, Garret wondered if they would ever get any closer to their goal.

Haskell had allowed Garret to use the field glasses to examine the clue, and the sight had put a spring in the blacksmith's step. He was sure it must be the children.

Another hour passed. The black sky was soon full of stars, and a low moon hung in the heavens, as if it had been sliced down the middle and the other half had fallen to earth. A low rumbling sound that had been gathering in volume all afternoon continued to get louder. They were all a little bemused by it, until Haskell told them there were waterfalls in these parts.

There were seven men left in the party, walking steadily by the light of a torch that Lem had lit and was carrying at the front of the group, beside Pius Garret. Suddenly, the torchlight fell on a large dark object at the water's edge. Lem Sykes broke into a ragged run, and Garret was soon beside him, jogging the last few yards to the clue that had eluded them for two hours.

Garret dropped to the ground and sighed. 'Help me,' he said to Lem.

The two men took an arm each of the still body and dragged it clear of the water. A moment or two later, other hands picked up the legs, and they soon lifted it on to the shingle bank and placed it carefully on a blanket that someone hastily spread there. Garret unrolled the blanket from his pack and covered the body with it. Then he lifted the head and began to slap at the cheeks.

'Let's take a look at him, shall we?' asked Masefield Haskell, removing his jacket and rolling up his sleeves.

The clue on the bank, half in the slow-moving river, was none other than the unconscious body of Trapper Watkiss. Haskell had seen the bright red of the old man's knitted underwear. Watkiss had removed his jacket and shirt when the flames had begun to penetrate, but his underwear had not been burned.

Trapper Watkiss had jumped off the cliff into the waterfall when he couldn't beat the fire out of his hair. Pius Garret looked down at him, glad that he had avoided slapping the side of his face that was red and blistering. Some of the old man's hair and beard were also missing, burned away in the fire. Trapper Watkiss did not regain consciousness, but Haskell soon turned to the men and pronounced that he was, indeed, alive.

The search party split up to forage for firewood. There was soon a large pile of it on the shingle riverbank, and Garret lit a fire in no time. Trapper lay in the warmth, and Garret removed most of the old man's wet clothes, before wrapping him in blankets. Haskell concocted a poultice using the silty river mud and some crushed leaves and smeared it on to the burns on Trapper's face. Then he covered it with a handkerchief, tying it under his chin.

'Where are the children?' asked Garret, his head in his hands. 'What have you done with the children, old man?'

'We're on the right track at least,' answered Haskell, trying to allay the blacksmith's fears. 'Trapper was sent to find the children, and we found Trapper, so we must be travelling in the right direction.'

'If Trapper found them, why aren't they here?' asked Garret. 'Maybe they died in the fire . . . Or maybe they washed up somewhere else. We should keep searching!'

'You could be right, I suppose,' said Haskell, stroking his chin, deep in thought. Then he jumped up. 'Let's do it,' he said, determined that Garret should not wallow in the idea that the children had been burned to death. 'We can check this bank of the river tonight and the other bank tomorrow.'

Two of the men kept watch over Trapper Watkiss, while the other five lit a torch each and began to scour the shingle beach, working their way towards the edge of the roaring waterfall. Garret walked into the spray as it misted up around him, but his torch began to fizzle and smoke, and was eventually quenched.

They found nothing.

Finally, Pius Garret was the only member of the search party awake. He sat with his legs crossed, looking into the fire and wondering where his children might be. He hoped against all hope that he might still find them alive.

'Where'sh me troushersh!'

Garret was so taken aback by the cry that he was on his feet almost before the exclamation had reached his ears. By the light of the fire, he could see Trapper Watkiss sitting bolt upright, clutching several layers of blankets to his naked and extraordinarily hairy chest. Then the old man brought a hand up to his cheek.

'Whatsh wrong with me fashe?' he shouted.

Garret walked briskly over to the old man. 'You're safe,' he said. 'We found you in the river. You've been burned.'

'My fashe?' asked Trapper, glaring out of the one eye that wasn't covered by Haskell's handkerchief.

'It's been salved and bound,' said Garret. 'That's why you're struggling to speak.'

'Too tight,' said Trapper, tugging at the handkerchief. He stopped pulling at his bandage when he realized that he was exposing his naked torso and clutched the blankets up to his chin again.

'I'll loosen it for you,' said Garret. 'Only calm down or you'll wake everybody.'

'Who'sh everybody?' asked Watkiss, looking around.

'Mr Haskell, who bandaged your face, saw Jake yesterday,' said Garret. 'He reported the sighting to Mr McKenzie, and we organized a search party.'

Watkiss frowned at Garret, but said nothing.

'Did you find the children?' asked Garret.

'Wretched boy,' said Trapper. 'Turned out to be a girl.' Then he stopped talking, and his face paled in the firelight. 'Oh lord . . .' he began.

'What happened?' asked Garret, drawing a little closer to reassure the old man.

Trapper Watkiss turned his face until his good eye was staring wildly at Garret.

'There be dragons!' he said.

Garret thought Trapper was going to faint, again, before he had found out whether Eliza and Jake were alive. Instead, the colour rushed back to the old man's cheeks, his eyes flashed and he began to tell his story, painting himself as the hero.

'So the children are safe?' asked Garret.

'Didn't you hear me?' railed Trapper Watkiss. 'If the dragons don't get 'em, the Injuns will. The whole settlement might have burned to the ground by now, and good riddance. Shame about those Appaloosas, though.'

Garret took a deep breath and asked again, 'When you last saw them, were the children alive and well?'

'When I last saw them, the children were being held prisoner by the Natives,' said Trapper Watkiss. 'Now, where's me trousers? And what's for breakfast?'

39

Never before had a white boy been marked by a Thunderbird. The Natives had recognized the marks on Jake's arm, and they had treated him according to their rituals, but not all the Natives had been willing to accept him into their tribe.

Yellow Cloud and Tall Elk took some time explaining this to Jake as they sat together in a teepee. Eliza had been taken gently away by White Thunder, who promised that no harm would come to her while she was at the settlement. Eliza was shocked by the events of the afternoon, but, for once in her life, she did as she was told, especially after Jake gave White Thunder a broad smile.

Jake was then allowed to bathe, since he was still filthy from tumbling down the muddy slope, despite his wash at Haskell's camp. He was given a set of clothes, including a pair of buckskin trousers, softer than silk, and a matching jerkin. He felt a little naked without a shirt, but the sleeveless garment fastened in front and showed only his shoulders and arms. Besides, all the Native men wore them.

At dusk, Yellow Cloud and Tall Elk led Jake to the biggest teepee at the centre of the settlement. It was called the Lodge, and all the important tribal business was done there.

The skins of the teepee were covered in designs of flying Thunderbirds of various sizes and colours, and painted flames climbed up the skirts of the tent. White smoke drifted out of the smoke flaps, which were decorated with constellations of stars that Jake didn't recognize and a great red circle where the moon should have been.

As they approached the Lodge, Jake could hear talking and laughing and the voices of children playing. When he entered, between Tall Elk and Yellow Cloud, the large group of people within fell silent.

Jake was the last guest to enter the teepee, and the most important. Chief Half Moon, still wearing the silk top hat, beckoned, and Jake walked towards him. When Yellow Cloud told him to sit next to Chief Half Moon, he did as he was told. Chief Half Moon reached his hand across his body and lightly touched Jake's arm, tracing the line of his tattoo.

Jake was not afraid, but he was a little in awe of the impressively dressed old man, who had grey streaks in the glossy hair that hung in long strands from the brim of his hat.

On his other side, Eliza grabbed hold of his right hand and squeezed. White Thunder hovered behind them with a basket of food. Jake wanted to speak to her, but he didn't dare offend the Chief, and everyone else was silent, as if waiting for something.

As they ate, Chief Half Moon spoke solemnly to Jake. He had very few words of English, but Yellow Cloud translated, and they managed very well.

Yellow Cloud explained the Natives' tribal connection with the Nimi'ipuu and that they were called the Cloud People. He explained that they lived separately from other tribes because of the Thunderbirds and because they hunted in the forests of the Bitterroot Mountains, which were inaccessible and inhospitable. He also explained that the Thunderbirds allowed them to cross into the Land of the Red Moon where they spent the winter months away from the snowy mountains.

After an hour of eating and listening, Jake began to feel frustrated. He respected Yellow Cloud, but he couldn't see how this information was relevant to him.

'What about the wagon train and my family?' asked Jake. Yellow Cloud looked at Chief Half Moon, who nodded slowly before turning back to his meal.

'I saw a dragon attack my family,' said Jake.

Yellow Cloud shook his head sadly.

'I saw the fire,' he said. 'I organized a rescue party. We had nothing to do with the attack.'

'The wagons didn't catch fire on their own,' said Jake. 'What about the legends? We were warned the dragons would come.'

'When we arrived at the wagon-train camp, we found only burning ruins,' said Yellow Cloud. 'We saw charred wood and a few dead. You were lying in shallow water, not badly hurt.'

'You should've left me to die with my family,' said Jake.

'You would not have died from your injuries,' said Yellow Cloud. 'The sickness came later. You must understand, we had to bring you to the settlement.'

'I don't understand at all,' said Jake.

'You are one of us,' said Yellow Cloud. 'Some of us believed it when you first arrived; others needed proof.'

'What proof?' asked Jake.

'The proof you gave them today,' said Yellow Cloud. 'My people have never seen a white man marked by the Thunderbird. Some of them did not want to believe it.'

'My burns,' said Jake, rubbing his arm without thinking.

'Not just the burns,' said Yellow Cloud. 'Chief Half Moon allowed you to be tattooed, allowed us to perform the rituals, but some questioned how you could be one of us. Why hadn't the Thunderbirds chosen a Nimi'ipuu boy? Our questions seemed to be answered when you went home to your own people. You would have died here. We did not expect to see you again.'

'I came back to find out about my family,' said Jake, 'and to prove that I had seen a dragon.'

'A dragon?' asked Yellow Cloud. 'I did not know you had a word for the Thunderbird in your language. Perhaps our two peoples are not very different.'

'We are very different,' said Jake. 'My people don't expect dragons to be real.'

After the meal, more of the Natives entered the tent. There was no longer room to sit, except for Chief Half Moon and his guests, but they too stood when the chanting began.

Chief Half Moon turned to face Jake, and, as he spoke, Yellow Cloud translated.

'You have come to us, our brother. Your Thunderbird spirit protects you. Your vision quest is completed. Your spirit has bestowed your powers upon you.'

Chief Half Moon reached for Jake's left hand and frowned when he found it bound in dirty bandages. He spoke quietly to Tall Elk.

Jake looked at Yellow Cloud, but the Native gave nothing away. Then he tried to catch Eliza's eye, but her head was bowed, almost as if she was at prayer.

Tall Elk moved between Chief Half Moon and Jake. He took Jake's left hand in both of his and began to unwrap the bandages. Jake wasn't sure the wounds had healed, and Mrs Garret had told him not to touch his bandages. He looked into Tall Elk's eyes, but the Native seemed calm, so Jake allowed him to continue to remove the bandages. When the last of the rags fell away, Jake looked at Tall Elk and saw the colour drain out of the Native's face.

Tall Elk looked from Jake's hand to his face and then at Chief Half Moon. The Chief half-raised one eyebrow. Then he looked into Jake's face, and Jake thought he saw a tear in the Chief's eye. He decided it was an odd thought and he must be mistaken.

Chief Half Moon took Jake's left hand in his left hand and raised it so high above the boy's head, so suddenly, that Jake was on his tiptoes, at full stretch.

There was an audible gasp as the Natives saw his hand, and Jake wanted to know what it looked like too. He had not watched while Tall Elk unwrapped the bandages, and now his hand was above his head, and everyone else could see it. The collective gasp of so many Natives made him anxious, and he felt his face reddening.

Chief Half Moon began speaking again, and Jake listened carefully to Yellow Cloud's translation.

'The boy sees through the eye of the Thunderbird. He is marked for greatness. He will bring the power of Thunderbird medicine among us.'

Then Chief Half Moon gently lowered Jake's hand and let go of it, after squeezing it in a way that Jake felt was almost affectionate.

Jake watched as the Chief removed a beautiful beaded bracelet from his nut-brown wrist. The large bright red gem at its centre gleamed brilliantly. It flashed reflected pink light against the skin walls of the Lodge as the Chief held it up for all to see.

Tall Elk took Jake's left hand, palm down, and held it before the Chief so that he could fasten the bracelet securely around Jake's wrist.

'We welcome you, our brother,' Yellow Cloud translated. 'We welcome you to the summer land of Smoke Mountain, and we welcome you to the winter land, the Land of the Red Moon.'

As the first of the ululating calls of joy from the oldest of the Native women began to ring out, Jake was finally able to look at his hand. He was mesmerized by the bracelet and by the beautiful red gem, which reminded him of another. Then he turned his hand over and looked at his palm.

Almost the entire flat of Jake's hand was covered in an intricate pattern. Pink puckered skin was interlaced with yellow scars, all curling around a central circle marked in a darker curving red ridge of skin. The marks wove around in a spiral, the flame shapes getting smaller towards the centre, overlapping.

The marks reminded Jake of something, but he couldn't think what. He stared at his palm for so long that his eyes began to smart. As he finally blinked, he saw an image in his mind's eye. He looked at the scars on his hand again, and then squeezed his eyes deep into his face so that the image in his mind was burned there forever.

Jake saw a beautiful, circular jewel. He saw overlapping green enamel scales. He saw a deep, glowing red gemstone. Jake opened his eyes and turned to Eliza.

'It's like my mother's brooch,' he said. 'Why do the scars on my hand look like my mother's brooch?'

'You're seeing what you want to see,' said Eliza. 'Your mother is dead, or gone at least. Everything is bound to remind you of her.'

'She was wearing her brooch the day of the wagon-train fire,' said Jake.

'My point precisely,' said Eliza.

As Jake let his arm drop to his side, the red stone of the bracelet fell to the inside of his wrist, where his father used to take his pulse. Jake was suddenly aware of a gentle throb in his arm that echoed the pulsing light of the gem.

'What's happening to me?' he asked himself, so

quietly that he wondered if he'd only thought the question.

'Nothing,' said Eliza, standing beside him. She took his hand. 'In the morning, we'll go home, or Mama will never forgive me.'

'I don't know,' said Jake. 'What if my mother is still alive? What if they can help me find her?'

Eliza dropped Jake's hand. She didn't want to argue with him, but she wanted to go home to her family, and she didn't want to be blamed for her father losing another son. They had all suffered enough.

'I'll make them take you home,' Jake said. 'I promise you can leave first thing in the morning. I have to stay. I have to find out about my family. I have to know if a dragon killed them.'

The celebration inside the Lodge lasted for about another hour, and then the Natives made their way in a ragged line out of the teepee to a large fire at the heart of the settlement. They sang and danced long into the night, while Yellow Cloud, Tall Elk and Chief Half Moon sat with Jake, discussing his role in the tribe. White Thunder led Eliza across the teepee, laid her down and covered her with a blanket. The girl was exhausted by her adventures and was convinced that her dreams would be less fantastical than real life.

40

'If you wish,' translated Yellow Cloud, 'we will call you brother and train you in the ways of our people.'

'What about the dragons?' asked Jake.

'You will be paired with a Thunderbird,' said Yellow Cloud. 'The ritual is simple and painless. The Thunderbird will choose you, respond to your call, to your command stone.' He pointed at Jake's wrist where the jewel continued to give off a warm red light.

'Must I become a brother?' asked Jake.

Yellow Cloud looked surprised and didn't translate the question for Chief Half Moon.

'We will not compel you to become our brother,' he said, 'but no one has ever refused. It is a great privilege to join the brotherhood. You are very important to us as one who sees through the eye of the Thunderbird. There is only one such in a generation.'

'I cannot become your brother,' said Jake, his chin dropping to his chest.

Chief Half Moon had not understood the conversation between Jake and Yellow Cloud. Nevertheless, he took the boy's chin in his hand and lifted his face, locking his gaze on Jake's eyes.

Yellow Cloud translated. 'You fear the Thunderbird,' he said. 'You fear the Thunderbird that destroyed your wagon train and killed your family. We fear it too. That is why you must join our brotherhood.'

'Then I have every reason to go back to McKenzie's Prospect,' said Jake. He wanted to wipe his face on the sleeve of his shirt, but he wasn't wearing a shirt. As he lifted his left arm to his face, he looked again at the tattoos. He blinked his tears away and sniffed hard.

Tall Elk sat down behind Jake and placed his hands on the boy's shoulders. He spoke in calm tones, and Jake began to relax as the sounds of the words washed over him.

'The Land of the Red Moon is home to the Thunderbird. They are many in their homelands and they do not all belong with our people. There are other forces that mean to do harm.'

'What forces? What land?' asked Jake.

'We do not know all that there is to know,' Yellow Cloud translated from Tall Elk's words. 'Thunderbirds have attacked before, raided many tribes and wagon trains.'

'You didn't say killed,' said Jake, turning to Tall Elk, even though Yellow Cloud was translating. There was urgency and hope in Jake's voice. 'You didn't say the dragons killed, you only said they raided. Do you know if my family's dead? Their bodies weren't found.'

'We do not know,' said Tall Elk in his broken English, before returning to his own language.

'We know that the Thunderbirds take as much as they destroy. We know that they take things to the Land of the Red Moon, but we do not know why.'

'What is this place?' asked Jake. 'There is no red moon.'

'Only the Cloud People can pass from this place to the Land of the Red Moon, and only the Thunderbirds can take us there.'

'Then I can go,' said Jake, excited by the idea that his parents might still be alive. 'If my parents were stolen by these dragons and taken to this place, I can rescue them.'

'It is unlikely they are alive,' Yellow Cloud said, 'but if you become our brother you will see the Land of the Red Moon one day.'

'Why can't I go now?' asked Jake.

'The Cloud People travel a great distance on foot

to our winter training camps to work with the Thunderbirds. We have a settlement close to the Lakes of Fire. It is a short distance from our winter training grounds to the Land of the Red Moon. We return with the first snowfall.'

'That could be weeks!' exclaimed Jake. 'I can't wait weeks!'

Yellow Cloud smiled. 'You see with the eye of the Thunderbird. We will begin your training tomorrow, and when the first snow falls you should be able to ride your Thunderbird to the winter training grounds.'

I see with the eye of the Thunderbird, thought Jake. *I see with the eye of the dragon*. He was suddenly aware of how important this could be in his quest to find his family, and of how important it could be in his life.

'We will also give you a tribal name,' said Yellow Cloud.

'What will it be?' asked Jake. 'I see with the eye of the Thunderbird.'

'Yes,' said Yellow Cloud.

'Dragon Sight,' said Jake.

'What?' asked Yellow Cloud.

'Dragon Sight,' said Jake again.

'I do not know how to translate for Tall Elk,' said Yellow Cloud. 'What does "dragon sight" mean?'

'It means,' said Jake, 'that I see with the eye of the Thunderbird.'

*

Jake wanted to celebrate with the Natives around the fire, especially after his long conversation with the elders. He had finally decided to join them, but it was late and he was tired, and Eliza was already asleep. He did not argue with Tall Elk when he walked Jake across the Lodge and made him lie down on the matting there, before covering him with a blanket.

Jake was asleep almost before he laid down his head, but not before he had looked once more at the scars in his palm and closed his left hand around the glowing red gem hanging from his wrist.

Yellow Cloud and Tall Elk sat talking about their new little brother and remembering their own initiations. They'd been boys once, sent on their vision quests to find out what kind of men they would become. At about Jake's age, they'd walked into the mountains, alone, as all boys did. There they had encountered their personal fates and found their spirit guides. The lucky ones, Tall Elk and Yellow Cloud among them, became brothers of the Thunderbird. Their spirit protectors from the invisible world gave them their calling. Yellow Cloud was a great scout, who travelled far and wide, meeting people and building connections. He'd bonded with one Thunderbird, and it was his duty to care for his mount and to train other riders.

Tall Elk also had the scars of the Thunderbird

spirit, but he was their wise medicine man, blessed with the skills to perform the tattooing rituals and to heal the burns inflicted by the Thunderbirds. He was a rider and a teacher, and an advisor to Chief Half Moon.

Neither Yellow Cloud nor Tall Elk had ever seen the eye of the Thunderbird marks before. Chief Half Moon had seen them once in his grandfather's hand, but Eye of the Storm had been buried before Chief Half Moon had been sent out into the mountains on his vision quest. For most of the Cloud People, the eye of the Thunderbird marks were simply legend. When Chief Half Moon had raised the white boy's hand, all of their questions had been answered. He was not only one of them, he might grow up to be the greatest of them.

41

'You must lead us to my children,' said Pius Garret.

'Not without a couple of dozen strong men with guns,' said Trapper Watkiss. 'I can take you to the Natives, but, you mark my words, we need guns and lots of 'em.'

'I've had dealings with the Natives before,' said Garret. 'They're not violent.'

'They've got horses and weapons, and they kidnap children clean away,' said Trapper. 'Those great beasts they ride! They make fire! They're pure evil!'

Trapper Watkiss struggled to put his clothes back on under the blanket. His long underwear was dry and his breeches had not burned through, despite the sooty stains behind. He had to borrow a shirt and jacket from the men, and, with the addition of the wrappings around his head, he looked even more bedraggled than usual.

Trapper slid his hand into his pocket, under the blankets, and felt around for the bracelet he'd stolen from the Native he'd stabbed. His fingers touched the cool stones, and he smiled. He had finally found the jewels and the settlement for Nathan McKenzie. If they could only get rid of the Natives, the mountain and all the riches hidden in it would be theirs. The children would be his excuse for invading the Native settlement, but first Trapper Watkiss had to get back to McKenzie's Prospect.

'If you want those children back safe in town,' he said to the men, 'we'll need to get up a raiding party. Do you want to fight the Injuns when there's a dozen of them to one of you? I won't let you do it.'

With that, Trapper Watkiss got to his feet, cast a glance at the rising sun and set off back along the riverbank, heading towards McKenzie's Prospect. He was not surprised to hear the men gathering up their belongings and kicking over the fire, ready to join him on his walk home.

As they approached McKenzie's Prospect that afternoon, one by one the men peeled off to walk home. There was no need for them to return en masse to the mercantile. Trapper Watkiss would report back to Nathan McKenzie, and they would spread word of the rescue party among their friends and neighbours. Menfolk from all around the town would meet outside the saloon on Main Street at dawn the following morning to plan the rescue.

Trapper Watkiss and Lem Sykes walked into the mercantile at dusk to find Nathan McKenzie sitting on his stool, filling his pipe. He didn't get up to greet them, but he did stifle a laugh at the sight of Trapper Watkiss.

Trapper frowned hard at Nathan McKenzie and stood next to him, looking at Lem.

'Go home, Lem,' said McKenzie. 'Your mother's got supper ready.'

Lem stood in front of the old men for a moment, perhaps expecting them to say more, but when they said nothing he turned and left. McKenzie locked the door of the mercantile and then sat back on his stool.

'Well?' he asked.

Trapper smiled at his boss, his eyes twinkling, and reached into his pocket. He pulled out the bracelet with its gleaming gems and held it up in front of McKenzie.

McKenzie smiled back at Trapper and then took the bracelet and began to examine the gems on it.

'Where do we get more like this?' he asked Trapper.

'That's the beauty part,' said Trapper, and he began to tell his story, finishing with the plan to take a rescue party back to Smoke Mountain. They could kill the Natives and drive the Thunderbirds away to rescue Garret's kids, and look like heroes in the process.

Nathan McKenzie slapped his old friend on the back. Then he broke into a hearty belly laugh, which Trapper Watkiss couldn't help joining in with.

42

Jake woke as dawn was breaking, to the sounds of the Natives hooting and hollering. He rose from his bed on the floor of the Lodge and went outside. Yellow Cloud, Tall Elk and Chief Half Moon greeted him, along with two other boys.

Eliza followed him out of the Lodge, where White Thunder joined her and led her to a group of women at the edge of the circle of men.

'This is Jake's day,' said White Thunder. 'We will stay with the women and prepare our feast.'

'We must go home,' said Eliza urgently. 'Papa and Mama will never forgive me, and they will never forgive you.'

'There is nothing to forgive,' said White Thunder simply. 'Tonight we will feast, and tomorrow Yellow Cloud will return you to your people.'

A hush fell over the settlement as the group of Thunderbird riders formed, each with his gem bracelet and his mount, and all of them brothers.

Jake and the two Native boys, who were both taller

than Jake and probably older, were soon surrounded by the men. They were introduced as Rolling Thunder and Grey Wolf, newly returned from their vision quests.

Rolling Thunder spoke a few words to Yellow Cloud, who answered them by glaring at the boy and saying something quickly and in a firm tone of voice. Both the boys blushed and lowered their heads. Yellow Cloud placed his hand deliberately on Jake's shoulder as if it was a sign. Then two more riders stepped forward and placed their hands on the shoulders of the other two boys, claiming their apprentices.

Tall Elk raised his hands in the air and spoke some words that Jake didn't understand, but which made his heart skip a beat. It was going to be a very special day. Jake was going to take a step closer to finding his family. When the short ceremony was over, Tall Elk led the group to the Thunderbird enclosure, and the three riders and their apprentices entered.

Jake soon realized that none of the boys had ever ridden a dragon, and he was astonished that they seemed afraid. He watched the first struggle to mount a beast, despite help from its rider, and the second was pale and his hands were shaking. The riders coaxed and soothed the apprentices and the dragons for twenty minutes before the two boys were settled on their mounts, their riders seated behind them.

Jake was the last to mount, and the other boys' jaws dropped as he climbed on to Yellow Cloud's dragon with the ease and grace of a practised rider. Jake pushed his hands into the feathers at the nape of the beast's neck and felt Yellow Cloud's torso behind him and his arms to either side as the rider took up his position. Jake felt as if he had come home.

The dragons rose into the air and made large lazy circles in the sky. Those left behind looked up at the dragons, hollering and hooting, celebrating the first rides of the three new apprentices.

As the noise subsided, the dragons turned to fly west over the forest. They flew higher than Jake had flown when he'd ridden with Yellow Cloud through the clouds and up to the settlement, but he felt totally secure. He watched the ground beneath getting further away until it was a dark green and grey patchwork of mountains and forests.

Jake also watched Yellow Cloud's hands. The Native had taken clumps of feathers in his fists, holding his hands upright so that his thumbs were uppermost. His hands worked in unison. When Yellow Cloud tilted his hands to the left, the Thunderbird turned left; when he tilted his hands right, the Thunderbird turned right.

Jake soon noticed that the movements were more subtle. By tipping, tilting and rotating his hands,

Yellow Cloud was not only able to signal the dragon to sail left or right but also how far in those directions it should turn, as well as its position in the sky relative to the ground. The flexing of the rider's leg muscles seemed to regulate acceleration, from a gentle hover to speeds that Jake knew were impossible in a wagon or even on horseback. The dragons were also able to fly fast for some time, unlike a horse, which could only gallop fast for a mile or two before it tired.

Jake hoped that the flight would never end. After about an hour, he noticed that the dragons had slowed down and were circling. The long, lazy, sweeping arcs almost made him feel like they were drifting down to earth.

He looked over the dragon's shoulder at a landscape that was full of the most extraordinary colour. The land opened up into a broad, shallow canyon, and he looked down into a steaming pool of purple mud, which looked like a great eye in the landscape. As they pulled around in a sweeping curve, Jake saw the surrounding land forming an expanse of orange dust that glinted and glistened in the sun.

He guessed this place must be higher even than the waterfall, as the dragon had not dropped nearly so far as it had risen in the sky on leaving the settlement. Another sweeping circle closer to the ground showed Jake a modest settlement with several small teepees and a corral, to the east of the canyon.

Jake knew at once that his dragon was in that corral, waiting for him. He could feel it in the warm pulse of his wrist as the gem of his bracelet rested there. He couldn't wait to sit on his own dragon's back.

Sweeping gently down, a dozen yards from the ground, Jake was amazed to see the great purple pool, the rich, dark mud bubbling on the surface. It looked, to him, like a huge cauldron sunk in the ground. He breathed deeply of the steam that rose off the mud, which smelled of the sulphur in his father's ointments. Jake's heart ached for a moment, and then he remembered that this was all part of his quest to find his pa and ma and Emmie.

The dragons approached the ground at a steep angle, extending their hind legs to take their weight. Then they dropped down on to four paws so that their riders could dismount. Rolling Thunder almost fell off the dragon he'd ridden in on, dropping to the ground, pale and wretched. Two Natives picked the boy up and took him to one of the teepees.

It took Grey Wolf's rider several minutes to coax him off the dragon, as he clung to its neck, his head buried in the feathers. He shook all over, rooted to the spot.

Jake felt sorry for the boys, but he was determined they were not going to spoil all the wonderful new experiences he was having. He even believed that Julius Greengrass would envy his amazing adventures. The only dragon that Greengrass had ever ridden was a mechanical one, and not the real thing at all.

The apprentices were taken to the teepee to recover. There was fruit and water, but, after he'd taken as much as he wanted of each, Jake was eager to get back to the corral, to be with Yellow Cloud and the dragons.

Jake tried to help Rolling Thunder and Grey Wolf to recover, but he didn't speak their language, and they didn't seem to want his help. He quickly decided to leave the boys alone and find Yellow Cloud, so he ducked out of the teepee and made his way back to the corral. As he approached, all of the dragons, including a pair of smaller, younger ones, stopped what they were doing and quietened. They lifted their heads and looked in Jake's direction in silence. Taking their lead from the dragons, the riders left the corral.

'There are but two young Thunderbirds ready for their riders,' said Yellow Cloud, who was standing inside the corral with the dragons.

'For the others?' asked Jake, gesturing towards the teepee where the two boys were recovering.

'They expected only two,' said Yellow Cloud.

Jake didn't care. He knew in his heart that one of the young dragons in the corral was meant for him.

He looked up at Yellow Cloud and then opened the gate of the corral and walked inside to stand beside him. Then Jake began to remove the bracelet from his left wrist.

Yellow Cloud reached down and took Jake's wrist, looking hard into the boy's face. Yellow Cloud could feel the throb in Jake's arm and the heat in his tattoo. He let go of Jake and nodded once, slowly, not taking his eyes off the boy's face. Jake took the bracelet from his wrist and held it by one end in his left hand.

The dragons that they had ridden on lay down in the corral and placed their heads on the ground. Their riders watched in awe. The two young dragons watched Jake, their heads high in the air. Jake swung the bracelet above his head until a rich, warm sound whistled from it, like a perfectly sung note that might shatter glass.

The two young dragons walked towards Jake, side by side, stopping within a few feet of where he stood. They pawed at the ground, swishing their tails and tossing their heads. Then they flexed their wings, making the scales gleam and shimmer. Finally, they snorted puffs of sulphurous breath from their nostrils, which formed yellow clouds in the air. Suddenly, both of the dragons lowered their forelegs to the ground and placed their heads flat on the earth.

'Both?' asked Yellow Cloud. One of the other riders spoke a few urgent words to him, and Yellow

Cloud nodded, answered and turned to Jake. He was too late.

The larger of the two dragons, with its sulphur yellow and sapling green splashes of colour, lifted its head off the ground and breathed a great puff of sulphur at the other one. The smaller dragon had irregular patches of glossy forest green. It blinked its eyes and closed its nostrils. Then it made a low humming noise, keeping its head on the ground in respect to its master. The larger dragon dipped its head and then lifted it again, lunging at the smaller creature, its forked tongue flicking between rows of razor-sharp teeth.

Jake took one deliberate step forward. He lifted his left hand, clenched his fist and brought it down sharply on the larger dragon's snout. The beast mewled as it dropped its head back on to the ground.

'It is our custom for the Thunderbird to choose his rider,' said Yellow Cloud. 'I have never seen two Thunderbirds choose one rider.'

'Am I to ride neither then?' asked Jake, defiant.

'You must choose,' said Yellow Cloud. 'Choose wisely, my brother.'

Jake did not need to be asked twice. He opened his left fist and fastened his bracelet back around his wrist. Then he placed his left hand, palm down, on the little green dragon's snout. Somehow, he knew that he was destined to be its rider. The creature opened its eyes and breathed a yellow whiff of smoke from its nostrils. When Jake removed his hand, the little dragon stood up, and the Native riders whooped and hooted their approval.

Jake heard a faint holler from behind him and turned to see Grey Wolf standing at a distance, watching.

'What will happen to the other dragon?' he asked, turning to Yellow Cloud.

'I have never seen a rider reject a Thunderbird,' said Yellow Cloud. 'He might not be fit to ride.'

'I could introduce him to Grey Wolf,' said Jake, gesturing to the Native boy.

Yellow Cloud exchanged a few words with the other riders as Jake reached up to pat his dragon on the flanks. The dragon leaned down, placing his head in Jake's arms. Jake looked up to see Grey Wolf staring, wide-eyed, at him.

'We shall see,' said Yellow Cloud to Jake. Then he beckoned the boy over, and Grey Wolf walked to the corral, tripping over in his hesitation.

Within ten minutes, Jake had successfully introduced Grey Wolf to the larger of the dragons. At first, the boy was afraid and the dragon reluctant, but Jake handled the dragon as if he was its master, and the creature responded to his silent commands.

Half an hour later, Jake was alone with Yellow Cloud and the little green dragon as the other riders worked with Grey Wolf.

'May I call him Match?' asked Jake, rubbing his dragon's snout.

Yellow Cloud looked at Jake sternly.

'Did I do something wrong?' asked Jake, embarrassed.

'We follow customs when we give a beast or a man a name. What is Match? Naming is a serious business and cannot be undertaken lightly.'

'I'm sorry,' said Jake. 'Matchstruck is my favourite writer. I used to read his books all the time. I wanted to remember him today because something amazing has happened.'

'We will talk to Tall Elk and Chief Half Moon,' said Yellow Cloud, 'and an appropriate name will be selected.'

'It's a funny name for a man,' said Jake, 'but when a match is struck it makes fire.'

'How does it make fire?' asked Yellow Cloud.

'I don't know . . . sulphur?' asked Jake.

Yellow Cloud looked blankly at Jake.

'Maybe they're magic,' said Jake. 'They smell like a dragon's breath.'

'Then I can think of no better name for him,' said Yellow Cloud, smiling.

43

After being introduced to his Thunderbird, Grey Wolf felt tired and overwhelmed. He soon returned to the teepee with the riders.

Jake wanted nothing more than to begin his training in earnest, but, once Match was named, Yellow Cloud insisted that they all needed to eat. They should also check on Rolling Thunder and make sure that Grey Wolf rested.

'To come to this place and to meet your Thunderbird is difficult and tiring work,' said Yellow Cloud.

'I'm not tired,' said Jake.

'No,' said Yellow Cloud, 'but we have travelled far and the other boys have suffered.'

Jake realized that he must do as he was told and went quietly with the others back to the teepee. Rolling Thunder seemed to have recovered some-what. He smiled nervously, and the colour returned to his cheeks.

'He looks happy,' Jake said to Yellow Cloud.

'He is relieved not to find his Thunderbird today,' said Yellow Cloud.

Jake was shocked.

'This is the most exciting day of my life,' he said.

'For many it is the most frightening,' said Yellow Cloud. 'The riders are chosen by their spirit guides, but their paths are often difficult. You are the lucky one.'

Jake certainly felt lucky. He waited for Yellow Cloud to eat and rest, but, as soon as he thought he was idling, he stood up.

'I'm ready,' he said.

'Ready?' asked Yellow Cloud.

'For my first riding lesson,' said Jake.

They left the teepee and walked towards the corral. The three boys stayed outside, while the three riders led their Thunderbirds out, leaving the two young dragons to rest. There followed a short demonstration of the correct way to mount a dragon, where the rider should place his feet and how to hold the neck feathers.

Grey Wolf and Rolling Thunder watched, intent, as the riders went through their paces. The three dragons launched into the air and made slow, sweeping circles above their heads. Then they flew out in the direction of the great purple pool. The boys followed on foot, walking for ten minutes across the orange sand.

Jake noticed several times that the sand beneath his feet felt gritty, like broken glass. It glinted and glittered as the noonday sun shone down on it. He bent down to scoop the sand into his hand and let it filter out through his fingers, leaving the two largest stones in his palm. They were orange and clear like sugar boiled up into hard candy. Jake put them in his pocket and jogged to catch up with the others.

When the boys arrived at the poolside, the dragons were already submerged in the wet mud. The thick purple liquid rolled down their necks and off their wingtips. The Native riders who had been tending the young beasts before they were paired were also there, doubling their numbers.

'Why are we here?' Jake asked Yellow Cloud. 'I thought I was going to learn to ride.'

'All things in their time,' said Yellow Cloud. 'It is important to be relaxed when learning. A long walk is very calming.'

'I have taken a long walk,' said Jake. 'Am I to ride back with you?'

'When a Thunderbird has been paired with its rider, it is better not to ride another,' said Yellow Cloud.

'So I'm not riding back to the corral with you?' asked Jake.

'No,' said Yellow Cloud, grinning at him.

'What's so funny?' asked Jake. Yellow Cloud laughed, showing his straight white teeth.

'Don't laugh,' said Jake, smiling slightly. His eyes shone as he took the bracelet from his left wrist and held it high over his head.

Yellow Cloud stopped laughing abruptly, and all eyes turned on Jake. He began to swing the bracelet, and, when it reached a certain speed through the air, the beautiful, clean note sang out. Jake swung the bracelet for several seconds, as the Natives watched, aghast.

When he thought it was time to stop, before he began to look foolish, Jake dropped his arm and fastened the bracelet back around his wrist. All the time, he kept the fingers of his left hand crossed. All the while his left arm had been tingling and throbbing, and, even after he had replaced the bracelet, Jake could feel a strong pulse in his palm. The sensation was so strong, in fact, that Jake looked down at his hand. He was amazed to see a strange light shining out from the ridged circle at the centre of his palm, as if his hand was burning and blistering all over again.

Then he heard it, and so did the Natives. Without hesitating, they all lifted their hands to shield their eyes from the sun and watched as Jake's little green dragon flew hard towards them. It stopped only when it was right over them and then dropped down as close to Jake as it could manage. The little dragon lowered itself on to all fours and rested its head on the ground at Jake's feet.

'So,' said Yellow Cloud, 'the lesson begins.'

'Good,' said Jake. He wanted to sound confident, but he was so excited his cheeks were flushing, and he couldn't keep the smile off his face. He could also feel butterflies of anticipation in the pit of his belly, and his hands were sweating.

Jake touched Match on the head, and the dragon stood up for him. He reached up and placed his left hand on the dragon's neck and his left foot on its knee. Then he hoisted himself up and gripped the little dragon's feathered nape. In one fluid movement, he hauled himself on to the beast's back. Jake's hands were close together in its neck feathers, his back was straight and his feet rested in the grooves where the beast's forelegs met its body.

Yellow Cloud walked around the Thunderbird to check that Jake was sitting correctly in the rider's position. He was amazed that he didn't have to make any adjustments to the boy's posture.

Making sure that Yellow Cloud was clear of Match's forelegs, Jake increased his grip on the neck feathers. Match lifted his forelegs and arched his back into the rampant position. Then he began to unfurl his scaly wings, the feathers at the alula joint fluttering as he spread them to either side of his body.

The astonished Natives, including Yellow Cloud, hooted and whooped. A much-recovered Rolling Thunder even stamped a little dance in the sand, kicking up shiny, glinting grains.

'You will soon be riding like a true scout of the Cloud People,' said Yellow Cloud, genuinely impressed. 'Now we must return to the corral. You must learn to care for Match. He will be your companion for life.'

Jake thought he was listening to his teacher's wise words and was almost as surprised as everyone else at what happened next. While Yellow Cloud was talking, Jake felt the muscles in his hands flexing slightly. By the time Yellow Cloud had completed his speech, Jake could feel the muscles in Match's back and shoulders responding to his touch. With just a little more pressure from Jake's hands, Match lifted his body further into the air. Then, with two or three measured steps and a beat or two of his wings, the little green dragon left the ground.

Jake kept the pressure in his hands and then transferred it from one hand to the other. Still climbing into the sky, Match began to turn a wide arc. The riders stared up at him with horror, pride and wonder.

Yellow Cloud couldn't believe his eyes and thought that Jake would soon bring his Thunderbird back down to earth. He began by smiling, but, after a few minutes of Match making bigger and higher circles, Yellow Cloud reached up and beckoned to them to land. Jake saw Yellow Cloud waving, and he wanted to wave back, but he was concentrating and didn't think he was quite ready to fly one-handed.

He soon became bored with the lazy circles and decided that, if he flew back to the camp, the others would have to follow him. Jake steered Match around until he was facing in the direction of the corral, and then he straightened his hands and increased the tension in his grip. The little dragon climbed higher into the sky. Instinctively, Jake pushed his knees deeper into Match's shoulders, and suddenly he was travelling much more quickly. They were soon flying almost as fast as he had flown with Yellow Cloud on their journey to meet Match.

'Go on, boy,' said Jake. Match didn't need any verbal encouragement, only Jake on his back, controlling his movements, but it felt good to talk to him nonetheless. Jake thought about the boys in the wagon train, who'd ridden their horses every day. If they could see him now, they would be as jealous of him as he had once been of them.

Match and Jake were quickly out of shouting range. Soon, they wouldn't be able to see Yellow Cloud waving at them. The Native removed his bracelet from his wrist and began to spin it to command his Thunderbird out of the mud pool. Within moments, Yellow Cloud rode into the air on Match's trail. He was followed by the other five dragons, and Rolling Thunder and Grey Wolf were left to walk back to the corral.

44

Jake was over the corral sooner than he had imagined possible. He was exhilarated and loving every minute of his first solo ride.

He leaned into Match's neck and rested his cheek there for a moment. In that instant, Jake felt a tingling in his arm and hand, like he'd felt before, except that it seemed to extend throughout his body. His head was soon full of a warm feeling. He closed his eyes in a slow blink. He felt a rush of blood in his head and heard a sudden roaring *whoosh*. He felt a warm, numb sensation in his limbs, almost as if he was swimming without water.

Jake shook his head and opened his eyes. His view had changed entirely. He couldn't see Match's neck in front of him or feel his back beneath him. He could not feel his hands in the feathers at the nape of Match's neck or his feet tucked into the dragon's forelegs. He blinked again, and, for a split second, he was just a boy, clinging in awe to a dragon. In his next blink, he was Match and Match was him. He saw through the dragon's eyes. He didn't need to steer because the thought processes that worked his limbs now controlled Match's wings.

Jake flew past the corral and had no intention of landing. Everything was new and exciting. He was flying, and it was the best feeling in the world.

As they flew, high over the mountain ranges, Jake knew it was bitterly cold, and yet he didn't feel the freezing air against his skin. He was aware that he was flying very high, and yet he didn't feel breathless in the thinning air. Jake was no longer flying the dragon; the dragon was flying Jake. It knew exactly where it was going, and it needed to take him there, and Jake trusted Match with his life.

First, Jake and Match flew west with the sun high above them. Then they dropped in the series of slow circles that all the dragons used at take-off and landing. Jake looked around at a great gleaming wilderness with more bubbling mud pools. There was also a glimmering turquoise lake of clear water, sending great gouts of steam into the air. It was like nothing on earth that Jake had ever seen.

Suddenly, a great fountain of hot water erupted from the turquoise lake. It shot up close to them and then rained down, hot and bright, warmer than summer showers and as heavy as any downpour. Match rumbled and snickered, and Jake knew that he was smiling.

They swept lower over the wilderness and back over the geyser just as it erupted again. This time, Jake couldn't help laughing too. The hot rain beat down on them, and the sulphurous steam wove around them.

After one more slow turn, Match picked up speed. Jake expected that they would fly back to the corral, but he trusted the little dragon. He allowed him to steer his own course while Jake enjoyed the ride inside Match's head.

Match followed the ridge of rock at the edge of the wilderness, picking up speed, but staying low. As he swept close to the escarpment, Match's turn almost flipped him on his side. His wings stretched wide, but were positioned almost above and below his body, following the rise of the ridge. Jake was thrilled with the feeling of the ground surging up towards him as their angle of flight got steeper.

Jake was about to whoop and holler like a Native. He understood their joy, and he wanted to celebrate. As he opened his mouth, he was suddenly aware of his hands in Match's neck feathers and his feet wedged into the top of the dragon's forelegs. He could feel the wind in his hair and the forces holding his body against Match's neck. Jake's eyes widened at the view. Then they squeezed tightly shut, and his throat constricted, turning the holler into a terrified scream.

'Aaarrrghh!'

Jake heard the sound go on and on . . . and on. He was still screaming long after he expected to be dead. Match was flying towards a sheer black rock face. The curve of the ridge had come to an end, and there was no way out.

Jake heard his scream fizzle away, and he blinked and opened his eyes. He did not know how Match had found a cleft in the vertical face of black rock, but he had. The little dragon had found a gap barely wide enough for them, and he'd tilted his body on to its side and was flying through it.

Jake panicked, kicking his feet and tugging the feathers at the nape of Match's neck. If he'd been more experienced, Match might have ignored Jake's frantic instructions, but this was their first ride, and, just as the boy panicked, the dragon panicked too.

Jake screamed again, this time with his eyes wide open. The scream bounced off the rock cliffs as Match tried to straighten up before they'd emerged on the other side of the stone tunnel. When they did emerge, the dragon straightened up too quickly and went into a lopsided tailspin. It ended with Match cartwheeling into a great blue sand dune.

Jake let go of Match's neck feathers and flew the last few yards before landing, without his dragon beneath him. He hoped the sand would be soft as he flipped over to land on his back next to the crumpled heap of Match's body. Jake was winded, and he grunted as he tried to sit up. He was more worried about Match, though, and he scrambled through the glassy blue sand to the dragon.

'Match, are you all right?' he asked.

Jake took Match's head in his arms. The little dragon blinked at him and puffed a little yellow sigh. Then he thrust with his legs until he was sitting on the dune next to his rider. He flexed his right wing easily, but when he tried to flex his left, his forked tongue appeared between his teeth.

Match was in pain. Jake scrambled around the dragon's left side and looked up at the alula joint of the wing. Then he stepped on to Match's foreleg and lifted himself on to his neck, facing his tail rather than his head. Match lowered his wing, and Jake took a good look at the joint. The feathers had been torn away and there was some blood, but nothing was broken.

Jake climbed off Match's neck, patted him on the head and went to find something to help the little dragon. The place they had landed in was beautiful and it was worth taking the opportunity to look around and get his bearings while the little dragon rested.

45

Jake took a proper look around, and his jaw dropped. Right in front of him hung a huge crescent moon, ten times the size of any moon he had ever seen, and a bright vermilion red.

Jake looked west and there was the sun, beginning its slow descent to the horizon. He looked at the great red crescent moon, and then towards the sun again, and he realized that something was wrong . . . That many things were wrong.

The sky was not blue or streaked with the orange and pink of a glorious autumn evening. It was mostly green, streaked turquoise and purple around the clouds, but the clouds were yellow and the sky was green. The sun was too big and not bright enough and was speckled black as if it was cooler than it should be.

Jake's mouth hung open as he gazed at the green sky with its enormous red moon. Then he cast his eye along the vast horizon. He recognized nothing. The shapes of the trees were wrong, the formations of the mountains were unfamiliar, and the sand was blue.

Jake had not thought about it when he'd landed, but the sand really was blue. He thrust his hand into it, sifting it through his fingers as he had done with the orange sand at the corral. He was left with two smooth, glassy beads. He compared one of them to the beads on his bracelet, and, although he couldn't tell for sure, he believed they were the same.

Jake heard a faint sigh and turned to see Match trying to clean his wound, flicking his forked tongue at it and puffing little yellow sighs. If Jake had been wearing a shirt, he would have torn off a strip to clean Match's wound, but he was wearing the Native buckskin trousers and jerkin.

He stumbled off the dune and looked around. Jake could smell sulphur in the air. He knew that there was warm water, and he trusted the sulphur in it would clean Match's wound thoroughly. His father had often used sulphur ointments on wounds. He just needed a rag or maybe the leaves of a plant.

Jake walked along the sandy ridge that linked several dunes and brought him closer to the hot pool. Then he began to stride down the slope, sideways, the sand shifting away in mini-avalanches wherever his feet fell. That's when he saw a piece of wood sticking out of the sand, but it wasn't flotsam and jetsam, not driftwood. It was a piece of worked wood, which had been sawn, planed and sanded, and had a bolt through it. It had also been burned.

Jake dug around the wood. The sand was not difficult to shift, and he soon uncovered something recognizable. It looked like the side-rail of a wagon, a small wagon, maybe a chuck-wagon. Then he saw the stitched edge of a piece of cloth. When he pulled it, more sand rolled away, and Jake knew it was the edge of a singed wagon canopy. He bit and tore at the cloth until he had a square of it, bigger than a handkerchief. He crabbed his way down the rest of the dune, bringing more sand down with him, and then jogged to the pool.

When he dipped the cloth into it, he could feel the searing warmth of the water and smell the healing sulphur. He soaked the cloth over and over, so that it was clean. Then he turned to walk back to Match and could not believe his eyes. Where the sand had spilled down the dune under his feet, all sorts of objects had been uncovered, or half-uncovered, that Jake hadn't noticed before. He could see the top half of a wagon wheel, a driver's bench, sticking out from the side-rail, and several canopy hoops were clearly visible, although some were charred.

Jake forgot the canvas in his hand as he began to climb the dune. He displaced more and more sand as he went from object to object, uncovering them all.

The wagon was small, and there were harness straps for one ox. There was a dented coffee pot and a small barrel of salt meat. Then Jake saw a splash of red on the sand. It was more cloth, and, when he tugged on it, he pulled out a set of knitted red underwear. Then he spotted more wood jutting out of the dune. It was a carved piece of scrollwork that belonged to an instrument. Jake was convinced he recognized the wagon and knew who it belonged to.

He made his way to the scrolled nub of wood that stood in the sand. He pulled it gently, shook the sand out of it and looked at it longingly. The last time he had seen this fiddle, Pa Watkiss had been playing it, and his ma had been singing. It was the day he'd met Yellow Cloud, the day before they had crossed the river. It was the last evening he'd seen his family alive and well and happy.

Jake sat in the sand, surrounded by what was left of Pa Watkiss's little wagon. There was not another one like it in the whole world. He remembered seeing the wagon lifted clean off the ground during the fire. He thought it had exploded. He thought the little wagon had hopped into the air. Then Jake remembered that he hadn't seen it land. It had simply disappeared. He tried to work out what might have happened. There was no sign of Pa Watkiss.

There was no sign of his ma or pa or Emmie, but the sand dunes were vast and could be hiding anything.

Jake wondered if he should begin to dig. Then he heard a loose canopy flapping against itself, and his heart missed a beat.

46

Jake turned at the familiar sound, half-expecting to see another wagon in the insane landscape.

What he actually saw was Yellow Cloud riding his Thunderbird through the gap in the rock and swooping down towards the dunes. There was more movement in the air, and Yellow Cloud was followed by five other Native riders astride their various mounts.

They looked glorious in the haze of golden sunshine, bathed in the warm light from the great red moon. Their scales gleamed and glistened, and their wings beat the air with a sound like the rumble of distant thunder.

Yellow Cloud wasted no time in cleaning Match's wound. He filled his hands with mud from one of the bubbling pools and smeared it on to the alula joint.

'The feathers are lost,' said Yellow Cloud, as he dressed the wound while Jake held Match's head. 'It will heal, but you should not have ridden so far, so fast. You have frightened him.'

Yellow Cloud was gentle with Match, but fierce with Jake, and the boy blushed. There was a strained silence between them for several moments. Then Yellow Cloud spoke more gently to him.

'What did you feel when you flew?' he asked.

'What do you mean?' asked Jake, blushing to the roots of his hair.

'You felt it, didn't you?' asked Yellow Cloud, smiling.

'It was as if I was Match and he was me. It was as if we were one person, one dragon,' said Jake, speaking so fast he was almost tripping over his words.

'How did you fall?' asked Yellow Cloud.

'One minute it was just me and Match flying together,' said Jake, 'and the next we were separate. I didn't know where I was and . . . I panicked. I didn't mean to, but suddenly I was just a boy who didn't know how to ride a dragon, and I didn't know how to land, and . . .'

'You have learned in an hour what it takes a year for many riders to learn,' said Yellow Cloud. 'There is only shame in wounding your Thunderbird.'

Jake took Match's head in his arms once more and laid his cheek on the top of his head. He felt his tattoo tingle and itch, and his hand throbbed.

Match made a little mewling noise and lifted his head. Jake looked into the dragon's deep, red, fathomless eyes. He did not blink and neither did Match, and suddenly Jake was looking out at his own eyes. He thought it was his reflection, but then he watched himself blink. Jake screwed up his eyes, and, when he opened them, he was looking at Match again.

The little dragon growled and then stood up in one easy movement. Match followed Jake and Yellow Cloud to the steaming pool where the other dragons were bathing and playing, and wasted no time joining them.

'What is this place?' asked Jake, spreading his arms to take in all the extraordinary scenery around them. As he did so, a strange two-legged creature with a high collar around its neck and white scales ducked under Jake's arm and waddled towards the water's edge. 'And what is *that*?' he asked, incredulous.

'We are close to our winter training grounds,' said Yellow Cloud. 'Our camp is a short ride over that ridge and into the valley beyond.'

'The Land of the Red Moon,' said Jake. 'I didn't know it was somewhere else. I thought it was just a fancy name. I should have realized because I didn't think dragons were real either.'

'What do you think now?' asked Yellow Cloud.

Jake wanted to talk about his family and about

finding Pa Watkiss's wagon in the dunes, but he wasn't sure what to say.

'I don't know what to think,' he said. 'Except . . . I think my family could be alive. I think they might have come here.'

'Why do you think that?' asked Yellow Cloud.

'I know who these things belonged to,' said Jake, pointing at the stuff he'd found in the dunes. 'I knew the man that drove the little wagon and the ox that pulled it. He played that fiddle when my mother sang.'

Jake's throat closed up, and he swallowed hard. The day had been full of such amazing adventures and now this. He didn't know whether to be happy or sad.

'These things were not here last winter,' said Yellow Cloud. 'I have not seen them before.'

'I didn't mean to say that you had anything to do with it,' said Jake, horrified. 'I didn't mean you had taken my family. I just want to know if they're really dead.'

'We must return,' said Yellow Cloud, getting up abruptly and turning his bracelet in the air until it sang. 'We will talk to the elders. They will know what to do.'

When all the dragons had shaken the healing waters from their wings, scales and feathers, their riders began to mount them. The water had washed

Match's wound, and new skin and scales were gleaming pale yellow in its place. Jake could even see the buds of new feathers emerging from the joint.

'You see,' said Yellow Cloud. 'They heal.'

Jake wasn't sure he'd be allowed to fly Match, but then he remembered his father's wise words: 'When a man falls off a horse, it is better he gets straight back on again, neh?'

'Ride with me,' said Yellow Cloud. 'I will be behind you all the way.'

Jake mounted Match and brought him up into the air. A few seconds later, he was surrounded by the other dragons and their riders, and Yellow Cloud was right behind him.

They flew along the ridge and back through the cleft. Jake watched the two riders in front of him line up their dragons. Then they disappeared into the narrow gap between two rock faces, turning their bodies as they entered. Only a minute away from the gap, Jake's eye was drawn by a deep shadow falling across him and a portion of the ridge beyond. The geyser released a great gout of steam, which clouded around him in a yellow haze, and yet Jake was convinced that he had seen something.

Less than half a minute from the fissure in the rock, Jake knew that he must guide Match safely through. He looked left and right, and there, against the rock ridge, he saw the great ragged shadow of a wing unfurling. Jake turned his head to see which of the dragons was casting the shadow. His quick, darting gaze was met by a pair of huge, fierce, magenta eyes.

Jake knew that the cleft was only a second or two away. His hand tensed as he prepared to turn Match on his side, and his eyes faced dead ahead so that he could complete the manoeuvre. There was no time to think about great black shadows or fierce magenta eyes. There was no time to wonder at the scale of the beast he had seen. There was no time.

Jake took a deep breath, turned his hands hard left and flipped Match at an angle so they could pass between the two sheer cliffs of rock. A minute or two later, Jake was back in the world of the small pale moon, where the sand was orange and the mud purple. It seemed ordinary compared to what lay beyond the narrow rock passage.

47

Somewhat cleaned up and back in his own clothes, Trapper Watkiss stood beside Nathan McKenzie on the steps of the mercantile.

'We have to save our children from the evil Natives,' said Nathan McKenzie.

Trapper Watkiss looked out over a sea of faces. Thirty or forty men and boys had gathered outside the mercantile to form a posse. They all had weapons, mostly rifles, and some had lengths of rope. Many wore serious expressions, but some looked almost gleeful. For them, frontier life was only interesting when there was conflict, which wasn't nearly often enough.

Pius Garret, who wished for the safe return of his children more than anyone, looked pale and doubtful.

'I don't like this,' he said to Masefield Haskell. 'The Natives aren't evil, and I see no reason to go to war with them.'

'You want your children back?' asked Haskell.

'More than the world,' said Garret, 'but Jake ran

away because he lost his family. Eliza ran after him because she felt guilty, as well she might. There was no kidnapping.'

'And yet,' said Haskell, 'the children have not returned home, and Mr Watkiss was the last person to see them.'

'Trapper Watkiss,' said Garret, 'is in Nathan McKenzie's pocket. I wish I knew what he was up to.'

'He's up to finding gems in the hills where the Natives reside,' said Haskell. 'Hence my job as surveyor and geologist.'

Pius Garret turned to Haskell, his eyes wide, and his jaw dropping. *So the rumours are all true*, he thought. After a moment, with Nathan McKenzie's speech in full flow, he asked, 'Can I rely on you to be the voice of reason, Haskell?'

'I'm a scientist,' said Haskell. 'What else would I be?'

'Thank you,' said Garret, and, before Masefield could answer, he said, 'Thank you for everything.'

'We must drive the Natives away from our mountains! I wish you all good hunting!' shouted Nathan McKenzie at the end of his rabble-rousing speech. Most of the three dozen or so men stamped their feet, waved their weapons or cheered, and several did all three. Pius Garret and Masefield Haskell didn't agree with McKenzie and the rabble, but they hoped some good would come from the search.

A large group of men does not move fast, and it took most of the day for the posse to reach the place where Trapper had been found, burnt and unconscious. The long walk, some of it single file along narrow paths, had taken the fight out of most of the men, and now they were faced with a sheer cliff.

'How are we going to climb that?' asked one incredulous farmer, pointing at the wall of chalk. He was broad and stocky, and ill-equipped for such a climb.

'I came down it,' said Trapper Watkiss. 'So there's sure to be a way up it.'

'We found you unconscious in six inches of water,' said one of the original search party, 'and the light's fading.'

'Perhaps we should send up our best climber,' said Garret, 'as a scout.'

'So the Natives can kidnap him?' asked Trapper. 'We need to go in, guns blazing, and roust them out of the mountains.'

'If there's a path up the cliff, I'll find it,' said Haskell, 'but I'll need some help with ropes.' Trapper Watkiss looked him up and down, taking in the floppy hair and the tweed suit, and sneered.

'I'll help,' said Garret, picking up a coil of rope that had been dropped on the shingle along with some of the tools and guns. Haskell took a small pickaxe out of his pack, and the two men approached the cliff.

An hour later, a large fire was burning brightly, and most of the men were sitting in groups, eating and waiting. It was almost dusk, and Haskell and Garret hadn't climbed very far. Some of the men had decided that nothing was likely to happen until morning and were sharing drinks from the flasks of liquor they'd brought with them. They soon grew rowdy and aggressive, and some of them were spoiling for a fight with the Natives, just as soon as they could find them.

48

Jake returned to the Native settlement to a hero's welcome. Tall Elk and Chief Half Moon formed a welcoming party as soon as word reached them that the boys had completed their first day's training, and there would be a feast to celebrate their safe return.

As they gazed into the sky, in the last of the late afternoon sunshine, the Natives were astonished to see a young dragon among the other mounts. They began to holler and chant as the Thunderbirds circled overhead, and broke into gleeful ululations as they saw that Jake was flying his own dragon.

As Jake dismounted, Eliza rushed over to him. She was so confused that she didn't know whether she wanted to thump him or embrace him. In the end, she smiled and punched his right arm. She looked at his left one, but didn't dare to punch it, not even in jest.

'Say hello to Match,' said Jake, and the dragon dropped down and placed his head on the ground at his master's feet.

'Hello, Match,' said Eliza. 'Pleased to meet you.'

'You're not afraid?' asked White Thunder.

'I was the first time,' answered Eliza, 'but, if Jake isn't afraid, why should I be?'

'Why indeed?' asked Yellow Cloud as he came to stand next to Jake.

'Did you see it?' Jake asked the Native.

'Did I see what?' asked Yellow Cloud.

'In the Land of the Red Moon,' said Jake. 'I didn't have much time to look, but it was big and black, with purple eyes.'

'I saw you in front of me,' said Yellow Cloud, 'but nothing else. We will talk again tomorrow. Tonight we will feast and celebrate.'

'We're going home tomorrow,' Eliza said fiercely, turning away from Jake. Then she turned back to White Thunder, and the women led the riders back to the Lodge for the feast they had spent much of the day preparing.

As Jake and Eliza sat side by side, Eliza said, 'They've been talking about you all day. They say you're special.'

'Not me,' said Jake, 'Match.'

'Didn't you see their faces when you were flying over our heads? Didn't you hear the singing and cheering?'

'That wasn't for me,' said Jake.

Before Eliza could explain, there was a sudden

commotion, and several Native scouts burst into the Lodge. Within moments, Yellow Cloud, Chief Half Moon and Tall Elk were on their feet, and then more of the men began to leave the Lodge.

'What's going on?' Jake asked White Thunder.

'I'm not sure,' she said. 'They're talking about many white men coming. They're talking about war.'

'Trapper Watkiss spent years trying to find this place,' said Jake, 'and, in the end, we were brought up here on the dragons.'

'They're climbing the cliffs,' said White Thunder, listening to the men as they prepared for the attackers. 'They talk of Flame Beard bringing white men with ropes and guns and torches.'

'That's what the Natives call Trapper Watkiss,' said Eliza.

'He shot at the dragons in the forest,' said Jake, 'and he stabbed Black Feather. Why would he come back? Why would he bring a posse?'

'They're coming for you,' said Eliza, shaking with anger, 'and it's all my fault.'

'I must stop it,' said Jake, looking around for Yellow Cloud. Some of the Natives were armed with bows and arrows, or with spears or knives. They started to leave the settlement on horseback, taking the long path through the clouds to the riverbank. The Thunderbird corral was full of riders mounting their beasts ready to fly out to meet the angry mob.

'*We* must stop it,' said Eliza. 'I'm coming with you.'

Jake spotted Yellow Cloud about to mount his dragon, and he ran over to him, followed by Eliza and White Thunder.

Jake swung his bracelet in the air, faster and faster, until it sang out the only note that was audible in the hubbub of the corral. All the dragons, mounted or not, turned in Jake's direction. In another moment, Match was at his side.

'They're coming for you because Trapper Watkiss told them we were here,' Jake told Yellow Cloud. 'I don't know what else he said, but you need me and Eliza with you.'

'Women do not ride, except in an emergency,' said Yellow Cloud, gesturing to the girls.

'This is an emergency,' said Jake. 'They'll kill you if they think you've harmed one of their women, but if they see Eliza they might stay calm.'

Yellow Cloud thought for a moment, while Eliza crossed her arms and glared at the Native.

'You will ride with me,' he finally told her. Then he said something to White Thunder, who turned to walk away.

'Where's she going?' asked Eliza.

'Women do not ride,' said Yellow Cloud.

'If I've got to ride with you,' said Eliza, 'she's coming too. Otherwise, I ride with Jake.'

White Thunder smiled at Eliza and waited for

Yellow Cloud's reply. He made no answer, but reached his hand down to help her up on to his Thunderbird. There was room in front of him for both girls.

Eliza could feel White Thunder trembling behind her. She took the girl's hands and pulled them firmly around her waist. Then she placed her arms over White Thunder's. White Thunder breathed deeply, and the trembling stopped, but she yelped when the Thunderbird took off. Eliza was determined not to be afraid again, but she thought she might have been, if it hadn't been for White Thunder.

In the time it took both girls to mount, Jake and most of the others were already circling over the settlement. Yellow Cloud wove bigger circles than the others, rising slowly so as not to scare Eliza and White Thunder. After half a dozen circuits, he had risen up beyond the others. Then he signalled and turned, and began to lead the dragons out over the waterfall.

The dragons, almost a dozen of them, flew in unheard and unseen by the posse.

Some of the men had drunk too much, and a number of scrappy fights had broken out. They had lit a large fire, and several torches had been wedged into the ground and were burning brightly. The sky beyond was black and impenetrable, and the stars were not visible with so much light from the fire and torches.

The waterfall continued to spill thousands of gallons of water over the precipice every second, creating a backdrop of sound, like nearby thunder.

As Jake flew over the waterfall, he realized how clever Yellow Cloud had been. The posse would not hear them coming. Jake couldn't even hear Match's wings beating and flexing beneath him over the deafening throb of the water. He couldn't feel the wind caused by the speed of flight, but he could feel the sting of a million water droplets as the drifting mists assailed him.

Jake wondered whether he had ever felt so good.

49

The posse had become so rowdy that the men had forgotten about climbing the cliff to the Native settlement.

When it grew too dark to continue, Garret and Haskell returned to the fire. They had stalled for time and begun to formulate a plan to stop the search party attacking the Natives. Before they knew what was happening, the posse of men from McKenzie's Prospect, with Trapper Watkiss among them, was well and truly surrounded.

No one heard the beating of wings as the dragons flew down from the north, and no one saw the Natives on their Appaloosas riding in from the south. The first that many of them knew about it was when they heard a shot being fired. The Natives on horseback began hooting and hollering, and raised their spears and bows in defence.

'Injuns!' shouted Trapper Watkiss, grabbing his spare rifle, another old Hawken just like the one the Natives had taken from him.

The old man was a good shot, but it was dark, and he was tired and panicked, and the burns on his face were sore. His aim was off, and his first shot flew wide.

While Trapper got ready to fire again, Pius Garret stepped in and caught the rifle barrel in his strong right hand.

'We talk first,' he said. 'I won't attack these people for no good reason.'

But most of the men had joined the posse because there was bound to be a good fight, and they checked and loaded their weapons, and urged each other on.

Then Yellow Cloud and his Thunderbird flew over them. The light from the torches and the fire gleamed off the scales on the creature's belly. Its wings beat, long and slow, and it came around in a large arc, followed by the other dragons. The men on the ground gazed up at the extraordinary creatures in awe and wonder, rooted to the spot, and totally incapable of raising their weapons.

'What did I tell you?' asked Trapper Watkiss, jumping up and down in a frenzy. 'There be dragons!'

Garret's hand dropped from the barrel of Trapper's gun, and the old man raised it to his shoulder, aiming it at Yellow Cloud's dragon. Haskell realized that something extraordinary was happening and kicked Trapper's legs from under him. The old man landed on his back with his feet in the air, gasping for breath, but not before the gun had gone off.

The rifle had been pointing almost vertically into the air. There was a sudden cry of pain, and a puff of yellow flame and grey smoke lit up the sky. A dragon had been hit. It spasmed in the air, flexing its neck and legs, and its wings contracted. In its pain, it sparked up a burp of flame that lit the scene in mid-air.

The men gasped as they heard a strange, squawking scream. It looked as if the dragon was going to fall out of the sky, as it dropped through the air, convulsing, but its Native rider soon steadied his mount. He urged it to spread its wings, and finally, the dragon swung away to land beyond the group of Appaloosas. The Natives on horseback stopped hollering and drew closer, raising their bows and spears at the posse.

'We talk first!' Garret said in a clear, loud voice.

Then someone jogged towards him. The crowd was so quiet, watching the injured dragon, that they heard the runner draw closer. Jake threw his arms around Garret and beamed at him. Then he waved at the rest of the men, both arms high in the air.

'Don't fight!' he shouted into the crowd.

Jake looked at Yellow Cloud on his dragon, high above them, and beckoned for him to descend.

Yellow Cloud landed his dragon thirty yards away, beyond the Natives on horseback, out of sight of the white men and out of reach of their bullets. Close by, the injured Thunderbird was being tended by his rider. Trapper Watkiss's bullet had grazed its neck, but the wound was not serious.

Yellow Cloud walked through the group of Appaloosas to the Native riding the lead horse. He spoke to the rider and stood beside the horse, unwilling to get close to the angry white men.

Eliza accompanied White Thunder until the Native girl was safely mounted on the horse of one of her cousins and then went to stand beside Yellow Cloud. She believed that no one would shoot at him if there was a risk the bullet might hit a white girl instead.

Garret saw his daughter and, without any thought to his safety, ran through the posse and across the shingle that separated them from the Natives.

'Eliza!' he cried.

Some of the Natives raised spears and bows again, but Yellow Cloud lifted a hand to shoulder-height to halt their attack.

Garret scooped Eliza up in a huge embrace full of relief and forgiveness. He could be angry later. For now a huge weight had been lifted from his shoulders, and he was simply delighted to see her.

He held a hand out to Yellow Cloud, and the Native shook it without reservation. Then Pius Garret took his daughter's hand and began to walk back to the posse. He just wanted to take Eliza and Jake home, and forget all about the trauma of losing them.

He was halfway across the shingle when Trapper Watkiss burst through the posse, his gun raised. Several of the men behind him also raised their rifles, and there were angry murmurs.

'Murderer!' shouted Trapper Watkiss, waving his gun at Yellow Cloud. 'You tried to kill me!' The old man tore the bandage off his face and threw it to the ground. 'My face is proof that you harmed me!'

The rider behind Yellow Cloud lifted his spear to shoulder-height, and his shout echoed through the air. As the Native's cry drifted away, a tense silence fell. Those were the crucial seconds when decisions might be made that could not be reversed.

'Stop it! Stop lying!' Jake shouted, running through the posse. He turned back to face the mob, ready to take a bullet for Yellow Cloud.

'Twice you've tried to shoot the dragons, Mr Watkiss!' said Jake so that everyone could hear him. 'Why would anyone want to kill such amazing animals? This is the second time you've attacked Yellow Cloud, a good and noble man! When you had no gun, you stabbed Black Feather! If he had died, I would have killed you myself!'

Trapper Watkiss searched for some justification for what he had done, for a way to explain his fear and loathing. One or two of the men behind him took their guns from their shoulders and held them, casually, at their sides.

'Evil creatures burned my face!' said Trapper Watkiss when he could think of nothing else to say.

'You stabbed one of these amazing beasts and shot another,' said Jake, 'and yet you're still alive, old man!'

'Jake,' said Pius Garret, taking a step towards the boy. Eliza squeezed her father's hand.

'He knows what he's doing,' she said. 'He's not a boy any more, Papa.'

When he was nose to nose with the gun and bathed in the light of the torches, Jake turned his left shoulder to Trapper Watkiss and the posse so they could see the burns and the tattoo covering his arm. The scales of the wing danced in the flickering firelight.

'I was burned too,' said Jake, 'marked by a dragon, marked as a rider. If you kill a dragon, if you kill a rider, you might as well kill me. I am their brother.'

Several of the men began to shuffle forward, craning to see what the boy was talking about. Someone gasped, and more guns were lowered.

'You must trust the Natives and witness the

wonders that they can perform,' said Jake. 'You must see the dragons at work. You must believe.'

Eliza and Garret walked up behind Jake. 'He's right,' she said. 'Dragons aren't just a myth.'

'Look again,' said Jake, gazing up into the dark depths of the sky. The dragons circled overhead, scales glinting and gleaming in the firelight.

50

There was a great rumbling roar, and a flash of flames swept across the sky, as if a comet was passing close to the earth. Several of the posse gasped, and some of them raised their guns again.

There was another roar, and another burst of flames, and, as their eyes adjusted, they saw what was happening in the sky above them. Flames lit up the dragons as they wove through the sky, their great lazy circles broken with jinks and twists as they avoided the gouts of fire.

To the north, a darker, heavier, more dangerous shape was suddenly visible.

'Yellow Cloud!' Jake shouted.

Yellow Cloud ran to him, and they both looked into the sky as another gout of flames passed overhead. In the second or two of searing light, Jake saw what he had dreaded. He saw the great, black, riderless shape of a vast dragon. It was three times the size of any of the Natives' beasts and its eyes sparked magenta as its face lit up with the flames that poured from its gaping maw.

'That's the beast that set fire to our wagon train!' said Jake.

With another great roar, the huge dragon flexed its massive, ragged wings and flew off towards McKenzie's Prospect.

'Evil!' shouted Trapper Watkiss. 'It's the devil and no mistake!' The old man clutched his face and danced an odd, manic jig. He was terrified, almost out of his skin, holding his gun with the stock pushed into his hip.

'Oh, for goodness' sake!' said Masefield Haskell, who was fed up with Trapper Watkiss and his shenanigans. The geologist thrust his hand out to grab the barrel of Trapper's rifle and slapped the old man's face hard. Trapper stopped shouting and jigging about, and clutched his cheeks with both hands, looking at Haskell as if he was a naughty child and the geologist was his mother.

Haskell thrust the gun at Lem Sykes, urging him to take charge of Trapper before he did any more damage. Lem Sykes simply smiled and poked Trapper Watkiss in the back with his second-best Hawken rifle.

'Pleasure, sir,' he said to Haskell.

'It's heading towards McKenzie's Prospect!'

exclaimed Jake, pointing at the great black dragon disappearing into the night sky. He took his bracelet and swung it until the clear, high note sang out, and silence fell over the posse. Then Yellow Cloud did the same.

When the notes had drifted away on the breeze, Haskell stepped between the posse on one side and Garret, Jake, Eliza and Yellow Cloud on the other. The Native horsemen had also drawn closer.

'I think we can all agree,' said Haskell, turning to Yellow Cloud, 'that you are in charge, sir.'

'The great black Thunderbird has come from the Land of the Red Moon,' said Yellow Cloud. As he paused, another voice began to speak, a high, light voice. White Thunder was translating for the Natives.

'It does not belong here, and yet it comes. It burns and kills and destroys. It will soon be over your town, spreading its flames and harming your people.'

'What can we do?' asked Haskell.

'We must defend McKenzie's Prospect,' said Yellow Cloud.

'You heard him!' said Haskell, raising his voice and his right arm for emphasis. 'Put your guns away and pair up with the Native riders.'

'Look!' shouted Lem Sykes. Everyone turned as a burst of light hit the horizon. Something in town was on fire.

'Hurry up!' shouted Haskell.

The white men lost no time in pairing up with the horsemen, who steadied their Appaloosas as their guests mounted. The horses would be slowed down by the extra weight, but riding was still faster than returning on foot. Only Haskell, Garret, Trapper Watkiss and Lem were left on foot.

The horsemen began to gallop off in the direction of McKenzie's Prospect, and another flash of light sparked off the horizon.

The dragons began to land on the shingle where the horsemen had been.

'Oh my!' said Haskell as he saw a dragon close up for the first time. Yellow Cloud's mount was the first to land, and Match set down beside him. The dragon with the grazed neck landed a few yards behind them, and then all the others landed, one at a time.

'You fly alone,' Yellow Cloud told Jake firmly.

'I wanted to take Mr Garret,' said Jake.

'I will take the blacksmith,' said Yellow Cloud.

'May I?' asked Haskell, an impossibly broad smile spread across his face.

Yellow Cloud gestured to one of the dragons, and Haskell jogged over to it and took the hand the Native rider offered without a moment's hesitation.

Trapper Watkiss stamped and screamed, and tried to run off into the night, but Lem was enjoying his role of jailer and taking his task very seriously. He had hooked a length of rope around Trapper's hands and tied them behind the old man's back, so that Trapper was on a leash.

'Won't never get me on one of those evil beasts!' shouted Trapper Watkiss.

'You can walk,' said Lem Sykes, poking the barrel of the Hawken rifle in Trapper's back again, and, with that, the young man began to drive the old man towards home.

51

The mercantile was locked, and the saloon was almost empty when the first strike came.

The posse had been gone all day, and the oldest and youngest men, and the women and children, were all that remained in McKenzie's Prospect when the first ball of flames shot through the air.

No one saw the first strike hit Merry Mack's cottage on Main Street. She cooked for the saloon and sold eggs out of her little house. She was feeding the chickens and dropped the dish of grain on the ground as the shingles on her roof lit up and then began to burn.

Within minutes, Main Street was full of people.

'Lightning strike, that's what Merry said,' one woman told another as they pumped water into the horse trough outside the saloon. A long line of mostly women passed buckets of water to Merry Mack's cottage. Then they passed empty ones back to be refilled.

Nathan McKenzie walked up and down the line,

leaning on his walking stick, trying to take charge of a system that was already running perfectly well without him.

'Douse the passage,' he shouted. 'We must safeguard the mercantile!'

Merry Mack's cottage stood next to the emporium, with a wide passage between them, and McKenzie was determined that the fire shouldn't spread.

'Douse the passage?' one woman whispered to the old man beside her. 'I'll douse him if he says that one more time.'

The man grunted his approval as they exchanged buckets for the twentieth or thirtieth time. There was no time to light torches, and no need while the roof was burning. As the flames fizzled out, the towns-people worked by the light of the moon.

Suddenly, the moonlight was gone. Several of the people, wiping their brows and taking a breath, looked up to see why. They expected a thundercloud had come in behind the lightning, but there was only blackness above. Then a great trail of fire lit up the animal that had produced it.

Above the roofs, spreading its wings in a steady hover, hung a great black dragon, spitting fire down on the saloon. It had great flaring nostrils and a maw like a dog's, full of sharp white teeth. Its eyes flashed magenta in the light of the flames.

Nathan McKenzie leaned heavily on his stick,

which bowed under his weight. His chest felt like solid rock as he tried to exhale the fear away, but he only managed a sigh.

'Arm yourselves!' he shouted, thrusting a key into the nearest hand. 'Unlock the mercantile and arm yourselves.'

Scared and horrified by the sight of the monster hovering, the old men could think of nothing better to do than follow Nathan McKenzie's instructions. They armed themselves with the guns in the mercantile and loaded them from the boxes of ammunition under the counter. Then Nathan McKenzie lined the men up on the steps of his emporium and urged them to fire up at the beast.

'My God!' he said. 'The boy did see a dragon!'

The great black dragon banked and turned, before pausing above the saloon, hovering like a mythical beast on some ancient shield. Then it breathed a bolt of flames at the shingles on the saloon roof, and the dry, grey wood caught fire as if it was tinder.

'Kill the wretched beast!' shouted Nathan McKenzie at the top of his lungs.

Several of the old men began to take potshots at the dragon's belly, but any that hit their target ricocheted off the glossy black and grey scales, as if off plate armour.

'Shouldn't we douse the fire?' asked one of the boys, who had never been a very good shot.

'We must guard the mercantile,' shouted Nathan McKenzie.

Merry Mack's cottage was left smouldering and the firefighters turned their attention to the saloon. It was a big two-storey building, and the women and children carrying the water were already tired. Half a dozen sleepy bodies tumbled out of the saloon, coughing and wheezing, and one of the women that served at the counter vomited on the boardwalk. Some of the firefighters dropped their buckets and went to help lead the survivors clear.

It was soon obvious that the saloon would burn to the ground, despite the best efforts of the townswomen. Some of the men on the steps of the mercantile, their useless weapons raised against the beast, slipped away to help to douse the wooden boardwalks so the fire wouldn't spread down Main Street.

'Keep shooting!' McKenzie shouted at the remaining band of riflemen on the steps of the mercantile.

Still hovering, the great black dragon turned away from the saloon, twisting its neck and turning its body. It was backlit by the flames that licked up and down the walls of the saloon, and looked fiercer and blacker than ever. Its magenta eyes glinted brightly.

Several more shots ricocheted off its chest as Nathan McKenzie shook his stick and berated the beast and his men for not being able to kill it. Almost as if he was answering McKenzie's shouts, the dragon bellowed a low, grumbling roar. Then the beast opened its mouth and exhaled another blast of searing yellow flames.

The men fled from the steps of the mercantile as the dragon aimed its fiery breath squarely at the front of the building, in utter defiance of the man who owned it.

'Get back here and kill that damned beast!' shouted McKenzie.

The front of the mercantile was on fire, and the door was open, so a great gout of flame began to set fire to the contents of the store.

Nathan McKenzie suddenly remembered that he kept a couple of barrels of gunpowder in the back of the mercantile, and he stopped shouting. His jaw dropped, and the flush of anger drained from his face, leaving it pale in the yellow light of the flames. All his instincts screamed at him to run, but, for a long time, his body wouldn't listen. When the message finally got through to his legs, his damaged limb failed him, and he fell sprawling to the ground.

As Nathan McKenzie fell, the mercantile store behind him began to spit hot rounds like firecrackers as the stock of ammunition lit up. Bullets cracked and popped and ricocheted around in the building. Several flew out over Nathan McKenzie's head as he lay in the dust, clutching his hat over his head and praying for all he was worth.

Then the entire store rocked with a roar and a bang so fierce that the townsfolk clutched at their ears to try to shield them from the deafening noise. A thousand burning splinters flew out of the mercantile. All the windows exploded with a crash, and shards of glass flew in all directions, tinkling to the ground yards away. The roof was shredded, lifting off the building in one piece, and then dropping back down, buckled and broken.

The creature dropped several yards, so that it hovered one storey above the ground. The townswomen huddled together, clutching their children and watching the devastation in fear and wonder. The beast beat its wings, fanning the flames that poured out of the mercantile, but it seemed to be concentrating its energy on the man lying at its feet.

It tossed its head and roared again, and McKenzie lifted his face just high enough to look into the dragon's purple eyes and great open mouth.

52

As Nathan McKenzie waited for his life to flash before his eyes, suddenly the dragon's head bucked and its neck twisted.

In that moment, he saw that the beast was not black, but dappled, black, grey and even white, like the Appaloosa horses that the Natives rode. He saw that it was covered in glossy, interlocking, iridescent scales, like a fish taken out of fresh water. He saw two rows of sharp, pointed teeth below a pair of perfectly round nostrils that exhaled curls of yellow smoke. He saw huge eyes of a colour that was neither pink nor truly purple. McKenzie's gaze was drawn deep into those eyes, and he thought that he saw something there . . . Something or someone.

The huge dragon didn't breathe fire, and McKenzie wondered why it hadn't killed him. Then it tossed its head and broke its gaze with McKenzie. It yowled and thrashed, and McKenzie saw the rash of arrows jutting out of the dragon's long neck, where a crest of blue-black, oily-looking feathers stood proud.

The burning mercantile lit up the night, and Nathan McKenzie saw half a dozen more dragons ducking and weaving intricate patterns in the sky as their riders loosed their arrows at the beast.

Another hail of arrows hit the dragon everywhere that its feathers grew, around its neck and feet, and at the joints of its wings. Its movements in the sky became crabbed and awkward. It tried to dodge the other dragons diving and wheeling around it, but couldn't. It roared one last almighty roar and then flattened its wings, extending them as far as they would go. It darted up through the posse of smaller dragons and emerged above them.

Haskell and Garret saw what the Natives had begun and aimed their guns at the beast's neck, hoping that bullets would do more damage than arrows. The great beast moved too fast, however, covering acres of sky, weaving around the smaller dragons and chasing them down.

The dragon that Trapper Watkiss had wounded was the first to fall. It was chased out of the sky by the heavy wing beats of the larger beast, sending the little dragon tumbling. It landed clumsily, but its rider was soon off its back and firing at the black beast.

One by one, the Native riders dropped to the ground and deposited their passengers. Eliza and

Garret found the rest of their family. Elizabeth and the boys had run into town when they'd seen the flames over McKenzie's Prospect and had been carrying buckets ever since.

Jake and Match were the last to fly over the town. They had no passenger to drop off and stayed in the air, watching events. They ducked and wove around the dragon that was nearly ten times the size of Match, keeping out of the beast's eyeline so they weren't attacked.

The dragon flew up and down and all around, but couldn't fix on a single target. It wanted to get away from the Natives, who were spoiling its efforts to destroy McKenzie's Prospect. It reared up, one last time, and flew high over the saloon and the mercantile. Jake flew Match below the dragon, between its back legs, so that it could see neither them nor the shadow they cast.

The dragon hesitated, and Jake was horrified when he realized exactly where the creature was heading. The great beast set its direction and began to fly east, towards the school.

As they approached the building, Jake noted the candlelight that shone from the large windows in the schoolhouse. Miss Ballantine was inside.

Jake urged Match onwards and upwards, and they appeared right under the dragon's chin just as its nostrils began to flare with sulphurous smoke.

The vast creature saw the little dragon at the edges of its vision and turned its head for a better look, while exhaling a comet of fire. The fireball just missed the front of the schoolhouse and clipped the roof. Jake breathed a sigh of relief. Then he saw the dragon turn and whirl around the back of the school, for another attempt at firebombing the building.

Jake looked in the direction of the schoolhouse door and then aimed Match at the side of the great dragon's head. They came in on its left and, once again, put it off its stroke. The dragon pawed the air behind Match as he darted away, dropping two or three yards by curling its wings up.

Jake did not need to steer Match at all. The little dragon simply read the boy's mind and went where his rider directed. Jake felt relaxed and in control, but also strangely excited as he realized that he was seeing through Match's eyes. The boy and the dragon were as one.

Match was smaller and faster than the great hulking dragon, and he had Jake in his mind to do all the thinking. He was soon buzzing around the big beast, which swatted at Match, missing every time, and becoming increasingly frustrated. The little dragon darted and ducked, avoiding three gouts of flames that seared the dusty ground outside the schoolhouse, but didn't scorch the building.

The fire in the roof was spreading, and, in between

keeping the big dragon occupied, Jake willed Miss Ballantine to get out of the school.

Match ducked down and flew along the side of the building, and Jake looked in at the windows, where he saw Miss Ballantine struggling towards the door. She was weighed down by something wrapped up in her arms. Relieved, Jake brought Match back up, and suddenly they were right in front of the dragon, which tried to swat them with one of its wings. The creature appeared to be tiring, weakened by the wounds in its neck. It tossed its head to dislodge the arrows embedded there as it wailed with frustration.

As they came around to the front of the building again, Jake finally saw Miss Ballantine struggling down the schoolhouse steps. Then he heard a rumble and a whoop, and suddenly Yellow Cloud was in the air beside him. He could also hear hoofbeats as the Native horsemen arrived at the scene and could see the townspeople hurrying up Schoolhouse Hill, carrying torches.

Yellow Cloud yelled at Jake, before peeling off and climbing to the west of the school, to draw the dragon away from Match. Jake had taken his eye off the ball and did not respond fast enough. He was back in his own head, instead of nestled in Match's mind, and the poor little dragon paid the price.

Jake clung to the feathers on the nape of Match's

neck as they fell out of the sky, spiralling towards the ground at an alarming rate. He tried to pull them up, but the evil dragon's huge wing had finally swiped Match, and he was winded and unable to recover in time.

Jake continued to pull up, hard, as Match hurtled towards the ground. Then, at the last second, he managed to get enough lift to prevent them ploughing headlong into the dusty earth. Match tumbled and rolled, flailing his wings and kicking up a long trail of dust as he skidded along the ground. Jake hung on to Match, and, by curling up as close to the dragon's neck as possible, he avoided anything worse than a few scrapes and bruises.

Miss Ballantine descended the schoolhouse steps, and Eliza and White Thunder ran to help her. The girls took some of the things from the teacher's arms and jostled them into position in their own. Only then did Jake realize what Miss Ballantine had rescued from the schoolhouse. The people of McKenzie's Prospect had built one school, and they could build another. Books, on the other hand, were precious, and most precious of all were the story-books.

As Miss Ballantine and the girls hove into view, Jake recognized the clothbound volumes that made up Miss Ballantine's collection of H. N. Matchstruck novels.

Two more dragons joined Yellow Cloud's mount in the skies over the burning schoolhouse. They flew in formation for a moment or two and then divided to attack the great dragon on all sides. Yellow Cloud flew over its head, making it wind its neck in a savage turn, as the second dragon flew around behind it, snapping at its tail. The third dragon came in low, scorching the scales off the beast's belly with a well-aimed blast of flames. The expert Native riders wove their mounts around the massive creature, taking it in turns to attack on all sides. The second dragon got close enough to scratch the beast's nose and duck away before it had a chance to breathe fire at it.

Then Yellow Cloud brought his mount down heavily on the big dragon's back, making it drop suddenly in the sky before it had the opportunity to spread its wings and recover. When it did, the third dragon swept in at an angle and buffeted the beast's wing so that it scrambled in the air and had to throw its body into a dramatic roll. The three little dragons continued to menace the huge creature for several minutes. It was an elaborate cat-and-mouse game. Once or twice, the great beast managed to strike back at the dragons with its claws and gouts of fire from its nostrils. It swiped and clawed, and they ducked and wove, tangling it in its own limbs and wings and tail. Eventually, after a long and exhausting battle, the huge creature was too confused and too angry to know what to do.

Finally, the great black dragon fell out of the sky. It was too low to spread its wings, and it landed on its back, in front of the school, with an earth-shaking crash.

McKenzie's men from the steps of the mercantile, and members of the posse, brought in by the Natives, opened fire on the dragon. It curved its wings around its body, and the shots ricocheted off its scales, sparking in all directions.

'Stop!' yelled Pius Garret.

The dragon had come down to earth between the townspeople and the school, leaving Miss Ballantine and the girls stranded at the bottom of the schoolhouse steps. They were right in the line of fire of any bullets that bypassed the dragon or ricocheted off its scaly hide.

Jake had made sure that Match was comfortable and then watched Yellow Cloud and the other Native riders bring down the dragon. He was horrified to see the townspeople firing their guns at the creature and even more horrified to see the beast's reaction. The great dappled dragon raised its head and turned to the schoolhouse, to Miss Ballantine, Eliza and White Thunder.

Jake was bruised and aching, and his hair and clothes were full of dust, but he couldn't just stand by and do nothing. He stumbled towards the vast dragon with the purple eyes, took the bracelet off his wrist and raised his arm high above his head. He began to swing the bracelet, and, by the time the note was singing, silence had fallen all around him. Jake stood a few yards in front of the monster dragon, between it and his friends huddled together at the bottom of the schoolhouse steps.

He screwed his eyes deep into his face, expecting to be incinerated at any moment, but that was still better than watching his friends die. When Jake could stand it no longer, he slowly opened his eyes. The dragon's head hovered a couple of yards away, its maw dripping acid saliva into the dust. Its glossy magenta eyes stared deeply into Jake's.

Jake felt something behind the dragon's eyes. He blinked and concentrated, allowing his mind to get lost behind them, just as he had with Match. Finally, he felt it. He felt what he had felt when he had looked into that same eye the night of the wagon-train fire, the night his parents were lost to him.

Jake summoned all the rage and hatred he felt for anything that could seek to destroy the people and the things that he loved. He didn't just think about Miss Ballantine and her books, or Eliza and White Thunder. He didn't just think about Pius Garret or his beloved Match. Jake filled his mind and his heart with all the things that he loved, but, more than anything, he thought of his family, of Ma and Pa and Emmie.

Filled with vengeance for them all, Jake took a deep breath and summoned all his remaining energy. Then he bellowed long and loud, 'Aaaaarghh!'

Jake's mouth and lungs concentrated all his loathing of the despicable beast into one great cry. It was partly a war cry and partly a mourning wail.

The vast dragon slunk back from Jake, making itself as small as possible, and then, its eyes still locked on Jake's, it unfurled its wings. With one great bound, and a fierce, sulphurous blast from its flaring nostrils, the beast took to the air. It sprayed its path with a great comet of flames and then followed the comet's tail high into the sky, turning west and disappearing into the darkness.

Jake was buffeted by its fierce, stinking breath. He felt suddenly hot and light-headed, and the wind from the dragon's wings felt like a hurricane pounding his chest. He fell to the dusty earth, his chest heaving, the bracelet clutched in his left hand. He had no energy to stand or to keep his mind working. He collapsed, all his efforts spent.

EPILOGUE

Nathan McKenzie sat in his sister's parlour and handed Trapper Watkiss the bottle of whisky that they'd been sharing.

'If you want me to keep you out of jail, you'd better do as I say,' said McKenzie.

'I'm the only one knows how to get to the Injuns,' said Trapper, and, with that, he pulled a bead bracelet out of his pocket and held it up for McKenzie to see, before snatching it away again.

'I know what's up in them mountains,' he said. 'The folks at the Hudson's Bay Company aren't going to be impressed with you losing the mercantile and the saloon, are they?'

'Are you threatening me?' asked McKenzie, grabbing hold of Trapper Watkiss by the front of his red knitted underwear.

'No, sir,' said Trapper, 'but we're partners now. You won't get what you want without my help.'

'Give me one of those gems,' said McKenzie, 'and I'll show it to the Hudson's Bay Company. They'll soon send reinforcements, and the mountains will be mine!'

'Will we get rid of the Injuns?' asked Trapper. 'Evil devils!'

'That's the first thing we'll do,' said McKenzie, holding out his hand for Trapper's beads.

'One day,' he said, 'Prospect will be McKenzie's Prospect again, you mark my words.'

Jake woke in a warm bed, his head resting on a feather pillow. He didn't open his eyes for a minute, but he could hear Pius Garret working busily in his forge, and he could smell bread baking and coffee on the stove.

'Sit down and rest, Eliza Garret,' scolded Elizabeth Garret. 'You've had more interruptions than one young person can be expected to cope with.'

'Well,' said Eliza, 'if anyone can deal with interruptions, Mama, it's you.'

'Tell us again!' said David.

'Yes, tell us how you rode a dragon, Eliza,' begged Michael.

Jake could tell, even with his eyes closed, that it wasn't early. In fact, it wasn't morning at all. The little window in the loft faced west and the sun, low in the sky, was shining into the room from that direction. He must have been asleep all night and all day.

He opened his eyes and rolled back the blankets on Eliza's bed. He was clean and dressed in Daniel's too-small pyjamas. He smelled his cuff, to make sure he wasn't dreaming. Then he remembered the fire and he remembered staring hard into the great dragon's eye.

I saw something there, he thought. *The same thing I saw the night of the wagon-train fire.*

Jake was out of bed, pulling his buckskin trousers on over his pyjamas, when Michael and David appeared at the top of the loft ladder. Eliza was right behind them.

'Get back into bed,' she scolded. 'Mama will be so cross if you run away again.' With that, they heard Mrs Garret's voice.

'Pius!' she called. 'Jake's awake!'

Jake was pulling his jerkin on over his pyjamas by the time Elizabeth and Pius Garret had climbed the steps and was looking around for something to put on his feet.

'I'm not running away,' said Jake as he stood in front of the Garrets in his pyjamas and the Native clothes he'd been given. If he hadn't looked so serious, they might have laughed at the sight of his strange combination of clothes.

'I've got to find out about that dragon. There's something inside it, something that makes it evil. It has something to do with my family, I know it does,' Jake said, speaking too quickly, his face flushing.

'That's enough now,' said Mrs Garret. 'You need to calm down. Supper will soon be ready.'

'Why don't you sit with Jake,' Eliza asked her father, 'and I'll bring up a tray?'

'Thank you, Eliza,' he said. 'That'd be grand.'

Garret and Jake ate their meal, and Jake stayed quiet and patient while they talked about everything that had happened while he was asleep.

'Haskell decided to stay in Prospect,' said Garret. 'He's beside himself about the Land of the Red Moon.'

'You heard about that?' asked Jake.

'Yellow Cloud told us you'd been there. Haskell was very jealous.'

'The next time I see him,' said Jake, 'I'll make up for it by thanking him for something, twice.'

'He wants more than that,' said Garret, laughing. 'He wants you to persuade your friends to take him there.'

'They're your friends too,' said Jake.

'I expect you're right,' said Garret. 'I don't want to see another one of those dragons for a while, though. It's too much excitement for a simple blacksmith.'

There was a long pause while Jake chewed thoughtfully. He didn't want to upset Garret, but he had something to say.

'Miss Ballantine said she expected you back in school as soon as you're able,' said Garret, before Jake could speak.

'What about the school?' asked Jake. 'The roof was on fire.'

'Everyone helped put out the flames. Natives stood side by side with townsfolk,' said Garret. 'It could have been much worse. There was no shortage of water or willing hands.'

'So the books survived?' asked Jake.

'Miss Ballantine would've died before she'd allow the books to burn,' said Garret. 'She told me to say, "The library is still open," whatever that means.'

'What about the mercantile?' asked Jake. 'And the saloon?'

'We'll soon build another store and another drinking hole in Prospect,' said Garret. 'The only person who made any money out of them was Nathan McKenzie, and I wouldn't want to be him at the next meeting of the Hudson's Bay Company.'

'Will he be all right?' asked Jake.

'People like Nathan McKenzie always come up smelling of roses, no matter how much horse manure they fall into,' said Garret. 'Talking of buildings, it looks like we're finally going to build a jailhouse in Prospect. Trapper Watkiss is holed up somewhere, but when he shows his face he's going to have to answer some tricky questions.'

'We're going to get a sheriff?' asked Jake.

'Who would you vote for?' asked Garret. Jake thought very hard, but he couldn't come up with a name. The only really important man in town was Nathan McKenzie, but Jake already knew that would change because, all through supper, Garret had called the town simply 'Prospect'.

'I don't know,' said Jake.

'About the bravest man in this town the past few days was Lem Sykes,' said Garret.

'Lem Sykes?' asked Jake.

'He was the only man stood up to Nathan McKenzie, and he had the most to lose doing it. He's lost his job, and his uncle's none too happy with him.'

'Is he old enough?' asked Jake.

'I'll tell you a secret,' said Garret, leaning closer to Jake. 'Lem Sykes is twenty-seven years old.'

Jake's eyes widened and his jaw dropped.

'I'll tell you another secret,' said Garret. 'Lem Sykes is more than a little bit in love with a certain schoolteacher.'

'Miss Ballantine?' asked Jake, surprised.

They were silent for a moment.

'I hope Emmie gets to meet Miss Ballantine one day,' said Jake quietly.

'I hope so too,' said Garret.

Jake pushed the last of his supper around his plate. Mrs Garret's meals were always delicious, but suddenly he felt serious and not very hungry, and he knew that he had to speak.

'I need to go back,' he said. 'The Natives might be able to help me find that dragon, which could lead me to my family, and there's Match to think about too.'

'I know,' said Garret, 'but, whenever you need us, you'll always have a home at the forge. We've talked about it, and we know you'll be spending time at the settlement, and with Match if you're going to grow up to be a rider.'

Jake breathed a sigh of relief.

'They chose me,' he said. 'I don't know what that means. I don't know if I should grow up to be a rider, or what my pa or ma would say about it. What I do know is that if I ever want to see my family again, I need the Natives to help me.'

'Yes,' said Garret, 'and I'll help you and so will Mrs Garret, and the boys love you, and I think that Eliza does too. Your pa would want you to have an education, though, and he'd want you to have somewhere safe to come home to.'

'The Native settlement feels like the safest place in the world,' said Jake, 'and right now doing sums and practising my handwriting doesn't seem very important . . . I'm sure Miss Ballantine will lend me all the books I need. My pa would tell me to follow my heart. He'd tell me to be my own man. The

Natives are wise, and I can learn a lot from them. Besides, I have to be with Match. I feel sure he and the Natives can help me find my family.'

Jake was more determined than he had ever been. He turned and looked out of the little window. Beyond, the vast red sun was setting across the great western plain. To Jake, it glimmered like the ruby in his mother's brooch. He resolved that he would find his family, no matter what.

ACKNOWLEDGEMENTS

Dan would like to thank Shannon Cullen, Ileen Maisel and his trail-riding pardner Andy, and express his love and gratitude to Nik for her support, assistance and forbearance during the writing of this novel.

Andy would like to thank Shannon Cullen for seeing the potential of a scribbled drawing and a paragraph of ramblings, Ileen Maisel for matchmaking, and Dan for twenty fun-filled years of making things up. We really are very lucky indeed!

DRAGON FRONTIER

RETURN TO

THE WILD WEST

WHERE JAKE'S EPIC ADVENTURE

CONTINUES!

HOLD ON TO YOUR SADDLES . . .
AND DON'T MISS THE NEXT THRILLING
TALE IN THE DRAGON FRONTIER SERIES.

COMING IN 2014

HOW TO DRAW A
DRAGON

BY ANDY LANNING
CO-CREATOR OF *DRAGON FRONTIER*

ANDY
LANNING

is a veteran comic-book inker and has worked on
almost every major superhero including **Spiderman**,
Batman, **The X-Men**, **Wonder Woman**, **The Fantastic
Four**, **The Ultimate Avengers** and **Superman**.

He has worked with **DAN ABNETT**, author of **Dragon
Frontier**, for more than twenty years. In that time they have
written some of the most famous superhero comics in the world,
including **Iron Man**, **Thor** and **The Punisher** at Marvel,
and **Superman**, **Batman**, **The Justice League of America**,
and **Wonder Woman** at DC Comics.

Now Andy uses his inking skills to reveal how to draw a dragon
– just like Match, Jake's dragon in **Dragon Frontier** . . .

Share your dragon picture with other fans at
Facebook.co.uk/DragonFrontier
(or ask an adult to do this if
you're not thirteen yet).

DRAGON FRONTIER

HOW TO DRAW A DRAGON

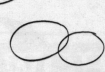

STEP 1:
A good starting point is to draw some basic shapes that form the framework for your dragon. The two lower rings form the body and the oval is the head.

STEP 2:
Continue with the framework by adding basic shapes for the neck, legs and wings. Always draw these bits in light pencil so they can be erased later. They are the basis for the details. In *Dragon Frontier* the dragons are four-legged (like horses) and are therefore easier to ride!

STEP 3:
Once you have the framework, you can begin to flesh out the dragon's shape in detail. Start with the head and neck – you can design this to look any way you want. This is a young dragon, like Match from the story, and is lean and fast so its head is more like that of a bird, streamlined and sleek. Use the line you've drawn in the framework as a guide and fill out the neck with curved lines. The underside of the dragon is a different texture to the topside: it's ridged and scaly, made up of tough thick skin to protect it.

STEP 4:
Next, add detail to the legs and body of the dragon. Again, use your guidelines and draw in curves. Notice that the dragon's legs are bent like those of a dog: double-jointed with a claw-spur on the elbow joint. The fourth leg is not seen as it is hidden by the other leg and the body. You can add as many or as few toes as you decide. This dragon has three toes on each foot, two at the front, one at the rear.

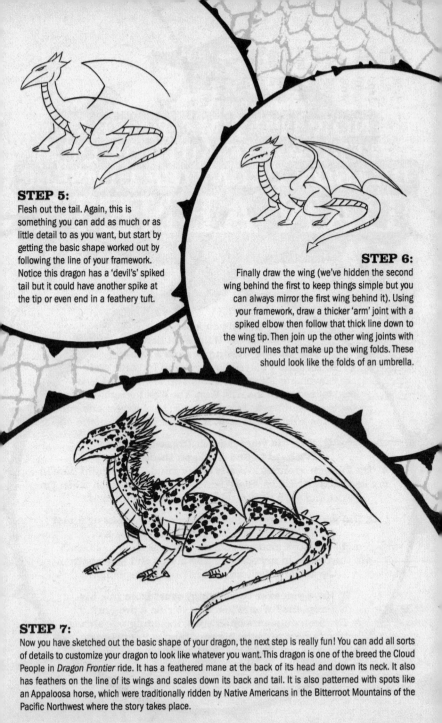

STEP 5:

Flesh out the tail. Again, this is something you can add as much or as little detail to as you want, but start by getting the basic shape worked out by following the line of your framework. Notice this dragon has a 'devil's' spiked tail but it could have another spike at the tip or even end in a feathery tuft.

STEP 6:

Finally draw the wing (we've hidden the second wing behind the first to keep things simple but you can always mirror the first wing behind it). Using your framework, draw a thicker 'arm' joint with a spiked elbow then follow that thick line down to the wing tip. Then join up the other wing joints with curved lines that make up the wing folds. These should look like the folds of an umbrella.

STEP 7:

Now you have sketched out the basic shape of your dragon, the next step is really fun! You can add all sorts of details to customize your dragon to look like whatever you want. This dragon is one of the breed the Cloud People in *Dragon Frontier* ride. It has a feathered mane at the back of its head and down its neck. It also has feathers on the line of its wings and scales down its back and tail. It is also patterned with spots like an Appaloosa horse, which were traditionally ridden by Native Americans in the Bitterroot Mountains of the Pacific Northwest where the story takes place.

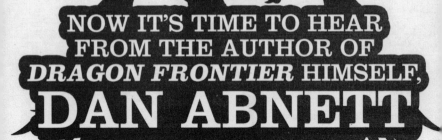

NOW IT'S TIME TO HEAR FROM THE AUTHOR OF *DRAGON FRONTIER* HIMSELF, DAN ABNETT

Q. Did you know a lot about the Wild West before you started writing *Dragon Frontier*?
A. As a kid I played cowboys and Indians, and my favourite TV western was *The Virginian*! I also liked to read about the Wild West. The West I imagined was probably quite different from the truth, but I have made sure that the West in this book is, at heart, very realistic.

Q. How did you research *Dragon Frontier*? It's hard to find a dragon these days!
A. The Dragon Frontier is really easy to find . . . It's right here in my imagination. That's where I do most of my research when I'm dealing with things that are not from our world.

Q. Did you take inspiration from any other books or films?
A. Yes, the western TV shows I loved as a kid, and I still love monster movies. The best dragon stories are the oldest, in my opinion. The myths and legends from the ancient civilizations are hugely inspiring.

Q. Have you ever been flying, apart from in a big aeroplane? Would you like to ride a dragon?
A. I've been on planes of all sizes, including one almost the same size as the bigger dragons in my book. Of course I'd love to ride a dragon . . . Who wouldn't?